COLD HEARTS
HOT SECRETS

SUE HAWLEY

Cover designer: James Price, The Author Market
Interior Layout: James Price, The Author Market
All rights reserved.
ISBN-13: 978-0-9997678-3-2

DEDICATION

This book is dedicated to all my siblings. They tolerated their little sister through the growing up years and encourage me each and every day.

CONTENTS

ACKNOWLEDGMENTS

I want to thank the gal who suffers through editing my manuscripts, Ella Price. She is a hoot to work with and I appreciate all she does. Also, James Price who designs the covers for the entire Peg Shaw series and formats the manuscripts. He always delights with the covers he provides. Sandy Lawrence, my publicist, who works so hard for the Peg Shaw books and has become a real friend. I also want to recognize my author community for their support and help.

CHAPTER 1

Finishing my required third cup of coffee, I surveyed my kitchen. During the last big case I worked for our township police department, the kitchen was shot to pieces by a drug dealing teenager. He, along with a friend of his, was mixed up with a nasty South American mob family by the name of Mendoza. Lucky for him the cops nabbed him before the mobsters got their hands on the little jerk. He made the mistake of bragging to his friend, within earshot of others, about shooting me in the shoulder.

Our kitchen needed a facelift, but I would've rather had time to plan the remodel instead of rushing through the process under those circumstances. I did enjoy our new, updated refrigerator and oven, so I was secretly glad I was finally pushed into making the changes. I was known for dragging my feet when any type of change was involved.

My husband, Andy, and I live in a small township northwest of Akron, Ohio. Once the 'Tire Capital of the World' due to both Firestone and Goodyear Tire Companies being located downtown, Akron is the largest city near us. Cleveland is about thirty-five miles north, and it sits on the southern shore of Lake Erie, one of the Great Lakes. It is home to the Rock and Roll Hall of Fame and the famous Cleveland Clinic. I know the city has a couple of sports teams, but I never bothered to pay attention to them.

Bath, our township, has been around since the late 1700s and at one time, it was home to wildlife and Indians. Some of those same Indians now reside in the woods at the back of our property—my life is complicated.

Our nearest neighbor, Amy Branch, is a retired high school science teacher. Together, we are consultants for the Bath Police Department. Most cases we work are simple and quick to solve. There have been a few that have been problematic, dangerous, and a pain in the butt. Amy uses logic to help with our work, while I usually depend on gut instinct. Deciding which method is more productive is a toss-up. We have agreed the combination of the two techniques is the reason for our impressive success rate. So far, we've batted one hundred percent, but I refuse to become cocky—it only takes one stinker of a case to ruin a perfect batting average.

Our immediate boss is the chief of police, Jack Monroe. The past few cases added gray to his hair and inches to his waistline. He tends to eat pie when the stress level climbs—I should buy stock in pie companies. He and his wife, Lori, along with Andy and I, sweated together through our kids' school years, but now we were safely on the other side of parenting. Andy and I have four boys who live scattered throughout the country. Our oldest, Adam, recently became engaged, and I was still hard at work accepting the fact I would soon become a mother-in-law. I try not to think about it … much.

"Hey Peg! How's your morning?" Bob asked happily.

Bob … is … um … a dead guy we work with while solving cases. He was actually the first case I worked for the police. He and his horrible wife, Elaine, were murdered in their bed. Turned out the culprit was on the police force, and Jack came close to having a meltdown once the guy was discovered—it wasn't pretty.

A few months ago, for some strange reason—which I blame on menopause—I suddenly acquired the ability to communicate with dead people. My Nana was the first to arrive, followed by Bob and Elaine. Bob, by now, was well aware of my three cup, morning coffee rule and followed it to the best of his ability. While he is irritating as all get out, I have a soft spot for him, but I make sure he remains clueless to the fact.

"Fine. What brings you around so early? Haven't seen you for a few weeks."

"I wanted to see how the kitchen turned out." He inspected the new appliances, nodding. "Looks pretty good. The oven sure is nicer than the old clunker you had." Bob usually looked like he just crawled out of bed. His dark hair was always in need of a haircut, he was disheveled, and wrinkled from head to toe. He'd been working on his appearance lately. My dad had given him a few pointers, which he obviously ignored today.

I narrowed my eyes. "There was nothing wrong with the other oven. A little outdated … maybe, but it worked fine.”

"Yeah, yeah … you hate change, but even *you* have to admit the kitchen looks tons better." Bob doesn't necessarily understand the concept of 'tact'.

"What have you been doing lately?" I asked mostly out of curiosity. Deadsville was still a mystery to us, and the little bits of information we picked up during cases was fascinating, especially to Andy. He loved hearing tidbits about the other side of life—I was usually irritated by what I heard.

"I joined a few clubs. I'm so excited to finally have a social life," Bob beamed. "Elaine wouldn't allow much socializing even when we were alive. Dead? No way!"

When we learned there were clubs, gatherings, parties, meetings, and jobs to do in the afterlife, I wasn't a happy camper. I wanted peace, quiet, and gold streets. Andy was intrigued and loved to learn as much as possible. I decided the less I knew, the better. I don't want to *work* or go to *meetings* over there … I want rest.

The phone rang catching my attention.

Bob smiled smugly. "It's Amy."

His abilities have increased amazingly since we first met. I couldn't decide if it was a good thing or not. He was proud of the fact, and he loved showing me how many new skills he had acquired—some were a tad creepy.

Amy's voice came on the line when I picked up. "Peg? I'm thinking of going to an extra class today. Want to come with me?"

I hesitated, caught off guard by her question. Was she out of her mind? "Um, no … thanks."

"Now Peg, you know the more we practice the better we'll become."

A few months back, Amy decided we needed self-defense classes. I hated them; she loved them. I still couldn't figure out how an eighty-something-year-old woman could beat the snot out of me each and every class. It took me a while to get comfortable with actually fighting back for fear of hurting her, even though I was the one bruised from head to toe. Even after I started defending myself against her, I lost battles and found myself on the ground staring at the ceiling more often than not. The guys who own the studio, where we take classes, enjoy watching the two of us spar. They get a kick out of Amy while I get kicked *by* Amy.

I glanced at Bob. "I have company."

"Oh … I'm sorry … it's so early for you."

"No problem. Maybe next time." I decided to ignore her 'early' comment. This time of the morning would be early for anyone.

She quickly changed the subject. "Bob was by earlier. I think he's a bit bored. I wouldn't be surprised if he shows up at your house soon."

I felt an eyebrow rise as I looked at Bob. "Thanks for the warning.

Enjoy your class." I hung up the phone as I continued watching Bob. "You've already been to Amy's this morning? Jeez, Bob … it's a little early don't you think?"

He waved a hand. "Amy gets up with the birds. Plus, she doesn't have a coffee rule."

My three-cup rule was known by everyone associated with me. It literally takes three full cups of hot coffee to wake up all my pieces and parts—aging sucks.

I shook my head as I rinsed my cup out and put it on the drainer to dry. Andy tried to talk me into a dishwasher while we were updating the kitchen, but I refused. I'd been washing dishes by hand since we moved into this house, and I saw no reason not to continue the practice. There was only the two of us, and it seemed like such a waste of money to install a dishwasher at this stage of our life.

The phone rang again, and I looked at Bob, but his attention was on the woods out back.

"Have you checked on your Indian pals?" Jack's voice boomed at me.

I threw my head back and sighed. "Why?"

"We have trouble."

The group of Indians who resided in my woods had been dead and gone for a long time. They were part of my protection team, so if I could detect them, we were in trouble. Depending on their level of agitation, I could gauge how bad the situation had become. I took a deep breath and turned toward the window. I gritted my teeth when I saw them milling around as they looked at the house—not good.

I turned my attention back to Jack. "What's the problem?"

Jack hesitated before speaking. "So you can see the guys?"

"Yep. They're not too upset, but they're definitely irritated for some reason."

"Damn. I'm coming over."

"Jack! I'm not even dressed yet. Can't this wait?"

He sighed heavily. "I'll give you half an hour to get dressed. Do you have any pie?"

I rolled my eyes … jeez. "You're gaining weight and don't need pie!" I snapped.

"I've lost a pound on the diet Lori stuck me on, and I'm starving." He actually managed to sound hurt.

I sighed. "Fine. I'll see you in a few minutes but give me the entire half hour." I hung up the phone and looked at Bob. "You have any idea what's going on?"

His face creased with worry, but he shook his head. "Nope. I really only came by for a visit. What'd Jack say?"

"Nothing actually. He'll be here soon, so I need to get dressed." I turned and headed for the bedroom.

"I'll keep an eye out," Bob called after me.

Once I was dressed, with teeth brushed and all, I ran my fingers through my stick straight hair, deciding I might need a cut soon. While Amy's gray hair was wildly curly, mine was the opposite. I quickly slapped a little mascara on my lashes, and decided it was enough—a full face of makeup was not needed for a morning meeting with Jack. I stepped back from the mirror and surveyed my image. I stand an inch over five feet tall in stocking feet. I dye my hair because I can't stand the mousy brown it turned years ago. I also have to acknowledge the extra inches around my waistline—four pregnancies didn't help my girlish figure much. I sighed as I gave up the inspection and returned to Bob.

Bob looked over at me as soon as I entered the kitchen. "Do you think I should tell Logan?"

Logan was a dead Indian who happened to be Bob's boss. He lived a long time ago, but since he wouldn't give any information about his life on earth, no one had any idea when or where he lived while he was here. Through the hierarchy on the heavenly side, Logan was given the task of keeping evil at bay on both sides of life. He gave out very little information; usually, only when circumstances became dire and my life was in danger. He played his cards tight to his chest, if he played them at all.

I shook my head. "Let's see what Jack has to say first."

Bob nodded, a look of worry still on his face.

"It's probably local crime and has nothing to do with Logan's 'big picture'." I tried to reassure him, but I wasn't sure how much good it would do.

Logan loved the *big picture*, and I wanted to scream every time he started lecturing about it. Good versus evil was an old story, but Logan had been fighting the good fight for centuries. Amy chewed his butt during our last big case, and I hoped she taught him a thing or two. He hated divulging any type of knowledge for fear of giving the dark side a speck of material to hold over our heads. Logan could be a real pain in the butt.

Jack knocked on the back door before I had a chance to grab the pie out of the fridge. I used to hide the pie, thinking the refrigerator was the perfect spot, but Jack sniffed it out during our first case. I decided it wasn't worth the bother to find a new spot to stash the darn things.

I opened the door. "What's up?" I didn't like his expression, but I kept my thoughts to myself.

"Break-ins … all over the damn township." He plopped his butt at the kitchen table and shook his head. "I usually wouldn't be upset, but the amount of homes being broken into is making me nervous."

I frowned. "Could it be kids? School started a few weeks ago, but I'm sure teenagers can make time for mischief."

He shook his head again. "That's exactly what I thought when it all started. We've been staking out various areas where we think they may strike next, but no luck. A couple of my officers have kept their eyes on the usual troublemakers, but nothing came of it."

I jerked my thumb toward the woods. "Something has the guys upset. Are you sure it's the break-ins?"

Jack shrugged, his frustration evident. "Have you talked to Logan lately?"

"Nope. I haven't seen him since the Mendoza mess was cleaned up."

Jack stared at me in shock. "You're kidding!"

I frowned. "No. Logan doesn't make social calls." I glanced at Bob who had the grace to blush.

Jack turned his attention to Bob. "Have you heard anything at all?" A couple months back, Jack was given the ability to see my dead folks. He was glad to be included in the small circle of people with the capability.

Bob shook his head. "Sorry, Jack ... I dropped by to see the new kitchen."

Jack looked around and nodded. "Looking good." He focused on the flooring. "I didn't know you were replacing the floor."

"Andy decided we might as well take care of the floor while we were moving the heavy appliances. I have to admit the old linoleum had seen better days."

Bob snorted. "That's an understatement."

I shot him a glance but kept my mouth shut. It was too early in the morning to start an argument with someone who could fade away if the discussion became too heated.

Jack's eyes strayed in the direction of the fridge, and I laughed. "Don't you think it's a little early for pie?"

He turned his attention back to me. "I haven't had time to eat breakfast, so pie sounds pretty good about now."

Grinning, I grabbed a plate, then retrieved the pie from the refrigerator.

"Make it a good size," Jack instructed. "Last time, you cut a skinny piece."

"Make sure Lori doesn't blame me for the fact that you're cheating to high heaven on your diet."

"Are you kidding? I'm not about to tell her I had pie for breakfast ... she'd skin me alive."

I shook my head in amusement as I placed the pie in front of him. "I'll make you some coffee."

One of my cherished small appliances was my one-cup-at-a-time coffee brewer. The little pod thingies could get expensive, but it was worth having a fresh brewed cup each time I wanted my favorite beverage.

After placing the cup next to Jack, I found myself peering toward the woods again. The Indians who lived there guarded the property for Logan and alerted him if there were problems. We had a few mistakes along the way, until Logan made sure they understood any intruders inside or outside were cause to contact him immediately. The arrangement worked pretty well, and I felt more secure knowing they prowled the woods between Amy's and our property.

Jack noticed the direction of my gaze. "Increased activity?"

I shook my head. "I'd feel a lot better if I couldn't see them at all."

Amy saw them all the time; I only saw them when trouble was brewing. Watching them mill around was disconcerting. I decided to take the advice I was given during the last case, so I headed toward the door.

Jack's eyes widened with concern as he swallowed a mouthful of pie. "Whoa! Where are you going?"

"I'll be right back." I made my way across the yard, irritated I forgot to change into sneakers. The morning dew was soaking my feet through my comfy slippers as I approached the small tribe. "What's up guys?"

Startled by my appearance and question, they looked at one another not quite sure what to do.

"I can see you, which tells me there's a problem. Trouble is ... I have no idea what's going on, but maybe you do." My foot started patting the ground as I felt my anxiety growing.

One of the men took a step forward. "You have never approached us before."

"Nope. Decided it was time to take the bull by the horns and discover information for myself."

He looked back at his friends nervously. Maybe they had orders never to talk with me. I might be breaking some sort of code of honor or trust Logan had in them, but I didn't care. If Logan wasn't going to show up and explain why I could see them, then I had every right to question them myself.

The man in front of me hesitated before he made up his mind. "There is a problem in the township. Many structures are being vandalized and items are being stolen."

I nodded. "Jack told me. It doesn't explain why you guys ..." I waved my arm in the direction of the woods. "... are so upset."

He glanced back at his friends, then looked back at me. "There must be a reason we are so unsettled. I believe the problem to be the people who are robbing structures." He paused as he thought a moment. "Whoever is involved is not local."

My eyes widened. "They're not kids from around here?"

He shook his head. "No."

"Where are they from?" I pressed—Jack would be interested to hear this bit of news.

The Indian shook his head. "Someone is behind the activity." He frowned. "We cannot see who … it is hazy."

"Hazy? What's hazy?" The conversation was becoming confusing to me.

He sighed. "I am sure Logan has explained we do not know everything."

I nodded. I was aware my dead friends didn't have all the facts, but that didn't mean I had to like it.

"There are many times the truth is hidden from our view. Even we did not know your police friend would try to harm you."

Owen had been on the police force and was even the town hero in many aspects. Too bad it turned out he was a sociopath who was murdering people throughout northeast Ohio for over a decade. I learned the truth at the last moment, and I came darn close to being slit open by his knife in my own backyard.

I shook my head, trying to clear it. "Thanks anyway."

The Indian nodded and turned to join his friends.

I trudged back to the house. Bob was nervously pacing back and forth on the back porch.

Jack had joined him, and they were watching my encounter with the Indians.

"Well? Do they know anything?" Jack demanded.

I shook my head. "Nope. Other than the fact that it isn't kids breaking into houses, they have no idea who the culprit is. He said something about it being hazy."

Jack frowned. "Hazy?"

"Yeah. I bet whoever is behind this has some connection to the afterlife."

A look of annoyance flashed across Jack's face. "Shit … another damn case where the bad guys have as much access to the dead as we do."

"Not necessarily. Remember Mom told me the criminals had no idea the dead were helping them," I reminded him. My mom should know since she was one of the culprits when it came to helping out bad guys.

He ran his hand through his graying hair, then turned to Bob. "How hard would it be for you to nose around and see if you can spot the jerks robbing houses?"

Bob rubbed his chin, deep in thought. "Not sure, but I could give it a go." He glanced at Jack. "You can't tell Logan though. Last time, there was a real stink when I helped you."

Jack held up a hand. "Promise … I won't let it slip this time."

During our last case, Jack 'borrowed' Bob to do a little spying for him without notifying Logan. Since Bob basically works for Logan, the situation caused some friction between the two men.

I sighed. "Why don't you just tell Logan. He'd understand."

Jack scowled. "Ha! He likes being in charge."

I shook my head as I made my way inside. I didn't want to be a part of their schemes. I knew a headache was just around the corner.

CHAPTER 2

Once Jack went back to the office, and Bob disappeared to do some spying, I decided a little house cleaning couldn't hurt. Sneaky spiders seemed to know they could exist much longer at our address than at Amy's. No bug in their right mind would dare cross her threshold—they knew better. She'd have them running so fast their little bug heads would spin. As I ran the vacuum cleaner through the house, I allowed my mind to mull over the newest wrinkle in township crime. I paused at the door of our oldest son's bedroom, which recently acquired a complete overhaul.

Bob and Nana worked together redecorating. The fact they're both dead gives them a huge advantage over those of us who still have heartbeats. Their ability to zip around town in a flash—looking for furniture, paint samples, carpeting, and curtains—was impressive. They also spent time searching the internet, but that required a living person hitting the 'next' button for hours while they looked for the perfect bedspread. I quickly lost patience being the page turner for the dead.

"It turned out pretty good ... didn't it?" Nana appeared to me exactly as I remembered her. Steel gray hair—which always looked as though she just walked out of her favorite hair salon with a fresh perm—sensible clothing, and a no-nonsense attitude. She basically raised me since my mom wasn't what would be considered 'mother of the year' material.

I smiled. "The room or Adam's visit?"

Nana grinned. "Both. She's a real sweetie."

Our oldest son, Adam, brought home his bride-to-be a few weeks ago to meet Andy and me. At the time, I was a nervous wreck trying to solve a drug crime case. Well … it was partly because I dreaded meeting the girl. Dad, knowing I was worried, verified she was a winner. When Adam walked in the door, it only took one look at her face and my gut told me she was the perfect match for him. Emily would fit nicely into our family.

"Yep," I agreed.

"You have to be careful nowadays. A lot of creepy people roaming around."

I nodded. "True. I appreciate everyone staying away during the visit. The last thing I needed was for my dead gang to be nosey."

Nana laughed. "Honey, we were all here. Even Henry popped in to check her out." Henry was another deceased guy who helped guard the house on our last case. He was from Atlanta, and he used to be a private eye back in the forties. I liked him at first glance, right down to his Humphrey Bogart fedora.

My mouth dropped open. "What? Logan also?"

The thought of the entire group of non-heartbeats milling around the house without my knowledge made my stomach knot. Andy and I deserved a little privacy … jeez.

Nana waved a dismissive hand. "Logan? No. He doesn't concern himself with romance stuff. He already had your dad check the girl to make sure she wasn't dangerous. Otherwise, he doesn't get involved with marriage plans."

I frowned. "Logan had Emily checked? Why? I knew Dad checked her out, but I thought it was for my benefit."

Nana began to fidget—never a good sign. "Just to ensure she was okay."

"In what way?" My gut told me that while there may not be a problem concerning Emily, there could be issues down the road. We have three other sons who would eventually want to marry.

Nana turned back to the curtains, inspecting every inch of the material for non-existing flaws. I recognized the dodge and refused to allow her to ignore my questions. "Nana!"

"Hmmm?" She looked at me innocently, pretending she had no clue what I was asking.

"This is important. You need to explain exactly why Logan would have Emily evaluated."

"Fine. I'll tell you even though I'm not supposed to say a word." She sighed. "Since you work for Logan, the bad guys on our side can maneuver someone, who is not necessarily healthy, into the boys' paths."

I sagged against the wall for support. The idea of dead creeps placing someone they are controlling in the path of my sons never entered my mind. Andy wouldn't be happy when he heard this complication. The poor guy was worried about our safety but now, I had to inform him of a new twist in our situation—he wasn't going to be a happy camper.

"Now don't get all upset. Why do you think your dad was sent to investigate her? Logan is pretty savvy about these things ... he thinks through all possibilities."

She was trying to make me feel better, but her words were having the opposite effect. I thought I would puke. I could feel sweat forming on my forehead and suddenly my inner temperature went wonky. Jeez ... a damn hot flash. The first one in weeks, and it had to hit now.

Noticing my discomfort, Nana nodded. "I told you those suckers weren't over. Menopause is unpredictable. It could take years to finally be rid of every symptom."

Ignoring her reference to my change of life issues, I sighed. "No one told me the boys could be dragged into this mess."

Nana watched me hesitantly. "You should've been able to figure it out on your own. I'm a little surprised Andy didn't realize ... he's pretty smart."

I ignored her slam on my intelligence and stuck to the issue which concerned me the most. "So, the boys could be in danger." It was not a question.

"Oh for heaven's sake! I told you ... Logan watches for problems. He sent people to guard the boys."

"Guard the boys?" I stared at her stunned. "He never said a word." Whether or not my stomach contents would stay put became a toss-up—I hoped they would.

Nana shrugged, unconcerned with my stomach. "Well ... he wouldn't. When does Logan ever give you more information than you need?"

The hot flash began to subside, but my anger was on the rise.

"He should've said something! I don't want the boys dragged into this mess!"

"Their involvement was inevitable. We have discussed the danger evil presents to everyone." Logan's voice came from the hall behind me.

I turned to face him. Every time I see Logan, I almost catch my breath. I have no idea what Indian tribe he was part of because he didn't divulge information easily. His attire was usually what I came to consider *Indian casual*—leggings, animal skin clothing, one braid in his long, black hair, and beads around his neck. His appearance was quite impressive in normal attire, but when he wants to make a statement, he's positively regal. The mayor of Akron learned the hard way that Logan knows how to awe anyone of his choosing.

"When were you going to tell me that the boys could be harmed?" I pushed myself off the wall and stood as tall as possible. When you are five feet, one inch you really have to stretch the spine, but I gave it my best try.

Logan studied my face before answering. "Peg, every living person is at risk. You should understand the dangers by now."

"But the boys are more at risk because I work with you, correct?" My temper was well known, and Logan endured my many flare ups with deliberate calm.

He gave a brief nod. "Possibly. I have provided each of your sons with protection."

I groaned. "Logan, I don't have the energy to worry about the boys being sucked into this chaos. It's bad enough Andy has to cope with my new lifestyle without dragging the kids into it too."

Logan turned to look out the window. I don't know what the guy would do if he didn't have a window to provide him with an excuse to ignore me.

Nana began to get nervous with our argument and tried signaling me to back off. I shook my head but remained quiet. In the past, I've out waited Logan when I wanted answers he was hesitant to give. It doesn't always work but today … it did.

"I believe we have the capacity to protect your sons satisfactorily. Their well-being is important to me."

"Why?" I demanded.

He turned to face me. "Because it is important to you."

Well, hell … his statement sure shut my mouth. I felt tears form, but I fought them back.

I sighed. "Maybe you decided at some point they will be part of your little army?"

Logan turned back to the window. I knew I pushed as far as possible for this chat.

"I must be going … work to do." Nana faded before I had a chance to stop her. She sure didn't want me to drag her into my squabble with Logan.

I turned my attention back to Logan. "Any particular reason you're here?"

"I believe Jack is facing township robberies."

"Yep. I talked to the guys out back, but they aren't sure what exactly is happening."

Logan turned to me, surprise written all over his face. "You have spoken with the men in the woods?"

I nodded. "Yep." There was no sense in informing him that Henry was the one who gave me the idea during our last case. I liked Henry, and I didn't want to cause him trouble with Logan.

Logan continued to stare at me, and I stared right back. I learned you have to hold your own with Logan. Amy proved she has a steel spine, and she is so much better at handling Logan than I ever have been—I usually blow a gasket while she uses logic to make a point. Logic and I have never been real good friends—I'm more of a gut instinct kind of gal.

After a few more moments of silent staring, Logan returned to window gazing.

I sighed. "Do you know anything about the robberies Jack should be aware of?"

He drew a deep breath. "I am concerned."

Uh oh. "About what?" If Logan was worried it was time for me to sweat more.

He inclined his head towards the woods. "They are reacting to the illegal activity."

I looked out back. "Yep … but at least it's only the normal guys." When situations became really complicated the Indians were joined by British soldiers, woodsmen, and even Vikings—it got pretty crowded out there sometimes.

He gave brief nod. "For now."

Jeez … talk about a pessimist. I continued unhindered by his attitude. "Jack might have the case wrapped up soon."

His eyes remained on the woods. "I fear the situation may prove to be complicated."

I narrowed my eyes. "How complicated?"

He turned toward me. "I am unsure of the nature of the problem." He frowned thoughtfully as he turned back toward the window. "The lack of knowledge causes uncertainty."

Yeah … I absolutely hated when Logan had limited information about a crime—it made my life miserable.

"Well … look at it this way … it can't be the mob because these are minor break-ins … plus, Sal would have inside info he would share. It also can't be teenagers because Jack's been keeping an eye on the usual trouble makers. The kids are back in school, and the robberies are being committed during the day. Your guys out back also told me it wasn't kids. So … we've knocked out two groups already."

Logan turned to look at me again. "Yes … I suppose we could consider your views as progress. Your logic is sound."

I snorted. "I don't use logic … it's common sense."

He ignored my comment and continued on. "However, I believe a few of the problems happened during the night hours. If not boys from Bath, the culprits could still be young."

I frowned slightly. "What makes you think boys are committing the crimes? Girls can be pretty vicious themselves." A thought suddenly sprang into my mind. "You don't think Mom is involved … do you?"

"Ah, Nell." He went silent, contemplating my question.

His silence prompted me to find out more. "Is she still locked up over in Deadsville prison?"

Logan winced at my use of the name I gave the other side. Heaven somehow ceased to be the word I used once I became aware of the lifestyle over there. The more I discovered, the more my view of the afterlife plunged—go figure.

"Yes, the committee has not arrived at their verdict concerning your mother. Elaine was recently released against my advice. There are strict guidelines we follow. She has not broken enough of the rules yet. Your mother, however, has proven she has questionable motives."

Elaine broke about a million rules in Deadsville and endured an interrogation by Sal, our local mobster turned good guy. It came as a huge shock to everyone, especially her husband Bob, that she was the niece of a mob king. She and her mother were despised by their family, so they had limited contact with them. That was the reason poor Bob never suspected her unsavory connections to the mob. Sal recognized her immediately, but her true problem was her friendship with my mother. Compared to Mom, Elaine was a babe in arms. Mom's rule breaking probably landed somewhere around the gazillion mark, and she was a huge troublemaker on the other side of life—it was a mess.

I scoffed. "Nice way of describing her selfishness and pure mean spirit."

Logan smiled but kept further opinions of my mother to himself.

I thought for a moment, then posed another question. "Do you think Elaine is capable of causing this much trouble?"

He nodded. "It is possible. She has learned much from your mother."

I rubbed my forehead—any thoughts of my mother gave me a headache. "What do you want me to do? Unless I have some type of info to go on, I have no idea where to start."

"Read Jack's files … it is a beginning." Logan began to fade and since I had no more questions, I waved. He smiled as he disappeared completely.

I heard my dad's chuckle coming from the hallway, and I couldn't help but smile. "Hey, Dad."

He grinned at me. "Hi, Twinkle Toes. Is Logan driving you nuts again?"

I sighed. "Dragging information out of the guy is like pulling chewed gum from the carpet … almost impossible."

Dad's grin grew wider. "Sometimes I believe he enjoys the banter he has with you."

I scowled slightly. "He sure doesn't appear to enjoy our little talks when my temper flares."

Dad shook his head, grin still in place. "Don't be so sure … he likes you."

I shrugged. Logan is a strange guy in some ways, but he has incredible control of his emotions. I was confident he liked me enough to keep me alive, at least most of the time, but I wouldn't bet the farm on the idea he liked me to the point of always tolerating my moods. Amy and I sort of ganged up on him during the major investigation and I could've sworn the poor guy was shocked by our attitudes. Serves the old Indian right … he was taking us for granted, so we blasted him for it.

I turned my attention back to my Dad and the case. "Is there any chance you've been snooping around the township for me?"

He shook his head, still smiling slightly. "Sorry, babe … I've been busy."

He had my full attention now. Seeing my dad after so many years was overwhelming at first, but I loved having him back in my life. He almost always wore the plaid shirt I gave him the last Father's Day we spent together while he was alive. He was a tall, beefy guy who played football in high school. I remember his dark hair and kind eyes, and he hadn't aged a day since I last saw him alive. Since the dead choose how they appear to us, it warmed my heart that he chose to wear something I gave him. His presence made me feel warm and safe.

"Busy?" One thing I've learned these past few months, is when the dead become evasive … it's time to ask questions … a lot of them.

He gave a brief nod. "Yep."

"Doing what?" I persisted.

He shrugged. "Work."

My eyes narrowed as I continued to watch him carefully. "What type of work?" Trying to get answers out of him was like pulling teeth.

His eyes twinkled with amusement. "Stuff for Logan."

"Stuff … anything I need to know about?" My headache was increasing, so I knew I was on the right track with my line of questioning, or maybe I was merely tired of having to drag information from my buddies with no heartbeats.

"Not at present." He sighed. "Sweetie … if anything pops that you should know about, then I'll tell you."

I scoffed. "Sure. I know how this works. I'm given details only at the last possible moment before someone blows my head off."

Dad laughed. "We aren't that bad."

I crossed my arms and stared at him, my stubborn streak was starting to surface. "I beg to differ. Jack has a conniption fit every investigation involving you guys. Logan doesn't bother telling us anything until he's forced to."

"He shared a lot last time," Dad reminded me.

"Yeah … after Amy and I chewed his butt out but even then, he hesitated."

Dad frowned slightly. "Be fair! Logan has a lot on his mind."

"I've heard that phrase too many times for comfort. What exactly is on Logan's mind?"

Dad shook his head. "I'm not sure, but he's certainly not happy."

Jeez … the last thing I needed was for Logan's head to be elsewhere. We needed him, and I wasn't going to pretend otherwise.

"Have you spoken to Jack? Logan wants me to study the files on the burglaries." I sighed, shaking my head slowly. "I doubt my eyes will pick up anything new. Jack's the expert … not me."

Dad chuckled. "Don't be so quick to downplay your abilities. You're the one who seems to find the problems."

I scoffed. "I don't find the problems, they seem to find me."

He grinned. "True. You do seem to attract the bad guys."

I moaned. "All I want is a nice, quiet life … boring is good."

Dad changed the subject. "Do you like Emily?"

I raised an eyebrow. "Yes, but she seems a little too good to be true."

He cocked his head. "Are you jealous?"

"No." I sighed heavily. "I want Adam to be happy. Emily seems to be perfect … a little too perfect."

He shook his head smiling. "There's no pleasing you today."

I continued on, ignoring his comment. "Andy loved her immediately."

His smile widened. "There ya go! You trust Andy's instinct, right?"

I nodded. "I have nothing against her, but Adam worships the ground she walks on. It just makes me nervous."

"I checked her out thoroughly … she's fine. She has a great job where she makes good money. She is also smart and can hold her own. Adam needs a girl like her."

I agreed, but I was feeling a little stubborn. "Maybe."

He grinned. "You're just being a momma hen."

I shrugged. "Probably."

"Hey, Peg?" Bob was back, and he sounded upset.

I frowned. "What's wrong?"

"The Vikings are out there." He pointed toward the woods.

My frown deepened as I looked in the direction he was pointing. "Oh, for Pete's sake … now what?"

CHAPTER 3

Dad disappeared, and I had a good idea where he went. I'd bet dollars to donuts he was in the woods talking with the guys. I hoped he discovered what had them gathering. The Vikings were usually the last people to show up when there was a problem—their arrival indicated the degree of seriousness. I wasn't thrilled that they were already present—things were escalating quickly.

I looked at Bob. "Do you have any idea what's going on around here?"

He shook his head, his face full of worry. "I don't think even Logan knows what the heck is happening. This is not a good situation."

I made my way back to the kitchen and plopped down in my chair. My fingers drummed on the table as I watched Dad talk with our new arrivals. It amazed me to learn the Vikings made their way so far inland hundreds of years ago. I sure don't remember any history lessons that taught such a juicy morsel of information.

"Peg, do you think the robberies have brought those guys here?" The concern in Bob's voice was as thick as molasses. For a dead guy, Bob sure worried a lot.

"I have no idea." My eyes were glued to the Viking talking with Dad. Their appearance was pretty much how I imagined—fur hats, wool tunics, and leather belts. Their belts had knives and other tools hanging from them. Their huge fur cloaks and the leather boots they wore looked warm. None of their clothing surprised me—they were from Scandinavia after all. It was way too cold there for me … I barely survive Ohio winters.

My fingers were dancing on the table, and my gut was in alert mode. Problem was … I had no idea what I should be alert about, and that made my stomach knot.

"Why are the Vikings here but not the Brits?" I wondered aloud.

Bob shrugged. "Does it make a difference?"

I rubbed my head for no reason other than to give my hands something new to occupy them. "Vikings are usually the last of the gang to arrive. If they show up, then the trouble is massive." I frowned. "But they are here before the Brits."

Bob was thoughtful for a moment. "Wow … I never knew there was an order to their appearance."

I sighed. "I'm not totally positive there really is, but they tend to appear in a particular order. Maybe it's a time frame deal rather than danger signal."

Bob's eyes were glued to the men in the woods. "Who shows up first?"

"Well … the Indians are always there whether I can see them or not. The Brits are usually the second to arrive, then the hunters, and finally the Vikings. I assumed they came in order depending on the level of danger. Now … I'm not so sure. Maybe it depends on when the guys were actually here in time."

Bob shook his head. "It can't be time frame."

I frowned slightly. "Why not?"

He pulled his gaze from the men out back to look at me. "Indians were here first, that's a given."

I nodded in agreement.

"However, before the British soldiers had a reason to come this far inland, you had hunters and trappers." Bob screwed up his face while he thought through old, forgotten history lessons.

"Damn … you're right."

He nodded. "Yep. My question is … why aren't there any American soldiers?"

I thought about his question for a moment. It never crossed my mind to wonder about the lack of American soldiers to add to the group out back. "Good question."

Bob glanced out back, then returned to deep thinking, which wasn't one of his strong suits. "We didn't really have any Revolutionary War battles here in Ohio. There was the siege of Fort Laurens back in 1778, but I don't think it counts. The War of 1812 is a little bit of a different story. Over near Toledo, there was the siege of Fort Meigs and of course the Battle of Lake Erie in 1813. It was one of the turning points of the war because it cut off the Great Lakes from the British, hindering their supply lines to their troops."

My mouth dropped open for a moment. "I had no idea you knew so much history." I was impressed with his knowledge.

Bob shrugged. "Elaine hated history, so I didn't talk much with her about it. Guess I got into the habit of keeping historical information to myself."

I was intrigued with this new aspect of Bob's personality. "Where'd you learn so much?"

"Books mostly, but it helps that we can travel in time." His focus was on Dad and the Vikings, so he missed my jaw dropping to the floor.

"You can what?" My voice raised to what would be considered yelling.

Bob frowned. "What?"

"You can travel in *time*?"

His face turned beet red. "Gosh, Peg … I shouldn't have told you … it's a huge secret." He looked around the room. "Please don't tell anyone … I'll get in big trouble."

"Since when can dead people time travel?" I demanded.

Bob sighed. "Peg, we live outside of time. Once you're dead you aren't tied to a physical world. The laws of physics don't apply anymore."

"But you are still in the universe, so physics would apply." As I spoke, I was trying to remember high school science class. Where was Amy when I needed her?

Bob shook his head. "Nope … we aren't *tied* to the universe. It's sorta complicated."

I stared at him while my mind ran around in circles. Finally, I was able to form a question. "How far back in time can you go?"

"It takes years to accomplish anything close to impressive. Personally, I can only go back through my life span. Logan probably has the ability to go back as far as he wishes … the guy has tons of talent."

My fingers started drumming on the table again. This new information would take me a while to digest. "Can you change events?"

He shook his head. "Gosh … no … even Logan couldn't manage that. Anyway, we aren't allowed to alter events even if we could."

"Bob, if there is a rule saying you can't alter anything, then it probably *is* possible."

Bob's face dropped. "I never thought of it quite that way before."

Poor Bob … he had a hard time connecting the dots sometimes.

I sighed. "Rules are put into place for a reason. If it was impossible there would be no need for the rule."

He nodded. "Yeah, I see what you mean."

I watched him carefully. "Have you ever tried to change anything?"

He shook his head. "I didn't give it a thought. I figured if they said we couldn't, then well … it wasn't possible."

Jeez.

"So … you were told you *couldn't*, not that it's impossible." I figured I'd clarify the situation for him.

He thought through my statement, then nodded sheepishly. "Yeah … you're right. I took it to mean it was hopeless to try, not that we'd better not change anything."

"Did Logan ever tell you anything about his experience with time travel?"

Bob shook his head. "He never discusses it … almost like it doesn't exist."

I frowned thoughtfully. "Does he know you can go back and revisit your own life?"

"Oh sure … just about everyone does it eventually." He shrugged. "It's sorta like living your life again except now you watch events rather than participate."

I smiled, shaking my head slightly. "Bob … sometimes you amaze even me with your simple way of looking at life."

He looked at the floor. "I'm not stupid, but I know I miss aspects of situations."

"I never said you were stupid, but there are times you don't pay enough attention to understand the circumstances."

He smiled. "Elaine always did say I didn't bother with any details."

I groaned. "If you can time travel, then Elaine probably can too."

His eyes grew huge. "Uh oh … I never thought she figured it out. I sure never told her."

My eyebrows raised in slight confusion. "Who told you?"

He shook his head firmly. "We aren't allowed to give the living that type of information."

He wasn't supposed to tell me about their ability to time travel either, but there was no reason to point out the obvious.

"I'm only asking because the same person probably explained the time travel stuff to her too … think of it as school orientation. You're given the rules and regulations, then told what's expected."

He nodded. "I will tell you it did remind me of school. There's a big meeting with all the newly arrived, and we are told how life goes on. It takes forever for those guys to explain the new chapter of life. At one point, I thought of leaving the seminar and finding something more interesting to do, but Elaine refused to budge. She wanted to find someone who would send us back to the land of the living."

I shrugged. "She believed her life was cut short, so she wanted someone to fix it."

He nodded. "Yep."

"Do you think she paid attention to this orientation meeting?"

Bob's face scrunched as he taxed his brain to remember the meeting in question. "I don't think so. She was so mad about the whole dead part her mind was pretty much focused on getting back here."

I thought about Elaine's friends on the other side and decided there was a huge chance someone like my mother probably filled her in concerning the time travel stuff—just my luck.

Bob came to the same conclusion. "Your mother probably told her."

I sighed. "Yeah … I agree."

"Well … on the bright side, she probably can't do much more than I can at this point. Even your mother couldn't push enough to force abilities."

Seeing my confused expression, he explained.

"It takes loads of time to learn simple essentials. Heck … when we first met you, we had no idea how to perform even the basic skills. Remember when I didn't know how to reappear to you?"

I nodded.

"We were way behind the curve, and I had to work really hard to achieve even beginner stuff." He shrugged. "Elaine didn't practice at all."

I snorted. "I bet she's honed her skills by now."

Bob shook his head. "Maybe, maybe not. Elaine is a smart lady, but she's not what I would call *active*. Your mother has tons of energy and zips around stirring up all sorts of trouble." He shook his head again. "Elaine doesn't lift a finger unless forced. When we ran our business, she drove me nuts waiting until the last minute to take everything to the accountant during tax season. We had to file an extension every darn year. You know how much an accountant charges for filing one piece of paper? Too much!"

Wow … I'd never seen Bob so worked up. Come to think of it, I'd never heard Bob talk much about his business while he … um … had a heartbeat.

"What happened to your business after … you know … the murder." I stumbled over the words, hoping I wasn't prying too much.

Bob shrugged. "Never gave it a thought to be honest. I did check on the house though. Whoever bought it sure keeps it in good shape."

I was a little surprised. "You never wondered what happened to your business?"

"Nah. I never did want to own a Porsche dealership." He paused as he thought back through his life. "Selling Fords would've been nice though."

I nodded. His comment reminded me of the only other time I've seen him angry rather than frightened concerning Elaine. During the investigation of their murders, Bob blew up big time at her, which I'm sure he paid for later.

"Once I found out about her family being the mob, I understood why she wanted a fancy car dealership and a big house. She grew up in that environment and was determined to continue in the same lifestyle."

I was thoughtful for a moment. "I'm surprised she married outside of the mob world."

"I've given this some thought, and I'll bet money none of their friends would date her much less go the marriage route."

"How'd you meet her?" I was honestly intrigued, which surprised the heck out of me.

He sighed. "One of my friends was dating her cousin. It was a blind date, and all I saw was her beauty."

I nodded. "Yep … a pretty face catches a lot of guys."

He shook his head. "It wasn't just that … she was fun back then. She had a pretty good sense of humor and enjoyed being around people."

I frowned. "What happened?"

He shrugged. "No idea. We got married, and I thought I was the luckiest man in the world. I was never what you'd call a prize catch, but here I was … married to a beautiful girl with a great personality. It didn't take long for it to change."

I frowned, slightly confused. "Did she think she was marrying someone with lots of money?"

He shook his head. "Nope. She said she saw potential, and she thought I'd make something of myself. I guess I didn't do it fast enough for her."

"She never wanted children?" I knew I was prying, but Bob never talked much about his life before, and I wasn't about to let the opportunity slip by me.

"Yeah … another little surprise after the wedding. She hated kids and wanted nothing to do with them. I was shocked. We'd talked about having a family, and she seemed all for it."

I sighed. "Bob … it sounds as though Elaine married you for a particular reason."

He frowned. "What do you mean?"

I gave myself time to gather my thoughts before I answered. "Look at it this way … Elaine was accustomed to a particular way of living. Nice house, designer clothes, expensive shoes, and flashy cars. Right?"

He nodded, but I knew he would probably miss the point if I wasn't extremely blunt, which would hurt his feelings. "What type of job did you have when you two were dating?"

His face cleared. "I was an auto mechanic. The money was decent, and she seemed …" His voice faltered as his eyes met mine, making me realize the penny had dropped. "She never loved me." His voice was flat, and I knew his ego had taken a wallop.

"I didn't say she never loved you." I was trying to give him a little bit of hope.

"You didn't have to say it." He sighed. "No wonder our marriage was rocky."

"I think it's important you take time and consider *why* she married you. It could help us cope with her now."

He nodded slowly. "Yes … you may have found the key to working with her." He looked at me. "Do you think if we understood her motives she might stop working for the … um … bad side?"

No way, but I kept that nugget of info to myself. "Ya never know."

He rubbed his brow. "Do you have any idea why she would marry someone like me?"

I studied him a moment. "Bob, you're a sweet guy. A little goofy sometimes, but sweet. You care about the people in your life, and you try your best to protect them. Don't judge yourself through Elaine's eyes. She had ulterior motives for marrying you, but it doesn't mean they were *bad* reasons."

He sighed heavily. "I assumed she loved me. Why marry someone and commit to a lifetime together if you don't love the person?"

I could think of a gazillion people who marry for stupid reasons, but I had no idea why Elaine chose Bob. I was convinced the answer would aid in dealing with her, but until we analyzed the situation, we would be in the dark. We had bigger problems to work through first. I looked at Bob. "Do you think you can put this on the back burner for the time being while we decide why I have Vikings milling around the yard?"

He nodded miserably. "Yeah … I'll try. Just sorta hit me, ya know?"

I smiled sadly. "I'm sorry Bob."

"It's not your problem, Peg. I'll think about it and maybe discover what Elaine was up to."

Dad popped back into the kitchen. "What's not your problem?"

I sighed. "Elaine."

He gave us both a questioning look. "Oh … Anything I need to know?"

Before Bob could start a long-winded explanation, I cut him off. "Nothing really new. Logan said she's out of heaven prison though."

Bob paled. "Oh, my gosh … I didn't know."

I frowned. "Logan didn't tell you? That's a little odd, don't you think?"

Bob shrugged. "He's a funny one. He really doesn't like to share much."

Dad and I exchanged a glance but kept our mouths closed. I could tell Dad was as surprised as I was that Logan hadn't warned Bob that his wife was on the loose.

I decided to pull the conversation back to the immediate problem. I looked at Dad. "What did the Viking guy tell you?"

"They aren't happy with the robberies. Given their history of invading their neighbors, if they think it's a big deal, then it's probably something to worry about."

I was getting more confused by the situation. "I'm having a hard time believing a few burglaries are so important. We've had problems before, and no one hit the panic button."

Dad was thoughtful for a moment. "Have you checked in with Jack?"

I shook my head. "Not yet. Logan wants me to read the files Jack has. He's hoping I find some type of lead. I think Logan's nuts, but going to the police station is on my list for today."

Dad nodded, then glanced at Bob. "Bob, why don't you join Peg. You may be able to contribute to their discussion."

I looked over at Dad, surprised, but I didn't argue. He must have a darn good reason for having Bob tag along with me. I wanted to smack him, but I knew it wouldn't do a bit of good since I have no ability to actually make physical contact with my friends from Deadsville.

Bob nodded but had none of his usual enthusiasm for our road trip.

Dad shot me a questioning glance. I shook my head, hoping he was able to decipher some sort of message.

I looked at Bob, deciding it was time to get moving. "Come on, Bob. We might as well get this over with. I don't think we'll discover any earth shattering information, but Logan is under the assumption we'll hit gold."

Preoccupied with his own worries, Bob looked up startled. "Where are we going?"

Dad frowned and looked at me again.

I sighed. "Jack's office to look at robbery reports."

"Oh … okay." He frowned. "Do you think it will help?"

I shook my head. "Who knows, but I might as well get my butt in gear and head to the police station." I stood and grabbed my oversized purse.

Dad cleared his throat. "Don't forget your cellphone." Dad missed out on cellphones and regretted not living long enough to enjoy the invention.

I nodded, then picked it up off the kitchen table. "Let me know if any of our other guys show up out back. I'm worried because the Vikings are already on site."

Dad nodded. "I agree."

Jeez Louise.

CHAPTER 4

It didn't take me long to make my way to Jack's office. It was only a mile or so away from my house. One of these days, I'd take the bull by the horns and walk there to give my body some much needed exercise—today wasn't that day. I parked the car a few steps away from the back door of the building, then made my way through the hallways of the police station. Our police force is small compared to bigger cities, but it was effective. The force has seasoned veterans who have been part of our community for their entire careers, so they understand the pulse of the people.

I waved at the dispatcher as I walked by, and she nodded. She still wouldn't crack a smile, but one of these days she'd thaw. Once it turned out Bob and Elaine's murderer was one our own, an admired cop, some of the staff transferred their shock at the discovery in my direction, so they were still uncomfortable in my presence. Jack assured me numerous times it wasn't personal, but it sure was uncomfortable.

I poked my head in his office as I knocked on the door. He was on the phone, but he waved for me to take a seat. I happily sank into the chair across from his desk. He bought it himself after sitting in a million office chairs to make sure he purchased one comfortable enough for any visitor's butt. I waited patiently for his call to end, by occupying my time with a quick glance around to see if there were any changes since my last visit. It didn't take long to decide there were no new modifications.

Once he hung up the phone, he leaned back in his chair and studied me until I began to squirm. "Any news?"

"Logan sent me to read the reports on the robberies." I shrugged. "I don't think it will do any good, but you know how Logan is sometimes."

He nodded. "Yep. He came by earlier, so I was expecting you. I agree you probably won't see anything we haven't, but a miracle could happen."

I sighed. "I'm not sure what he's expecting me to find."

Jack laughed. "I have to admit, sometimes you do stumble across new information. I've been over these files a hundred times, and I haven't seen anything worthwhile." He handed me a stack of folders.

I frowned. "Wow … more than I anticipated." I thumbed through them quickly, then looked up at him. "Have you heard of any other surrounding areas having the same problem?"

He pointed to the phone on his desk. "I just got off the phone with the police chief in Hudson. They've had a handful recently. Same scenario … minor robberies with no personal injuries."

Hudson is an upscale community about fifteen miles from our township. From what I've heard, the shopping there is great, but I hate the entire 'shop till you drop experience', so I'm no expert.

I looked around the office for Bob. I spotted him by the window, staring at the window frame. I knew his mind was on our earlier conversation.

I looked back at Jack. "Bob's here."

Jack glanced over and nodded. "Is he your guard?"

I frowned. "I'm not sure."

Jack's eyebrow raised, but he didn't ask for an explanation. Probably figured I'd tell him later.

I snapped my fingers as I realized I had information to share.

"I know these break-ins aren't committed by anyone in the township." I tapped the folders in my lap.

He watched me carefully. "Okay … I'll bite. How do you know?"

"An Indian in the woods told me. He mentioned they couldn't see *who* the culprit is, but they are positive no one from the township is involved." I sat back satisfied with myself.

A voice from the doorway interrupted our conversation. "Chief … I hate to interrupt, but we have a problem."

I looked up and smiled at Dougal MacMillian—my new favorite rookie. His tall stature and shock of red hair made it obvious he was from Scottish heritage, even if his name didn't register that fact with some moron. He fixed my peeling wallpaper in the kitchen, which ended up saving my butt during a big drug case we worked on together.

He threw me a quick smile, then turned his attention back to Jack.

Jack watched him warily. "What's up?"

Dougal looked a little grim. "Dead body this time."

Jack sighed. "Shit."

Dougal nodded. "Yes, sir." Smart man … he kept his remarks short and simple.

Jack shook his head in disbelief. "I'll be right with you."

Dougal nodded, then his face disappeared from the doorway.

"The Vikings must know more than they're telling you." Bob spoke with his eyes still focused on the woodwork.

Jack's eyes widened. "Vikings? You're kidding."

"Nope." I turned to Bob, frowning slightly. "What makes you think they're holding back? Dad talked with them."

Bob shook his head. "Something's off. I can't put my finger on it, but if they've already shown up, whatever is going on is big."

I looked at the ceiling and sighed. "Bob, I don't want a mess."

He shrugged. "I know."

Jack listened to our short exchange, his face etched with concern. "I'm used to bad guys withholding information but when the good guys start …" He shook his head. "… there is trouble brewing somewhere. Logan doesn't seem to understand that concept."

I drummed my fingers on the stack of folders in my lap. Logan must be involved somehow, but I couldn't decide why he would allow information to be kept from us again. He seemed quite concerned with the burglaries, and I had to believe he had a damn good reason in mind to pull any sneaky Pete stuff.

Jack stood and looked at me. "Are you coming?"

"To the crime scene? Sure." I stuffed the folders in my purse, then turned to Bob. "Are you planning on staring at wood all day, or are you coming with us?"

Bob turned toward me. "I'll meet you there if I can."

I frowned. "If you can?"

"I have an errand to run." For once in his life, Bob wasn't blabbing his plans.

I shook my head. "Fine." I turned and followed Jack to the parking lot.

Jack glanced at me. "Are you riding with me or taking your own car?"

I thought a split second. "I'll take my own. Where is this place?"

Jack looked at the paper in his hand. "Off of Ira Road."

"I'll follow you." I dug into the vast pit of my purse looking for car keys.

He nodded. "Sounds good."

I followed Jack, and due to the lack of traffic, I didn't have to be worried about losing him. Ira Road was a couple miles from the police station. It was a nice, straight road; it had few nasty twists and turns like many of the roads in the township. I forgot to ask if we were turning left or right at the light signal, but I wasn't concerned since his car was in plain sight.

I was worried about Bob's emotional state and Logan's lack of information. The last thing I needed was for both of them to fly off the rails during an investigation. I found my mind drifting as I reflected on both men. I almost missed spotting Jack's right turn onto Ira Road.

Ira Road had an old cemetery that was established in 1829. There were about two hundred recorded burials, and local lore claimed the place was haunted. I decided to have Bob check it out when we were done with this case—it might prove interesting.

We turned into a subdivision that was built about fifty years ago. Homes were modest but nice; a lot of them were newer than my farmhouse. Jack pulled up behind the police cruisers lined up. I spotted an ambulance— probably there to haul away the victim in the house. I took a deep breath when I realized this would be my first dead body. Well … newly dead. I was comfortable with my dead guys because they looked normal. I had no idea what was facing me inside the house.

Jack must've realized the same thing because he looked hesitant as I walked over to him. "Peg, you don't have to go in there. We've never had you witness a murder victim quite this way before."

I nodded. "I might as well see what I can handle." I felt my stomach lurch, but I was determined to push myself a little.

With a quick nod he started toward the house, and I trailed after him. I noticed Dougal beat us to the scene and was guarding the door.

He frowned as I approached. "Mrs. Shaw … are you sure you want to go inside?"

I shook my head. "Nope, but I need to at least be in there."

Dougal nodded. "Stay to the left when you go inside. The body is in the living room which is on the right. Don't let your eyes stray."

I nodded. "Sounds like a plan."

Jack scooted in while I was talking with Dougal. I took a deep breath, then headed inside. There was more noise than I anticipated—the source was a house full of cops and emergency rescue workers. They were practically bumping into each other as they went about their duties.

An officer was explaining things to Jack as I approached. "The struggle started in here."

Keeping my eyes busy on anything other than the dead body, I glanced around the room. Furniture looked new and at first glance, the living room held no photos that I could see. The color scheme was typical bachelor— bland and boring. I liked it. The guy was neat as a pin—no socks on the floor, no dust gathering in sneaky places, and the air was fresh as though he recently aired the house. The only mess was the one made by whoever murdered the poor guy.

Jack nodded as his eyes took in the scene before us. I never really had a chance to observe him in action, and I had to admit he was impressive. As Jack pointed to items on the floor, the officer continued. "We believe the vase and clock were knocked over during the fight. It appears the victim arrived home during the robbery."

Jack nodded again, his eyes never stopped scanning the room. I could almost hear the gears in his mind grinding as he inspected every nook and cranny without moving from the spot he seemed to be glued to. "Who was the owner?"

The officer glanced down at his notebook. "Mr. David Peters ... divorced, no children, age forty-two."

"Wow ... you have all that information this fast?" I was shocked.

After a quick glance at Jack, who nodded, the officer responded. "Yes, ma'am ... it's routine."

I surveyed the room slowly. To my untrained eyes, it looked like a mess and nothing jumped out at me. I stubbornly refused to look toward the area where the victim lay, but my peripheral vision made me realize Mr. Peters' entire body was covered with a sheet. I was thankful for the sheet, but I still forced my eyes not to stray.

Floyd's quiet voice spoke from behind me. "Hey Peg."

I turned to look at him. "Hi Floyd. I wondered if you'd be here."

Floyd was a crime scene cleaner and a great handyman. In his spare time, he redecorate Adam's boyhood bedroom. He made it into a lovely guestroom just in time for my son's and his new fiancé's visit. Floyd could also see ghosts, and he informed us of his ability when he was cleaning the crime scene at my house during the last case.

His eyes darted to Jack, then back to me. I shook my head. Logan insisted we keep Floyd's talents a secret; he wasn't even willing to let Jack know. Floyd nodded, then quietly waited until the cops were finished with their investigation.

I looked at him. "How long does this take?"

He shrugged. "Depends on the crime." He glanced around. "This one looks pretty cut and dry. They're almost finished taking fingerprints, then it's my turn."

"Do you see anyone?" I whispered, leaning closer to him.

He shook his head. "Not yet. I usually don't until it quiets down, and everyone leaves. For some reason, they don't like the chaos." He was careful to whisper back to me.

I nodded. Floyd can see and hear the victims of homicides as he cleans the crime scenes. He has his own rules ... such as never making eye contact with them or allowing them to know he is aware of them. Victims have a need to tell him everything that took place during their murders, but they didn't seem to realize he could hear them. Logan asked him to join our efforts, and I suspect his talents will come in handy.

"Call me later if you discover anything helpful," I whispered.

He nodded. "Yep."

Jack walked over to me. "Anything?"

I gave him a questioning look. "Such as?"

He waved his arms around. "I don't know … anything useful."

My eyes scanned the room again. "It's a mess. Otherwise … nothing."

Jack snorted. "A lot of good you are." He stomped over to the victim, and I averted my eyes.

Floyd leaned toward me. "Don't react, but Mr. Peters is over by the fireplace."

"Thanks." I slowly let my eyes wander through the room again, stopping when I spotted the dead guy. He was good looking in a Cary Grant sort of way. He was tall and slender but not too thin. He had light brown hair that was recently trimmed. I felt so sorry for him when I noticed the confusion on his face.

I looked back at Floyd. "Does he have any idea what's happened?"

Floyd shrugged. "He's probably trying to make sense of the situation. It seems to take them a bit of time before they realize they are dead. By the time the cops are gone, the facts settle and they start the process of accepting their murder."

I shook my head sadly. "It's so sad."

Jack turned and motioned for me to join him. I wasn't thrilled by the prospect, but since I've seen the man's ghost, I decided I could handle looking at his body.

I reached Jack in five steps, then he pointed to the body. "Do you know this guy?"

"What would make you think I know a total stranger?" My irritation started to climb, and I knew a hot flash was not far behind.

He shrugged. "Just making sure."

I threw him a dirty look, but he ignored my attitude.

I took a breath and shut my eyes. Slowly, I opened one eye, then the other. I frowned. The man did look a little familiar, but his name certainly didn't ring any bells. Since I just studied his ghost, I wasn't surprised I couldn't help Jack identify the guy.

Jack noticed the change in my expression. "So … you do know him."

I slowly shook my head. "No … not really. He looks familiar, but I have no idea why. Maybe I've seen him at the grocery store or gas station."

Jack's face fell. "Damn … I was hoping you would know something."

"Jack, this is a small township. We probably run into people constantly and don't bother to register the fact … post office, grocery store, bank …" I began rattling off the numerous places we see total strangers before he interrupted.

"Fine, I get it."

I cocked my head and studied his face for a moment. "Jack, did you really expect me to know the poor guy?"

He looked at the floor. "It was a long shot."

"What difference would it make? Even if I knew him, I don't know how you think it would help."

He looked me square in the eyes. "Peg, if *you* know someone, there's a good chance it's a lead." He held up his hands when I tried to argue. "Face it … you attract trouble like honey attracts flies. I was hoping you'd at least know who he was … it would've been a start."

I shrugged but worked hard to keep my temper under control. *I* didn't invite problems, they sorta found me all by themselves … jeez.

He read my face, then shook his head. "Don't get mad at me, but it's the damn truth!" He looked around and frowned. "Where's Bob? I thought he was joining us."

Surprised, I glanced around the room—no Bob in sight.

"He realized Elaine might not have married him for love, and it has him in knots."

Jack frowned, confused. "He's dead! Why does he care now?"

I sighed. "He's insecure enough without this piece of information roaming around his head."

Jack shook his head. "He's scared to death of her."

I nodded. "He's not alone."

We stood to one side as the paramedics hauled off the gurney that held the newly deceased Mr. Peters. As they passed, I caught a whiff of sulfur … Uh oh.

Jack noticed my expression. "What?"

I sighed heavily. "I could smell sulfur."

He looked slightly confused. "So?"

"The only other time it's happened is when Mom left the den. Nana thought she was being theatrical, but now I'm not so sure."

"Damn it! Even locked up in their weird version of jail she makes my job harder," Jack snapped.

I nodded, but my head was spinning. Was Mom somehow behind this man's murder? Had her powers increased to the point Logan could no longer control her? Had she enlisted Elaine to do her dirty work? The questions were endless, and my stomach was one big, fat knot. "I'll talk with Logan. I'm sure he's aware of her abilities, especially if they have expanded significantly." I was thoughtful for a moment. "How is she obtaining strength?"

Jack shook his head. "We need to get to the bottom of these robberies. The trustees are breathing down my neck, and this murder is going to send them into orbit."

Rather than a mayor, Bath Township's form of government is a board of trustees. A board of trustees was the first type of government under the Northwest Ordinance of 1787 way back before Ohio became a state. Almost two hundred years later, not much changed, concerning townships, under the state constitution. The trustees' responsibilities are to see to the basic needs of the population—road maintenance, police and fire protection, cemetery maintenance, zoning and trash removal. They didn't do anything earth shattering, but the trustees had the power to make Jack's life miserable when events upset them. Murder had a tendency to make them nervous, and they were never quiet about their feelings. I seldom thought about the board, but Andy paid close attention since he enjoys local politics more than I do. Amy's deceased husband loved to stir the pot of politics, so he caused more than one fight during township meetings.

I looked at Jack. "Is it my imagination or is the crime rate rising here?"

Jack's face grew grim. He rubbed his face, shaking his head. "Yep. Ever since we got involved with Logan ... the place is falling apart."

I nodded. "It sure seems that way."

Floyd cleared his throat. "Chief? You done?"

Jack nodded. "Sure Floyd ... thanks for waiting."

I winked at Floyd as we walked past him. He smiled and nodded.

Once outside, Jack turned to me. "Don't misunderstand me. I realize none of this mess is necessarily Logan's fault, but we used to be a quiet place for the most part."

I listened as my brain locked onto a thought. "Jack ... I think we are a mirror image of what is happening throughout the world."

Jack opened his mouth to respond but was cut off by Logan's voice behind me. "Very astute observation."

CHAPTER 5

"Damn it, Logan." Jack jumped when he heard Logan's voice.

"It was not my intention to startled you, Jack." Logan turned to me. "You are correct … Bath is a microsystem which reflects evil's activities throughout the entire globe." His arm waved slowly indicating the neighborhood. "This is merely a small example of the events which have only just begun."

My eyes became slits. "You mean to tell me this mess is only at the beginning stages for us?"

Logan nodded.

The sadness in his expression would've broken my heart if I wasn't so angry. "You never explained the turmoil quite this way before."

"It is important for all of you to have an understanding of what we will be battling over the next few years." He looked at Jack. "Your job will become increasingly demanding as well as crucial to the fight. I have been steadily building forces to ensure we are prepared."

"I know you believe we are at war." Jack frowned as he struggled to wrap his mind around Logan's words.

Logan sighed. "We *are* at war and have been for millennia. Many times, we have been within reach of victory only to have it snatched away at the last moment." He shook his head. "My plans have taken decades to accomplish, and I believe these last few battles will tip the scales in our favor."

I looked at Logan surprised. "Last few battles? We are near the end?"

He shook his head. "Time is not the factor. The war could easily last another thousand years. As the fight intensifies, the major battles will decrease as the enemy regroups." He pointed to the house. "Mr. Peters was a skirmish rather than a battle. There will be many more such skirmishes." He smiled. "Do not lose faith."

"Amy believes we will win eventually," I reminded him.

He gave a brief nod. "Yes … I agree with her wholeheartedly."

I studied his face for a moment trying to put my finger on the change I saw in him. His eyes were clearer and less filled with worry. His face lost the exhausted air which was so evident only a few weeks ago. "Something is different about you. You seem much more confident."

He nodded. "I have given much thought to Amy's council." He paused. "She is a wise woman with life experience. Many of us on our side were growing weary, but recent events have encouraged us and given our spirit new energy."

I was a little confused. "What recent events?"

He shook his head. "Maybe I will share with you another time. Now, we must continue the good fight."

"Hell, Logan … I know we have to keep going." Jack sounded disgusted by Logan's speech. "I don't have time for religious talk. I need to solve crimes, and I have a big, fat murder here. The trustees are going to blow a gasket."

"Logan, does Mom have enough power to be the cause of Mr. Peters' death? Elaine is out of your heaven jail and running around loose." I paused. "I smelled sulfur when Mr. Peters' body rolled past me."

Logan frowned. "Sulfur?"

I nodded. "The only other time it happened was once when Mom left my house."

Logan turned and stared at the trees lining the property. I decided to keep my mouth shut while he mulled over the information. I hoped his new-found energy wouldn't be squashed by my report of sulfur hanging around the body.

Logan didn't bother to turn as he spoke. "I will examine the possibilities concerning the sulfur. If Nell is capable of mischief while under secure confinement, our battles will intensify."

He paused and seemed to be waiting for comments from Jack or me, so my mouth opened. "Last thing we need are Mom's powers to be increasing. How in the hell is she gaining strength while locked in your prison?"

Logan sighed. "I will increase the shields around her immediately."

"Will it prevent her from having access to her friends, alive and dead?" Jack asked.

A small frown appeared on Logan's face. "I was confident the security surrounding her was sufficient."

Jack scowled slightly. "So what you're saying is … there is a possibility some of your guards could be working for Nell?"

Wow … it never ever would've occurred to me that Logan could've hired slime balls. He must've read my mind because he turned his attention back to me.

"Peg, it must be obvious by now that people do not become perfect in death. Trusted allies have to choose whether they remain fighting for good." He shrugged. "Rejection of beliefs is rare, but it does occur."

I felt a headache start to form, and I tried to ignore the slight pounding. "So these dead people just wake up one day and decide working for the dark side is more fun?" I could hear the panic in my voice. The last thing I wanted was for those I came to rely on to change sides. I needed Nana and Bob, not to mention Logan.

"I have no intentions of deserting the cause against evil," Logan said softly. "I have been battling for many centuries, and I refuse to turn away so close to the finish."

Jack watched Logan carefully. "Is it personal convictions or stubbornness that keeps you going?"

Logan smiled. "I would have to admit to both."

Jack looked at his watch. "I've got to head back to the station. Peg, do you need anything?"

I shook my head. "I'm fine now that the body is gone."

Seeing a physical dead *body* is not the same as seeing a dead *person*. I thought I handled it well, but my stomach contents were having a debate whether to stay put or make a hasty exit—I wasn't sure which side would win.

We watched as Jack's car followed the slight curve in the road until it was out of our sight.

I sighed. "I have to be honest with you … I'm nervous. If Mom can control her group while locked away, and dead people decide to change sides midway through a war … what's next?"

Logan shook his head at me as though I was a child in need of further instruction. "Peg, every situation in life has setbacks. Some are small and others quite large, but we continue on our path. You know well enough that life has twists and turns." His voice was calm, and I knew he meant well, but my headache was growing by leaps and bounds.

I glanced back at the house, allowing my eyes to wander over the bushes lining the red brick, waist-high planter filled with autumn colored flowers. A little early for mums in my opinion, but to each their own. I could see Floyd through the window, meticulously cleaning the crime scene. I knew from experience that when he was finished, the house would be spotless, and no one would guess it was the site of a gruesome murder. Floyd must've felt my eyes on him because he turned and nodded.

Logan broke the silence. "I believe our friend has gleaned information from Mr. Peters. This may be your opportunity to speak with Floyd."

I sighed, then took my pounding head and trudged toward the door. I expected Logan to join me, but when I glanced back he already faded. I rubbed my head as I opened the door. Mr. Peters was still talking to Floyd. I knew Floyd would never make eye contact or speak with a fresh spirit— he had rules.

Mr. Peters never acknowledged my arrival, he just continued talking. Floyd told me a few weeks ago that he quietly cleaned while each newly deceased person shared their death experience—usually death by murder. Many cases had the ability to be solved now that Floyd was part of Logan's army.

I looked at Floyd. "Anything interesting?" I didn't want to stem the flow of Mr. Peters' tale of woe.

Floyd shook his head as he began methodically placing cleaning supplies in the rubber tub he carried to each crime scene. "Nothing helpful. I don't think the poor guy has a clue what happened."

I nodded, keeping my thoughts to myself. I had a ton of questions I would love to ask the dead guy, but I wasn't sure what the protocol was in these situations. I walked through the area where the body was found and looked for anything we may have missed. The cops were damn thorough, but you never know when an insignificant item could turn into the motherload of information. I spotted a photo on the kitchen counter that I missed before. I studied the picture of a woman standing on a beach. I turned the black, wooden frame over, then used my thumb to pry the metal tabs enough to lift the back away from the frame.

Floyd walked over and watched me. "What are you looking for?"

I shrugged. "I don't know. There's writing on the back of the photo." I pulled the picture from the frame, then tried to decipher the writing. "Damn ... it's not written in English."

"Hey, put that back!" Mr. Peters' voice rang out behind me.

Uh, oh ... Mr. Peters was standing to my left by the time I decided not to engage. Floyd jabbed my arm, warning me to keep quiet. I pressed my lips together trying to keep my natural responses in check.

"I said to put it back!" Mr. Peters was getting angry quickly.

"I'm going to copy this down and see if Jack knows what language it's written in." I spoke to Floyd, hoping Mr. Peters would hear me. Rummaging through the nearest drawer, I found a pen and pad of paper.

"Why would you write down what's on the back? It's private property!"

Mr. Peters shouted.

Jeez … the guy was a pain in the butt. I'm no expert with the law, but I was pretty positive once someone's dead, personal property is up for grabs—at least it was a good enough theory for me to snoop.

I carefully copied the writing, then held it out to Floyd for his approval—I wanted another set of eyes on my copy to ensure accuracy. Once he nodded, I stuffed the pad in my purse and began the process of putting the photo back in the frame.

I looked at Floyd. "Do we know who Mr. Peters was?"

Floyd shrugged. "I have no idea."

"I'm standing right next to you," our dead companion informed me.

I raised an eyebrow. So … the newly dead man heard me. I looked at Floyd and noticed his worried expression. Tapping a finger on my chin I spoke. "I wonder if Mr. Peters was involved in the local crime wave. It could explain his murder."

Floyd closed his eyes as if in pain. I was on the edge of breaking his ironclad rules, but I figured those were *his* rules … not *mine*. Mr. Peters lack of response to my statement made my stomach knot. I struggled to keep my eyes glued on Floyd's increasingly worried face. My instinct wanted me to confront the dead man, but I suspected Floyd would faint dead away from distress. To keep my temptations at bay, I continued to wander through the room, searching for any new item that caught my attention. It didn't take long for me to spot a slit along the border of the built-in bookcase. My fingers traced the slit, but I couldn't find any type of hinge that would allow me to open the compartment.

"Leave it alone," Mr. Peters commanded.

I ignored him and continued to study the wood. I tapped my fingers, hoping for a spring action result. The small panel gave way on the last tap … bingo!

"You have no business nosing around here." Mr. Peters voice became stern, but I continued to ignore him.

I turned to Floyd, his eyes were as big as saucers.

I grinned. "Let's see what the guy was hiding."

"Leave it alone!" Mr. Peters growled.

I reached in and pulled out what looked like a leather wallet and a 9mm gun … jeez Louise.

Floyd groaned, and Mr. Peters sighed.

I flipped open the wallet, discovering it wasn't a wallet but identification of some type. I turned it, so I could read the ID and almost dropped the gun from shock.

"Floyd … we may have a problem, and Jack is going to have a heart attack."

Floyd didn't say a word, he just shook his head.

"Mr. Peters was apparently in the CIA, and this is his ID and gun. Jack needs to notify someone high up on the food chain about the man's murder."

I began digging in my purse for my phone. Why the damn thing always hides from me is a mystery. Finally, my fingers found it, and I yanked it from the depths of my purse.

"Don't call anyone!" Mr. Peters commanded.

I spun around, looking directly at him. "Why not?"

The poor guy stumbled back a few steps from the shock of my confrontation. "You can hear me?" he stuttered.

"Yep, and so can Floyd. Floyd meet Mr. Peters … Mr. Peters, meet Floyd. I'm Peg by the way."

Mr. Peters' face was a picture of shock and concern. "You can't allow anyone to know about my government position." For a dead guy, he was giving a lot of orders.

"Is your name actually Peters?" I could feel the snottiness growing by the second.

He scowled. "That's none of your business."

I decided to try to talk some sense into him. "Someone should be notified about your death. The fact that you were murdered may be of interest to your boss."

He stared at me for a moment, then turned to Floyd. "You could hear me the entire time I was talking to you?"

Floyd tried to ignore the question, but Peters wasn't about to let poor Floyd get away with pretending.

"I know you can hear me if she can!" Peters pointed a finger in my direction.

"Oh, put a sock in it." I glanced at him as I inspected his gun. "Is this thing loaded?" I released the magazine, then noticed a bullet was missing. "One in the chamber? Nice. Were you expecting trouble?"

Mr. Peter's frowned. "You know about guns?"

I sighed. "Yep … but I'm only a beginner. A guy I work with insisted I take training."

His frown deepened. "Who are you?"

I shrugged. "No one important." I tapped the leather case containing his identification against my chin. "There must be someone who needs to know you're dead." He started to argue, so I held up my hand to quiet him. "Have you bothered to notice I'm not asking you a lot of nosey questions? Or insisting you tell me everything? I'm not even demanding explanations. I respect the need for secrecy, but you need to cut me some slack here. Who do we notify?"

His face became stone, and I'd had enough. "Bob!" I yelled.

Floyd jumped, and Mr. Peter's frowned. "Who's Bob?"

I decided if he wouldn't answer my questions, then I wouldn't answer his either. A bit of tit for tat … tough beans buster.

I felt a slight 'pop' in the air, and I knew Bob arrived. "Hey, Peg. What's up?" Bob didn't even notice Mr. Peters. "Do you need any help with the crime scene?"

I pointed to Mr. Peters. Bob's mouth dropped open when he saw who I was indicating to with my gesture.

Bob looked at me hesitantly. "Peg … are you supposed to talk to the dead guys?"

"You're dead," I reminded him.

"Yeah … but I work with you." He threw his hand towards Peters. "He hasn't been cleared."

I opened the leather case so Bob could read the identification. He mouthed the letters silently to himself, and the penny dropped. "CIA? Are you kidding!"

I continued to watch Bob, uncertain of what we should do next. "I think he may already have clearance."

Bob shook his head. "The situation needs someone with more authority than I have. I'll get Logan." He was gone before I could stop him.

Mr. Peters frowned. "More authority? What's he talking about? Was he dead?"

I laughed. "Buster … you are about to embark on an interesting journey."

Floyd looked at me worried. "Peg, are you sure about calling Bob and Logan?"

I nodded. "Yep. We may have a bigger problem than we originally thought. Why would a CIA agent be living in Bath? We aren't important enough for espionage."

"I need to sit down." Floyd threw a glance at Mr. Peters who nodded his permission for Floyd to find a place to relax for a moment. Floyd's sense of propriety almost made me laugh.

I looked at Mr. Peters. "Do you have any coffee? Jack will have to be called back here and is going to need it once he arrives."

He refused to answer, so I began rummaging around the kitchen cabinets until I found the container. I rinsed out the coffee pot since I had no idea when it was last used, and I started a fresh pot. The aroma of coffee filled the air, and I almost didn't notice when Bob returned.

Bob watched me hesitantly. "Um … Peg … Logan said to call Jack."

I raised an eyebrow, but Bob shook his head and shrugged. I tucked my cell phone in my jeans pocket while I argued with Peters, so I dug it out and made the call.

Jack answered the phone almost immediately. "What now?"

I sighed. "You need to return to the crime scene."

Jack was silent for a few moments while he digested not only my words, but also my tone of voice. "I'm not going to be happy … am I?"

"Not sure. I have coffee brewing."

He sighed. "Damn … now I know it's bad."

I frowned slightly. "I didn't say it was bad, just that you need to get here."

"Does Logan know there's a problem?"

I sighed. "I'm not even sure it is a problem, but yes, Logan knows. He told Bob that I was to call you."

"Damn" he muttered.

"See you in a few minutes," I said, then hung up. I turned to Bob. "Why wouldn't Logan come?"

Bob turned red. "I'm not allowed to tell you."

I raised an eyebrow. "Committee meeting?"

Bob sighed. "Peg, you know the rules."

"Bob, you spill the beans constantly, so go ahead and tell me." My patience was wearing thin. My headache dissipated, but my stomach was knotted.

Bob shook his head. "My newest goal is to work really hard at keeping my mouth shut. You wouldn't believe how much trouble it causes when I tell you classified information."

Yeah, actually I *would* believe it. Bob let many cats out of the bag since we started working together. Some of those cats have been tigers. Since the poor guy can't keep a secret for long, I've been able to find out a few juicy morsels.

"Classified information? This guy is giving out national secrets?" Mr. Peters looked at us dumbfounded.

I glanced in his direction as I shook my head. "There are more fish in the sea other than national interests."

Mr. Peters stared at me. "Do you work for a foreign government?"

The question caught me off guard. After a moment of stunned silence, I burst into laughter which threatened to lean toward hyena hysterical … jeez.

CHAPTER 6

I got myself together as I watched Jack's police car pulling into Mr. Peters driveway. No sense in him thinking I was falling apart so early in the investigation—I'd save the hysterics for later down the road.

I looked at Floyd. "Floyd, Jack is still unaware of your involvement. Do you want to clean one of the bedrooms? You might find something interesting if you poke around."

Floyd nodded, and I knew he was thankful to be out of the situation.

I turned to Mr. Peters. "Look, Jack is chief of the Bath police. He's a good guy, so watch your manners. Also, he has no idea Floyd has special … um … abilities. You know how to keep a secret obviously, so keep this one until I tell you otherwise … got it?"

Logan made the decision to keep Jack in the dark concerning Floyd, and I wasn't about to cross him merely because Mr. Peters was CIA. He nodded in agreement, then I turned as Jack came storming in the house.

Jack's eyes immediately found me. "What's so important that I had to drive back?"

I pointed to Mr. Peters. "Meet the dead guy. Mr. Peters, this is Chief Monroe of the Bath police department." I poured Jack a cup of coffee, then set it on the kitchen table as his eyes widened at the sight of the newly murdered victim.

Jack plopped down in the chair, then reached for the steaming cup. "Anything to go along with this coffee?"

I laughed. "It's not my house, but I'll scrounge around." I looked at Mr. Peters with my eyebrow raised.

He shook his head. "No … I don't eat sweets."

Jack almost spit his coffee across the room. "You can communicate?"

I frowned. "Didn't you hear me introduce you?"

Jack shrugged. "I thought you were being snotty."

I shook my head in disbelief. "Jack … you can see the man standing right here with us."

Jack sighed. "I guess I'm getting too used to these dead people." Jack took a minute to study Mr. Peters, then he looked back at me. "What's the deal here?"

I threw the leather identification case on the table, then carefully placed the 9mm next to Jack's coffee cup.

Jack stared at the objects for a hot minute, his mouth dropped open and his eyes bulged with shock.

"Where'd you find these?" He finally managed to speak once his brain had kicked back into gear.

I pointed to the spring-action, hidden door. "Interesting don't you think?"

Jack rubbed his hand over his face. "Shit."

I gave a brief nod. "Yep … the guy was CIA, but he won't tell me who to notify of his death."

Jack picked up the ID, studying it carefully. "How much do you want to bet he was undercover?"

It was my turn to be surprised. The thought of undercover work never crossed my mind. I turned to Mr. Peters. "Well?"

He shook his head. "No comment."

Jack nodded. "Yep, he was undercover."

A thought suddenly popped into my head. "The ID matches his driver's license though. If he was undercover, wouldn't he use a fake name?"

"Maybe. David Peters is not an unusual name though." Jack shrugged. "It might be easier in the long run to use his real name, especially if he's worried about someone he knows being around to question his use of a false name. Maybe the driver's license is fake."

I looked back at Peters, but he wasn't about to clarify anything. I decided a cup of coffee sounded good, so I turned to grab one for myself. Before I could do anything I heard a distinct 'pop'.

I turned to see Logan standing there.

He looked at me and Jack. "Please forgive my tardiness."

Jack spoke before I had a chance. "Glad you're here, Logan. I think this is more your problem than mine."

Logan raised an eyebrow. "Explain please."

Jack shrugged. "He's dead … not my territory."

Logan frowned slightly. "He was alive until a few hours ago. I believe any information you could glean would help your investigation."

Jack shook his head. "He's dead now. A few hours ago, he wasn't even on our radar."

I knew from experience that Jack didn't necessarily enjoy dealing with dead people, especially when they weren't cooperating with him.

Logan gave a brief nod. "True. Now we are aware of the complication, and it is your township."

Jeez Louise … these two picked this particular moment to have a turf war? They were both trying to pass the ball and get the dead guy off their hands … it was ridiculous!

"For Pete's sake! You two behave. Logan, we need to know what Mr. Peters was doing here and if he was undercover. You need to decide if he's a good guy or a bad guy. Work together!" I could hear Amy's attitude in my tone. Hanging around her was rubbing off on me. I'm not saying I don't have an attitude of my own, but she has what I call her 'teacher voice'—it works wonders. Jack and Logan stared at me, then glanced uneasily around the room.

Logan cleared his throat. "Peg is correct. I apologize." He sighed. "I truly do not enjoy working with the government. Jack, I would appreciate it if you would find out whatever information you can about Mr. Peters."

Jack nodded. "I understand, Logan. The alphabets are a pain in the ass."

I decided the alphabets were the government agencies—FBI, CIA, NSA, etc. They all seemed to have their own form of law, and they tended to block access to information from the local police departments.

Logan turned to our newly deceased victim. "I gather you work for the government." He pointed to the identification in Jack's hand. "Sadly, the mere fact that you work for the CIA does not necessarily guarantee you are not working with our enemies."

Mr. Peters' expression was both stunned and furious. "How dare you infer I am a traitor to my country!"

Logan frowned. "Mr. Peters there is much more at stake than a mere country."

Peters shook his head in disbelief. "World affairs are in bad shape, and you stand there telling me there are more important situations? You are nuts."

Logan glanced at me.

"He means crazy." I translated. Every once in a while, Logan needs a little help with modern slang, and I am always happy to bring him up to date with the lingo.

Logan shook his head. "I believe you are gravely mistaken. You are no longer of this world, but the problems of this world are greatly influenced by the realm in which you now reside."

Logan turned to Jack, taking time to study his face. I could tell he was in the decision-making process, so I kept my mouth shut. Finally, he nodded to himself. "Peg, please ask Floyd to join us."

I raised an eyebrow, but I turned and trotted my butt down the hall to retrieve Floyd. Logan must've decided it was time for Jack to know about Floyd's involvement. Jack would blow a gasket once he realized he'd been left in the dark.

I snagged Floyd, then I headed back to my coffee. I glanced at Logan. "He's on his way."

We waited in silence until Floyd joined us. The tension I felt made me sigh. Jack and Logan had a history of disagreements, and I tended to side with Jack. Logan could be damn secretive, and it was irritating not to mention dangerous for us.

I warned Floyd of the fact that Logan probably planned to tell Jack about his ability. I could tell by the misery on Floyd's face that he wasn't thrilled at the prospect of Jack's potential anger.

Floyd nodded to Logan then Jack, but he didn't open his mouth.

Logan calmly looked at Jack. "Jack, I believe the time has come for you to be aware of the fact that Floyd can see and hear our side of the veil at every crime scene he sanitizes. He agreed to work with us once we were aware of his capabilities."

Jack's mouth dropped open for a split second, then snapped shut with enough force I was surprised his jaw didn't break into pieces. His eyes darted to me, and the anger on his face made me squirm. I took a sip of coffee, trying to ignore him.

He glared at me. "Thanks for telling me!"

I shrugged. "You and Logan have your own little pow wows. You don't tell me everything. Logan asked for us to keep it quiet, so I did."

He knew I was right, and that only made his irritation to grow. "Damn it, Logan … you could've told me."

"My decision was not meant as a sign of distrust. I am a cautious man for good reason." Logan kept so many secrets, so I didn't know how he was able to remember who knew what—sorta impressive if it wasn't so damn aggravating.

Jack looked at Floyd. "How long have you been able to hear and see these guys?" He pointed a finger at Mr. Peters as he spoke.

Floyd thought about the question. "Quite a while. It's not really something you tell many people."

Jack nodded. "Yep." He sat back in his chair, allowing his cop brain to work. Finally, he spoke. "Ever hear anything useful … like who murdered them?"

"Most of them are so confused they ramble for hours. Mr. Peters here …" He waved a hand in Peters direction. "… was so stunned by the turn of events, he talked mostly about his family."

I raised an eyebrow, then I looked at Peters. "Family? So there are people we need to notify."

Mr. Peters lips became a thin line. "No."

Logan studied the man, then shook his head. "You only have limited immediate family. Both of your parents have passed to our side. You have no children and no current wife."

Current wife … how many wives were we talking about here?

Mr. Peters watched Logan for a moment before speaking. "Family is not easy to have in my line of work. Some manage a family … I'm not one of them."

"Not to be rude, but how many wives have you had?" Even I had to admit the wife of a spy more than likely didn't have an easy time of it. How would you explain your husband's occupation to your friends? I shook my head, glad I wasn't the poor gal married to a spy.

"None of your damn business!" he snapped.

I was a little shocked by his snappy response. "You don't have to take my head off! Jeez."

Mr. Peters turned his head. I guess he was trying to prove how well he could ignore me. I shrugged.

Logan looked at our new ghost. "I would appreciate your cooperation, but it is not necessary. There are many avenues available." Logan turned his back on Mr. Peters, faced Floyd and smiled. "Floyd, thank you for your service to us. Believe me when I say we consider your unique abilities advantageous."

Floyd nodded but remained quiet—he wasn't stupid. The air was still thick with tension. I couldn't decide if Jack's mood or Peters' stubbornness was the main culprit, but I would be glad when everyone calmed down enough to work together—I could hope.

Logan kept his attention on Floyd. "Floyd, think back a few hours. What family could Mr. Peters have been referring too?"

Floyd nodded, then stared at the floor while he tried to remember the conversation. His head tilted slightly to his left, and his eyes appeared to glaze. Everyone in the room remained stock still as if one tiny move would break the spell of Floyd's memory. I didn't realize I was holding my breath until Floyd looked up at Logan. I exhaled heavily, then sucked in a huge gulp of oxygen.

"He has a sister in the township. He said something about her asshole husband. I got the feeling she's the reason he moved here." Floyd stopped, then shook his head. "He hadn't accepted his death yet, so he was a little muddled … ya know?"

Logan smiled and nodded. "Yes. The first few moments of death are confusing. Thank you, Floyd."

"Wow." Jack was watching Floyd with a look of awe on his face. "No wonder Logan wants you working with us." He rubbed his hands together. Obviously, his anger at Logan dissipated as he witnessed Floyd's assessment of Peters' rant. Jack looked at Floyd with new interest. "Did his brother-in-law kill him?"

We all looked at Peters who kept his eyes averted. Heads swiveled back to Floyd.

"Well?" Jack pressed.

"I'm thinking!" Floyd seemed to be getting antsy. We were pushing him. He never had to share this type of information before. He always kept the secrets of the dead, and now we were prying into those beginning moments of a dead person's emotions and thoughts. Floyd's sense of honor was at war with our need for information. Finally, Floyd shook his head. "I'm sorry, but I can't be sure. He did the usual ramble … they all seem to talk nonstop, and I can't catch every piece of information. I'm not used to having to pay close attention. Usually, I clean, and they talk." He shrugged.

Logan nodded. "The information you have provided will give us a place to begin probing." He glanced at Jack. "Do you have enough to commence?"

Jack nodded. "I'll start with the sister." He looked at Mr. Peters. "I know you want to keep your secrets, but Logan knows what he's doing. If you're a good guy, you can trust him. If you're batting for the other team, you need to take into consideration that Logan is a worthy adversary."

I almost fell over from shock when I heard Jack's glowing assessment of Logan. Those two fought constantly, but I guess deep down Jack knew Logan was fighting the same battles he was as the police chief.

If Logan was surprised at hearing Jack's words, he kept it to himself. He watched Mr. Peters carefully as Jack spoke, then he nodded his head in satisfaction at the conclusion of Jack's speech. "Mr. Peters, we have the capabilities of helping your sister if she is in need of assistance."

Peters looked up surprised. "You'd help her?"

Logan frowned slightly. "Why would you think otherwise?"

Peters shook his head as he looked at Floyd. "You sure I can trust these people?"

Why in heaven's name would he trust Floyd's opinion? Floyd saw my frown and smiled. "I'm the first person he saw after he was killed. It's not the first time this has happened. I seem to be a comfort to them."

I nodded, wondering if it was like when chicks assume the first living thing they see is their mother—life is weird.

Floyd looked at Peters. "Sir, I believe they are deserving of your trust and equally of your help. Anything you tell them will be kept in confidence, and they will get the job done. I've seen the results myself."

Peters seemed to hang onto every word Floyd spoke, then he sagged with relief at the end of his statement. Peters looked at Logan. "What do you want to know?"

Logan relaxed a tad and smiled. "I would appreciate any information concerning who killed you." Before Peters could answer, Logan held up his hand. "Maybe start with a general statement. The training you have received is an advantage. Rather than answer with your emotions, describe the scene through the lens of your disciplined mind."

Peters snapped his mouth shut, and nodded as he listened to Logan's advice. He closed his eyes, so I figured he was reliving the incident from hours before. Even though his eyes remained shut, his head turned as though he was viewing the episode as a bystander. He must have top-notch recall … I had to admit it was making me envious—I couldn't remember what I had for lunch most days.

With a final nod of his head, Peters opened his eyes and looked at Logan. "I was studying photos I took of my sister's husband. I've had the bastard under surveillance for the past few weeks."

Well, that sure blew our theory that he interrupted a burglary in progress. I held up a hand to interrupt him. "Does your sister know you live in here?"

Peters' eyes widened, and I gathered my question took him off guard. "Why do you ask?" His guard was up, which was enough of an answer for me.

I shrugged. "If she knew you lived here, it stands to reason that her husband would be a hell of lot more careful knowing you're around town."

Logan nodded, and his eyes turned back to Peters.

Peters took a moment before he answered. "Cindy or her husband has no idea I'm here. Their house is on Bath Road, which is close enough for me to keep an eye on her, but far enough so we don't pass each other on the road."

I raised an eyebrow. "The township is pretty small not to bump into each other."

Peters smiled. "I'm good at my job." He opened his mouth to continue when Jack was next in line to interrupt.

"Wait a minute … you mean to tell me you've been spying on your brother-in-law?" He pointed to the gun on the table. "Were you carrying during your little spy operation?"

Peters frowned. "I had no reason to be armed." He sighed. "Just because I'm an agent it doesn't mean I spy for a living."

"Bullshit!" Jack yelled. "I've work with enough of the alphabet gangs to know a desk jockey when I see one, and you ain't one." His face became red, and his hands were on his waist which emphasized the expansion of that particular area. The man really needed to stick to his diet.

Peters studied Jack's face, then made the decision to focus on Logan. "As I said, I was studying the photos when I heard someone behind me. I was caught off guard, which doesn't happen often, but I put up a damn good fight."

He looked around the room, his eyebrows raised in surprise. He turned to Floyd. "Thanks for cleaning up."

Floyd smiled. "No problem."

I thought it was strange how calm Floyd was throughout this process, and I wondered why. I looked at Logan, but it was obvious he was ignoring me and that only made my curiosity grow. I'd have to keep my eye on Floyd. I wouldn't put it past Logan to be running his own little training group without my knowledge.

"What's your brother-in-law's name?" Jack wasn't about to let a CIA operative ignore him if he could help it.

Without bothering to look in Jack's direction, Peters spoke. "Jim Morgan."

Jack scrunched his face as he allowed the name to filter through his brain. Finally, he shook his head. "I've never heard of him."

Peters shrugged. "I'm not surprised. He plays dirty, but he keeps a low profile."

I watched him carefully. "Explain dirty."

"Cindy has been miserable for years, but she refuses to leave the son-of-a-bitch." He shook his head. "I can't figure out why she'd want to stay."

Jack nodded. "Classic abuse scenario. Wife stays out of misplaced loyalty or fear … sometimes both."

"Before our parents died, they begged her to divorce him. She always made excuses."

I shot a look at Logan. If Peters parents were dead, then there was a good chance Logan could use them to help Cindy.

Logan obviously had the idea already churning around in his Indian brain. "How long have your parents ceased to live on earth?"

Peters gave him a strange look. "They both died in a car accident four years ago. Why?"

Logan waved off the question, but I knew the look on his face—he was plotting something.

CHAPTER 7

"Please continue describing your murder." He continue to watch Peters carefully.

A look of surprise crossed Peters face. "I told you … I was taken by surprise and fought back."

Logan shook his head. "For someone with your training, I find it hard to believe you were surprised by an intruder."

I decided to add my two cents. "Maybe whoever broke in here was part of the gang robbing houses in the township."

Logan nodded. "Your idea has validity." He turned his attention back at Peters. "Did you recognize the person?"

Peters shook his head. "Nope … but I know it was a man. Almost as tall as I am but heavier … he had a good twenty pounds on me."

I watched Peters carefully trying to decide what to say next. "One theory suggests you walked in on a robbery, but you said you were home going through evidence against your sister's husband."

Peters immediately went on the defensive. "What are you implying?" His voice was tight as a drum as he glared at me.

"Nothing." I was startled by his reaction. "Are you hiding anything?"

He shook his head firmly. "No."

I shrugged. "Fine."

Jack rubbed his chin. "I wonder if this guy had elite training of some sort." He looked at Peters. "Did you get the feeling he was as good as you?"

Peters eyes grew wide. "My instincts kicked in immediately. Your mind tends to go blank as you go through the motions. If you practice enough it's a little like being on auto-pilot."

I was relieved Amy wasn't with us to hear Peters' views on practicing self-defense. She would never let me forget his words. She's addicted to practice, and she drives me nuts with all the nagging.

Jack nodded. "Exactly. What did your instincts tell you about the guy?"

Peters was thoughtful for a few moments before answering. "He was good ... good enough to take me down." His eyes shifted again as he surveyed his living room. He shook his head. "I still can't believe it happened."

"So, you don't think your brother-in-law was capable of this?" I used my hand to indicate the room as I spoke.

"I wouldn't think so ... but to tell you the truth, I've never liked the dude. Something about him just doesn't sit right."

I nodded. I know about situations feeling 'off'. I've been caught in plenty these last few months, and my instincts were usually right on target. I looked at Logan. "What do you think?"

Logan's eyes shifted to me. "I believe the robberies are the reason your woods are filled with so many visitors. We need to determine who is committing the crimes and why."

I narrowed my eyes. "When we left it was just your Indians and the Vikings ... who has joined them?"

Peters frowned. "Vikings? What the hell are you talking about? Is that some type of code?"

I ignored him and kept my eyes glued on Logan's face.

Logan continued, ignoring Peters' question as well. "The discussion will continue at a later time. At the moment, Mr. Peters testimony is far more important."

I recognized evasive action when I saw it, and Logan was evading like crazy—I knew it was useless to press him on the point.

Jack was impatient to return to questioning Mr. Peters. "Mr. Peters, I need as much of a description as possible."

I frowned as an idea clicked. I scanned the room quickly, then looked at Floyd. "Did you find any pictures? Peters said he was looking through a stack of photos he had taken."

Floyd looked at me surprised, then he shook his head. "No pictures. You were here earlier ... did you see them?"

I shook my head feeling my jaw tighten. I looked over at Jack. "Do you think any of the guys snagged the pictures as evidence?"

Jack pulled his phone from his pocket and called the station. After barking a few questions and impatiently listening to answers, he hung up. "Nope … no photos of any type."

Logan was following his own train of thought. "Mr. Peters, you said your parents died in a car accident. Were you satisfied it was an accident?"

Peters' mouth dropped open as he leaned against the wall for support. I still didn't understand how dead folks accomplish physical acts, but I tried not to obsess about their little quirks. "I never gave it much thought. My sister called to inform me they were in an accident. I flew home for the funeral, then went right back to work. She handled the rest."

I watched him carefully. "Who handled their will? Your brother-in-law?"

He shook his head. "I have no idea. I signed a few papers she sent me but there didn't seem to be anything unusual." He paused. "I was a bit surprised she was named executor of the will. I assumed those duties were mine. My parents must've changed the will at some point."

Jack perked up hearing Peters' statement. "They changed their will? When?"

Peters shook his head. "I have no idea. There was a stretch of time when I was in and out of the country so much, maybe Mom and Dad decided I wasn't available enough for comfort. I wouldn't blame them."

I drummed my fingers on the table. "Your parents are dead, your creepy brother-in-law somehow gained control over their will, you're dead now, and the photos are missing." I shook my head. "How does any of this pertain to burglaries around here? It doesn't make sense."

Logan listened to my analysis, then nodded. "Do you believe they are connected in spite of the facts?"

My eyes closed as I tried to decide what my gut was telling me. After a few moments, I nodded. "I don't know how exactly, but I do have the feeling Peters is somehow involved with the break-ins." I looked over at our newly dead friend. "Do you have any ideas?"

"About your robberies? Nope. I had a lot of vacation time built up, so I took it all in one haul." He looked around the room. "I bought this house and have been tailing the jackass ever since."

I looked at Logan. "Then the jackass must be up to his neck concerning the robberies."

Logan nodded. "I believe you are correct." He looked at Peters. "I am not certain how your family is connected to the problems facing Chief Monroe, but I am convinced they are involved somehow. Would you be willing to help us?"

Jeez … another recruit.

Peters looked startled but after a moment, he nodded. "If you will help my sister … I will help you."

Logan nodded. "Jack, how are you able to help Mr. Peters sister?"

Jack rubbed his chin thoughtfully. "Well … I hate to bring up the obvious but if the husband is involved, then there's a good chance the wife is in the mix."

"What? Absolutely not!" Peters yelled.

Jack shook his head. "Sorry Peters, but years of experience have taught me wives aren't as innocent as people think."

I decided to counter Jack's claim. "Laura was." Laura Spanelli was not only innocent of being involved with her crazy husband's crimes, but she was scared spitless of the creep.

"Spanelli?" Peters narrowed his eyes at me. "What do you know about the Spanelli family?"

Logan, Jack, Floyd, and I exchanged uncomfortable glances. How could we explain our partnership with Sal? Sal was a mobster after all.

Finally, Jack sighed. "It's a long damn story, and we don't have time for it now." He held up a hand as Peters began to argue. "I promise to explain the mess in detail at a later date. For now, it's on the back burner."

Peters wasn't happy, but he accepted Jack's statement.

"Peg has brought up an excellent observation … Laura was innocent," Logan reminded Jack.

Jack nodded. "I know, but she was a rare exception."

"True," Logan agreed. "I will have Bob follow Mr. Peters' sister for a few days which will allow us to make an informed decision."

Peters frowned. "Who's this Bob fellow?"

"A trusted associate," Logan replied.

I was surprised he gave a little information to Peters. Logan never is one to share anything until forced by events.

Peters didn't seem happy with Logan's answer either, but he'd have to get used to Logan sooner or later—might as well be sooner.

I looked at the others. "If we accept the possibility that this guy is involved, the next questions is 'why'? Who is Jim Morgan?"

Jack looked at Peters. "Did you do a background check on the guy?"

Peters shook his head. "I tried but office time is scarce, and the matter was not something I wanted anyone else privy to … if you know what I mean."

Yeah, who wants their co-workers knowing the in-laws are creeps?

Jack looked surprised "Really? That would have been top of my to do list."

"You'd be surprised at how the government frowns on investigating people off the books. You get in big trouble if you're caught."

Jack's eyebrow flew north. "That would've stopped you?"

Peters' face turned brick red. "It shouldn't have. Hate to admit it, but I was on an upward career path, so I didn't want to rock any boats."

Jack nodded. "I understand … you like your job. I like mine too, so I get what you're saying, but …"

Logan cut Jack off. "I believe we have enough to begin positive movement. Jack, what is your assessment?"

Jack looked surprised at the interruption and the turn in the conversation, but he knew Logan well enough to realize it must be time to cut Peters loose. "I'll head back to the office and start pouring over a few files."

Logan nodded, then turned to me. "Peg, thank you." He nodded to Floyd, then faded.

Peters was shocked at his departure. "That's it? Now what?" He looked to Floyd and me for guidance. We looked at each other then back at Peters.

I hesitated, then spoke. "I'm sorry, but we aren't the welcoming committee. I have no idea how any of this stuff works."

Floyd shook his head. "I listen, clean, and leave. I never did know what happened next."

I rubbed my forehead. "I know someone who can help. Bob!"

Bob appeared. "What? Gosh, Peg … you sure are demanding today."

I pointed to Peters. "We don't know what to do with him."

Bob looked at Peters, then back at me. "Yep, on it. Come on sir … I'll show you the way." Bob took hold of Peters arm, then they faded slowly. Bob was trying to be nice by easing the guy into the next life, but Peters looked petrified—I didn't blame him.

Jack, Floyd, and I sat quiet for a few minutes as we mulled over the current situation.

Floyd cleared his throat, breaking the silence. "I should head out. I'm done here and there's a job waiting for me in south Akron." He shook his head. "Some days are crazy busy."

Jack nodded, then I walked Floyd to the door. "Thanks for everything … I'll be in touch."

Floyd nodded as he grabbed his bucket of cleaning supplies. I watched him walk to his truck and decided we were damn lucky to have Floyd on our side.

Jack joined me at the door. "We need to go. I'll lock up here and meet you at the station. There are a couple of reports you should see."

I looked up at him and frowned. "Reports? New ones?"

Jack hesitated a moment before answering. "It's hard to explain. You'll understand when you read them … come on."

Jack waited as I rinsed out the coffee pot and made sure it was unplugged, then he locked the door behind us before we headed for our cars.

I glanced at Jack. "Is there something you aren't telling me?"

He shook his head. "Nope."

It was obvious Jack wasn't in the mood to divulge a speck of information, so I gritted my teeth. He was getting as bad as Logan. I slammed the car door just to show I was not a happy camper, then crammed the keys into the ignition.

"You really shouldn't treat your car so badly." Dad's quiet voice came from the passenger seat.

I glanced at him. "Hi, Dad. Have you been lurking in the shadows?" I knew he wanted to pull my stress level down a bit, so I took a few deep breathes as I turned the key.

"Lurking has such an ominous sound … don't you think?" I could feel his grin even when I wasn't looking at him.

I smiled in spite of myself. "I despise when anyone keeps secrets. Do you happen to know what Jack isn't telling me?"

He watched me carefully. "I think your police friend wants your first reaction rather than giving you time to form an opinion that could turn out to be wrong."

I hated when the dead made sense. "Fine. It must be juicy for Jack to keep it under wraps."

Dad shook his head. "Not necessarily. Jack respects your gut instinct, and he probably trusts it more than Amy's use of logic."

I frowned. "Amy's logic is based on facts. My guts is based on …" I waved a hand around. "… nothing but instinct. I land in a lot of trouble because of it."

Dad laughed. "Yep, but you have to admit you're right more often than not."

I shrugged. "It's luck."

He smiled slightly. "There's nothing wrong with a little bit of luck."

We rode the rest of the trip in comfortable silence. My mind wandered, trying to piece together facts along with any holes we had in the case. How did a CIA guy, his brother-in-law, and our robberies fit? I shook my head, knowing at this point, I had no idea. As I felt my internal thermometer rise, I turned on the car's air conditioner knowing full well it wouldn't alleviate the hot flash. At least it would make me feel like I attempted to cool off.

Dad broke the silence after a while. "Have you talked with Sal lately?"

I frowned. "Not since my last firearm lesson."

Amy decided we needed to learn to shoot a gun during the last case. I thought she was nuts, but I had to concede when Dad, Logan, and even Jack decided it was a good idea. Her boyfriend and ex-mobster, Sal Spanelli, was giving us lessons. Logan wanted my sweet husband, Andy, to join us. His work schedule made little time for practice, but Sal made himself available to fit Andy's timetable.

He glanced at me. "What about Amy?"

I nodded. "Sure. We have self-defense classes two or three times a week. The old girl beats the snot out of me every time."

Dad chuckled. "You might want to consider calling Sal in on this investigation."

I sighed. "It's going to get sticky?"

He shrugged. "Maybe."

Jeez Louise … no one was interested in giving a gal a break today.

I pulled into a visitor's parking slot at the police station, then turned off the car. As I turned to ask Dad another question, I spotted Jack stalking toward my car.

"Come on … we don't have all day." He realized someone was with me and leaned down. "Oh … hey Dave."

Dad nodded. "Jack."

"Are you joining us?"

Dad smiled. "No … just having a little quality time with my girl."

I felt tears form but shook them off as I opened the car door. "Later, Dad."

"Twinkle Toes." He faded before I joined Jack for the short walk to his office.

I glanced at Jack. "Dad thinks we should call Sal."

Jack scowled. "Shit."

I nodded. "Yep … he knows something."

We made it to Jack's office with almost no one trying to get the boss's attention. I settled myself in my favorite chair and waited for Jack to shuffle through the pile of folders on his desk.

Once he spied the folder he was searching for, he held it out to me. "Do you want some coffee?"

I shook my head as I opened the file. "I think I've had enough for the day."

The file was thick, but I was able to thumb through the pages quickly. It was obvious the entire folder was filled with reports that only dealt with the township robberies. I went through the entire file three times before an idea hit me. "Do you have a map of the township?"

"Sure." He reached into his desk, then handed over a folded map.

Once I opened it, I spread it out on the floor and sat next to it. My bones and muscles thought I was nuts, but eventually I made myself somewhat comfortable. I grabbed my purse and began digging for a pen. Finding one took longer than I had the patience for, but I finally nabbed one. I grabbed the file and began plotting the addresses on the map. When my mission was accomplished, I sat back with satisfaction. "Finally! I found the link between the break-ins and Peters' brother-in-law."

Jack joined me on the floor. "What? How in the hell did you manage that?"

Using the pen as a pointer I showed him each house involved in a robbery.

He frowned. "Yeah … so what?"

I raised an eyebrow. "Whose address is smack dab in the center?"

He peered at the map and consulted his notes. "Son of a bitch! Jim Morgan's address."

I nodded happily. "Yep. His house is almost equal distance from each and every robbed address. Interesting … don't you think?" My eyes continued scanning the map as I spoke. I grabbed the file again, then entered the dates to match each robbery.

Jack watched me curiously. "What are you doing?"

I shrugged. "Checking if there is a pattern. Maybe we can predict where the next robbery will take place." Even after a careful survey of the dates, I couldn't find the pattern I had hoped to discover. "Damn."

Jack studied the map for a few seconds. "Andy might be able to help."

I looked up at him surprised. "How?"

Jack shrugged. "He's pretty good with charts and stuff. He was able to help once before."

I nodded agreement. "True." As I sat there, I tapped the pin on my lips, hoping the action would spur my mind to see some sort of order—no luck. I struggled to my feet and folded the map. "I'll take this home and see what Andy comes up with." I crammed the map into the cavern I called a purse.

"Good." He hesitated. "Do you think it's time to call Sal?"

I shook my head. "Wait until we have more to go on. If Andy can figure out a pattern, we have more info to give Sal."

Jack nodded. "Makes sense."

I glanced around, making sure I had all my things. "I'll call you the second I have anything to share."

Jack grinned. "See why I didn't want to say anything earlier? You came in here cold … no data to mull over on the drive here. I haven't even finished my coffee and you found a big clue."

I sighed. "Lucky me."

CHAPTER 8

Andy beat me home by a good half hour. We made a pact concerning dinner—when I'm working on a case, whoever hits the house first starts dinner. We were both sick of scrambled eggs or grilled cheese for dinner. I was also tired of fast food, except for my favorites which include the mall food court and my all-time beloved Treeline—where the hamburgers are to die for. Okay … so maybe I'm not as tired of them as I thought.

I walked into the house and the fragrance of broiled steak and fresh cut tomatoes filled the air. We were fortunate that Andy had rescued a couple of plants from the destruction the drug dealing teenagers had inflicted. Even with too much rain at the beginning of the season, my tomato plants managed to keep us happily slicing the juicy red treats for the past month. Andy must've harvested the last few survivors on the vines.

Andy was still handsome in spite of the aging process. At six foot, one, he stands a foot taller than me. He is still as trim and fit as the day I married him. His blue eyes remind me of Paul Newman every time I look at them. I have a ton of gray hair hidden beneath my grocery store hair dye, but gray barely sprinkled Andy's auburn hair. However, even he had to admit the last few months added to the gray count. He had his fair share of stress working with Logan.

Andy smiled at me as I rounded the corner to the kitchen. "Hey, sweetie … busy day?"

"Yep." I watched as he cubed an apple, and with a quick glance in the bowl, I realized he was making Waldorf salad … what a guy.

I gave him a quick peck on the cheek. "Do you need any help?"

He shook his head. "Nope … almost finished here."

The scent of the steak cooking made my mouth water. "When did you pick up the steaks?"

"On the way home. Logan showed up at the office to inform me that you were tied up with the robberies. Any luck?" He stirred the apples into the mixture, and my mouth watered even more.

"After dinner I need you to look at a map, but I'd rather eat than talk." I laughed, then headed to set the table while Andy finished the steaks.

One bite and I was in heaven. The beef melted in my mouth, and I sighed as the flavors of garlic, pepper, and steak hit every taste bud I owned.

We kept the conversation light as we enjoyed our dinner. I learned the hard way about talking shop while trying to enjoy a meal … it was a good way to get heartburn.

Once Andy's delicious meal was consumed, and the kitchen was back in order, Andy looked at me. "Ready for me to see the map?"

I sighed and grabbed my purse, finding the map in record time.

Andy studied my markings and times. "Am I searching for a pattern or guessing when the next robbery occurs?"

I shrugged. "Both."

He nodded, his eyes never leaving the map as they roamed between the addresses I circled. He grabbed my pad of paper that lives on a corner of the table, then reached for a pen. Within ten minutes, he had a graph drawn. He leaned back in his chair to study his handywork. When he was satisfied, he pushed the graph over to me.

I glanced at it, but we both knew he'd have to explain his ideas—he's the engineer. I looked at him. "Okay … tell me what you think."

He cocked his head, his eyes still on his graph. "There's a focal point."

I nodded. "Yep. Jim Morgan's house."

He looked over at me. "Jim Morgan?"

Damn … I hadn't brought him up to date. I took less than five minutes to explain the entire situation including the CIA guy and his family issues.

When I was done, Andy whistled and shook his head. "Wow … I thought the mob was a problem. Now we have the government?"

A few of our cases involved Sal, our reformed mobster. To add to the mayhem, we had a few newbies trying to resurrect the old-time mob families—too many *Godfather* reruns for their own good.

I nodded. "Yep. Logan and Jack are both disgusted with the CIA connection, but I don't think the government is involved … just David Peters. It's just a coincidence he's a spy."

Andy cocked an eye at me. "Really? You don't believe in coincidences."

I shrugged. "I'm willing to lie to myself until evidence proves otherwise. I don't think Peters was holding back on us. He really hates his brother-in-law to the point of taking a vacation and buying a house, just to nose around."

Andy continued staring at me until I began to squirm. He finally shook his head but didn't offer any argument. He tapped the paper. "If the center points to your friend's brother-in-law's house, then I would bet money he's involved. The timeline is interesting. Only a couple of robberies were done at night. I think they are watching the houses and choosing when the owners should be gone."

I sighed. "That's not good. If they are doing surveillance, it could point to pros at work rather than amateurs." I rested my tired head on my hand, but kept my eyes glued to Andy's graph.

Andy nodded. "I agree. What are they stealing?"

I opened my mouth to answer and realized I had no idea. "Jack never told me."

Andy glanced at the clock. "It's not late … call him."

I frowned. "Don't you think it could wait until morning?"

Andy shook his head. "It will drive you nuts until you have an answer. Go ahead and call."

I grabbed the phone on the table and punched in the number to Jack's cellphone.

He answered on the second ring. "Did Andy figure it out?"

I smiled. Jack tends to forget his manners when he's up to his ears in an investigation. "He drew a graph."

"I knew it! Didn't I tell you he was good at this stuff? His mind works differently than ours."

I ignored his high praise of Andy. "What are these guys stealing?"

"The usual … computers, TVs, DVD players."

I shook my head. Nothing in Jack's list was remarkable. "Is there anything torn up?" My fingers drummed a beat on the table as I waited for his answer.

He hesitated. "Torn up?"

"Like they were looking for something in particular."

Jack was quite for a moment while he mulled over my question. "What makes you think they were looking for something?"

My fingers stopped their agitated movement. I could tell by the tone of his voice he was holding back information. My eyes became slits as I worked to control the anger before it formed into a full storm. "Jack! Is there anything you aren't telling me?"

He cleared his throat. "We try to keep key elements out of the newspapers."

I could hear the caution in his voice, which only increased my temper gauge. "Jack, I'm not a reporter looking for a juicy story. I work for you … remember?" My teeth were clenched so hard, I was surprised I didn't break them into pieces.

My comment was met with silence. I hoped he was rethinking the lame-brained idea of withholding details. Since Jack whined to high heaven when Logan wouldn't tell us vital info, he didn't have a leg to stand on in my opinion.

Finally, I heard a deep sigh. "Peg, you know how I feel about departmental leaks."

"Since when do I blabber sensitive material?" I snapped.

"Okay … settle down." He paused. "Before I answer, I am interested in why you are asking the question in the first place."

I glanced at Andy, then down at the graph he drew. "I don't know … gut feeling I guess."

I could feel Jack's smile through the phone. "Told you … your gut works for you."

I scoffed. "My gut gets me in trouble."

"Maybe, but you have solid instincts. The houses have been searched. Doesn't look like a professional job though. At first, we assumed it was kids making a mess out of spite or meanness, but when every single place was ransacked we had to rethink our theory."

"So … it probably was a pro making the scene appear like a bunch of teenagers were making mischief."

He sighed. "It's possible. Are your guys out back still nervous?"

I shook my head. "It's too dark to tell. I'll check in the morning."

September is an early reminder that winter is just around the corner. I hated losing the late sunsets and warm air. Cool fronts moved in from Canada at alarming speeds, so we experienced increasingly colder nights. To confuse our bodies, the days were still so warm and sticky you'd swear it was summer. Early fall tends to be a roller coaster of temperature variations, and my sinuses were not amused. To add insult to injury, fall brought ragweed, leaf mold, and a host of other allergens to the party. Menopause not only brought hot flashes and night sweats into my life, but for the first time, I had allergies—getting older sucked.

Jack sighed. "Too bad. I've come to rely on your friends in the woods."

I knew how he felt. As much as I dreaded what I would notice when I checked out back, it was always a relief when I couldn't detect the Indians in the woods. I constantly found myself sneaking peeks every so often, just to be sure all was well.

"Yeah … they're a pain in some ways, but I know exactly what you mean." I paused, then looked back at the graph. My brain picked up some nugget of understanding, but I had no idea what message it was sending me. "What do you have on the agenda for me tomorrow?"

"Not sure yet. Get a good night sleep, and I'll call you in the morning."

I smiled. "Sounds like a plan." I hung up the phone, my eyes still glued to the graph. Maybe I'd figure it out after a solid rest.

Andy and I hit the hay earlier than usual. As I tossed and turned listening to Andy's snoring, I ordered my mind to settle down. As usual, it didn't listen to me. I finally drifted off but restful isn't what I experienced. When Andy's alarm blared at the usual time, I was relieved. At least the sun would appear soon, and I could start the day. Making my way down the hall for my morning ritual of caffeine, I heard noises in the kitchen. My heart almost stopped. I did an about face and headed back to the bedroom. I grabbed the phone and began to dial the police station.

"What's wrong?" Andy's voice was groggy as he struggled to wake up. He slept as sound as a log most nights, and he hit the snooze button numerous times before finally falling out of bed to start his day.

"Someone's in the kitchen," I whispered.

Andy shot out of bed, grabbing the gun Sal gave him out of the night stand drawer.

I felt my eyes widen. "I don't think you should charge in there with a gun."

He started for the hall. "It's better to have protection."

I frantically tried to think of an alternative to Andy putting himself in more danger. "Wait! I have a better idea." Andy paused looking at me. "Bob!" I called.

Within a matter of seconds, I heard a 'pop' in the room. Bob stood at the end of my bed, averting his eyes in case there was a stray boob in his line of vision. "What's up? It's early for you, Peg."

I ignored his comment. "Who's in the kitchen?" I tried to keep my worried voice a whisper.

Bob frowned. "Kitchen? No one. I was in there when you called, so I can guarantee it's empty."

I cocked my head, studying him a minute. "You were in the kitchen? Making noise?"

Bob's face lit up like a Christmas tree. "You could hear me? Wow."

I looked down at the phone in my hand grateful I didn't finish dialing the number for the police station. I sighed and hung up. "Bob, you scared the living daylights out of me!"

Andy returned his gun to the drawer. "I'm taking a shower."

I could hear the irritation in his voice. It was rare for Andy to be annoyed with Bob, but finding out your crack of dawn intruder is one of your ghostly pals obviously fit the bill.

I turned to Bob. "What were you doing in there?"

Bob's face turned scarlet. I asked Logan why the dead still have certain living abilities, such as blushing, but he refused to give me an answer—I guess it would remain a mystery. "I was practicing."

I sighed. "What were you practicing."

Bob loved adding skills to his resume, and he seldom bothered to consider the consequences of his actions. He has startled more than one person at the mall, performing his experiments to see how the living would react to his actions. Logan finally told him to knock it off ... well, probably in a nicer way than I would.

Bob rubbed his hands together. "You know how Logan, and even your mom, can make physical contact?" I nodded, so he continued. "I've been working hard to figure it out. It's tougher than you'd think."

I frowned slightly. "I heard voices. Who were you talking to?"

His face reddened more. "Um ... well ... to be honest, myself."

I cocked an eyebrow.

"It helps me concentrate." He sighed. "Sorta helps me focus."

Jeez Louise.

I headed back to my kitchen. "I need my coffee. Don't bother me for at least an hour."

"No problem," Bob called after me. "I'll use Adam's room."

I hesitated, then shook my head and continued down the hall. I'd deal with Bob later. I still needed to start my engines with caffeine.

The sun was peaking over the horizon, and I could see dawn spreading slowly through the woods. I decided I wouldn't be able to detect any movement in the trees for at least another few minutes. A cup of coffee should be the perfect amount of time before I could check the activity level of my guards.

I sat at the table and savored the peace and quiet. I knew it wouldn't last long, so I allowed myself time to appreciate the serenity before the day began. After I drained the last drop, I stood to make another cup of coffee, but I wouldn't allow my eyes to drift outside. Once the fresh cup of coffee was in my grip, and I had settled back in my chair, I drew a deep breath, then turned to face the wooded area.

The Indians were still agitated and looking toward the house nervously. My gut knotted, but I forced myself to continue sweeping the area with my eyes to see who else had joined them. I couldn't detect any Vikings, which was good news, but I spotted a few new players. I squinted, then leaned forward so I had the chance to make sure I hadn't lost my mind. Who the hell was the guy in a kilt? Not to mention a few in some type of hooded robes. I plopped my head in my hands and groaned.

"You have observed the new additions." Logan's voice came from behind me.

I didn't bother to lift my head. "Yep. Who are they, and why have they shown up now?" More strange people milling around outside was probably not a good sign.

Logan didn't answer for a moment. When he did, there wasn't a whole lot of comfort in his words. "As the enemies of the world increase their efforts, your guards must also increase. I have brought a deeper aspect to the field."

I turned my head toward him, frowning slightly. "Kilts and robes?"

His eyes never left his crew of dead folks out back as he nodded silently.

I knew a headache wasn't far off, and I wasn't thrilled with the band of knots in my stomach. I pointed to the woods. "So, who are the new guys?"

"Re-enforcements." Sometimes obtaining a glimmer of enlightenment from Logan was as easy as wrestling a tiger … jeez.

Not too long ago I could count on Bob spilling the beans. Lately, his fear of Logan's reaction to what could be described as misguided indiscretions curbed his enthusiasm for sharing. I was at fault for the misguiding due to my ability to needle the poor guy relentlessly without an ounce of guilt. Bob answered easily without realizing he was probably disclosing Logan's carefully guarded secrets. To my regret, Bob was more careful now.

"Let me put it another way … who the hell are the guys in kilts and robes?" I snapped.

A small sigh escaped Logan, but I ignored it. He turned to me. "It has been decided, for your own safety and peace of mind, to bring in additional …" He paused thoughtfully. "… layers."

I frowned. "Layers? Of what?" I had no idea what he was talking about, and the headache decided to make itself known. I rubbed my head waiting for him to answer.

"There was a time when people from the continent you call 'Europe' came to this land in search of a suitable area to hunt."

"I remember learning this stuff in school." I wasn't in the mood for one of his lectures, but I remained silent.

He shook his head. "They arrived much earlier than most understand. Their journey took them over an ice bridge, and it took a great deal of time to achieve success."

My brow creased as I tried to grasp his meaning. "Ice bridge? During an ice age? Wasn't it thousands of years ago?"

"Many ice ages have occurred, and more are possible." He shrugged. "Earth has a mind of its own regardless of man's ideas."

I thought a moment. "Were you alive then?" I figured it wouldn't hurt to dig a little about his past. Logan seldom allowed himself to share any data concerning his life on earth, and I might be able to pull a tidbit out of his cautious mind.

He smiled. "No. However, they did visit many times during the following centuries. Eventually, they left a small group of their people to continue the journey. I had the good fortune to meet them as I wandered."

I watched him curiously. "What were you searching for?"

He gave my question a few moments of thought before he answered. "Spiritual quests are best done alone. Truth is elusive, and many passed by without ever observing how close they had come to grasping it." He stopped talking, and I knew he was lost in his own memories. I kept my mouth shut, allowing him time to cruise down memory lane. After a few minutes, he continued as he indicated the newest members of the gang out back. "These men are from the Celtic tribes of Europe. I requested a few of the Druid members to join us."

I sat straight up the chair. "Celts? Druids? They were here at one time?"

I learned months ago that anyone Logan had guarding the woods, at one time or another, either lived here or passed through Ohio as they traveled. I understood the Indians—they had a village on the property hundreds of years ago, so there was a tie to the land. The British soldiers we had on occasion were also bound to the property due to Ohio being part of the England before the Revolutionary War. The Vikings were a surprise, but Logan explained they were here well before Columbus ever discovered America. Now, a new twist with Celts and Druids.

Logan smiled. "Yes."

I could sense by his tone of voice that he was pleased at my surprise. Logan enjoys his little secrets, and I had a sneaking suspicion he took great joy in shocking me with pieces of history no one learned in school.

I joined him at the window, studying the newest members of my guardians. The Celts clothing was much more brightly colored than I could have imagined. Their boots looked like leather, but which animal hide was anyone's guess. I had no idea if they had deer in Europe or not, but they may have made them while living in Ohio, which had a large deer population now. Logan didn't bother to explain, and I didn't bother to ask. The kilts were probably made of wool and while they matched my idea of a kilt, the design was not exactly tartan plaid I was accustomed to seeing in pictures. I leaned forward hoping to get a better look, but I knew I would probably have to be closer to make out the design. I could see the bright colors and the large pin which held their cloaks.

The Druids, on the other hand, wore plainer colors than their friends. While they did wear hooded cloaks, they weren't white as most people today would assume. Their clothing was totally hidden by the floor length robes, and each man's robe was a different color.

I was suddenly more curious. "Do the colors mean something?"

Logan shook his head. "Only a matter of preference. The colors have little significance. However, they do have a hierarchy, but their clothing signifies nothing."

I nodded and continued to stare. The Celts looked fierce, and their battle shields were well worn. I spotted more than a few rings on fingers, then noticed their hair was adorned with jewels as well. The Druids heads were covered, and their stance was confident. I could feel the power emitting from them.

I pointed to the Druids. "So … you decided we needed a little spiritual aid?"

Logan smiled. "Do you object?"

I shook my head. "Nope … every little bit helps."

"Do not underestimate the Druids. I learned a great deal of my powers from their teachings."

My eyebrows rose. "You studied with them?"

He hesitated, then nodded. "I was an apt student. They brought a new level of understanding to my attention, and I will always be thankful for their influence."

"Are they powerful?"

Logan gave a firm nod. "Very."

Jeez Louise.

CHAPTER 9

Logan left me to finish my morning ritual. Now that Andy accomplished his morning practices, it was my turn in the bathroom. I gave myself a once over in the mirror to check if any gray hairs were peeking through my favorite grocery store hair dye. I leaned close to the mirror for the inspection. Once I decided the gray would stay safely camouflaged for another few weeks, I dressed in comfy jeans and blouse. As an afterthought, I added a sweatshirt—fall can be tricky in northeastern Ohio, so layers are the answer. If the temperature turned warmer, I could always peel off the sweatshirt. I knew there was a nip in the morning air, so I wanted to be prepared for any temperatures the day decided to throw my way.

As I headed back to the kitchen, I could hear Bob in Adam's old bedroom muttering to himself. I stuck my head in the door to check out the situation. "Everything okay?"

He looked disgusted. "You wouldn't believe how difficult this stuff is."

I watched him curiously. "What stuff?"

He waved his arms in a circle. "You know I'm working to increase my abilities … right?" He stopped as he waited for my nod. Once he saw me acknowledge his work, he continued. "Let me tell you … it's harder than you'd think." He sighed. "Even your grandmother has more power than I do."

"Bob, Nana's been working on her skills longer than you have," I reminded him.

He scowled. "We've been dead almost the same amount of time!" He began to pout.

I have no patience with pouters. Instead of glaring at Bob, I gave my eyes permission to study the room. Bob and Nana prepared it for Adam's big homecoming with his fiancée in tow. I had to admit, for dead people, they did a damn good job. Floyd did the actual work, but they planned every bit of the redecorating. New paint job, carpet, and bedspread. Bob and Nana had a blast pouring over paint colors and bedspreads. Turns out, Bob has quite a bit of talent and Nana still loves projects. They made an excellent team if you discounted the ongoing arguments and difference of opinions. When it came time to overhaul the kitchen, to rid it of the damage done by a snotty teenager's gun, they were deep in the mix adding their own opinions concerning flooring, appliances, and any other idea that popped into their heads. At one point, I thought Andy might burn the entire house down just so they would shut up—it was a close call.

Since I had no advice to offer Bob's present problem, I shrugged. "I guess you just have to keep working on it."

Bob sighed. "That's exactly what your dad told me."

I smiled. "Well … he would know."

I heard the phone ring, and I knew it was probably Jack. I was grateful for the interruption, so I hauled my butt to the kitchen to answer it.

"There's been another break-in." Jack really needed to learn a few phone manners. When he's wound up, he seldom remembers how to start a normal conversation.

I grabbed Andy's graph and the map of the township. "Where?"

"Not far from our mystery CIA guy's house."

He gave me the address, and I circled the area on the map and tried my hand at the graph. "It still fits Andy's graph and falls within the circle keeping Jim Morgan's house as the center."

"Either the guy is being framed or he is the ring leader."

I was thoughtful for a moment. "Is there any evidence?"

"Nope. Do you think the CIA guy could help us?" He sounded a little too hopeful.

I frowned. "I have no idea where he is now. Maybe he moved on."

"Moved on? Where?" Jack's incredulous tone made me smile.

I shook my head. "I don't know the rules over in Deadsville."

Jack was silent for a moment. "Maybe Bob can roam around looking for him."

I sighed. Lately Jack was utilizing Bob to investigate and snoop. Logan frowned on the activity, but as long as he wasn't flat out demanding Bob not help Jack, everyone pretended the practice was fine. I tried to stay out of the fray but somehow always found myself in the middle of their schemes.

"You'll have to ask him yourself." I was hoping to distance my involvement.

Jack hesitated a moment. "Do I just call him?"

"Yep." There was no way I would inform Jack of Bob's presence in my back bedroom. I knew him well enough to know he would ask me to do his dirty work.

"He's pretty good actually." I had a sneaking suspicion Jack was working hard to justify stepping on Logan's toes by using Bob.

"Good to know." I was a little curious about what Jack had in mind even though I didn't want any part of the plans. "What exactly do you want him to find out for you?"

Even through the phone, I felt Jack's evasive attitude. "Oh, you know … snoop around a little. Maybe check out Jim Morgan's movements, and see who his friends are."

I frowned. "Why not use your guys? Sounds pretty routine to me."

Silence greeted my question. I out waited Jack—I was gaining skills in the silent treatment arena.

Eventually, Jack sighed. "The department doesn't have the means to sniff out any ghostly influence. Hell … it isn't easy for you and me, and we can usually *see* the damn dead guys."

I couldn't argue with him there. "Bob has a unique set of skills that you have access to as long as Logan doesn't find out?"

"Pretty much. I'm not stupid though … Logan is more than likely aware of how often I ask Bob to help. I think he turns a blind eye as long as I stay within certain boundaries."

My eyebrows raised in surprise. "What are the boundaries?"

Jack snorted. "Hell if I know … I figure the day Logan turns me to stone is when I'll know I crossed a line."

I burst out laughing. "A little over the top don't you think?"

Jack chuckled. "Logan's a little scary sometimes. I wouldn't put it past him."

I shook my head. "He has major powers for sure, but it doesn't mean he would turn on you."

Jack sighed. "He likes you."

"He respects you," I threw back at him.

My comment made Jack grow quiet for a few seconds. "You really think so?"

"Yep. He would've never given you the ability to see all the dead crew if he didn't trust you one hundred percent. You've earned the respect."

"He's still scary as hell sometimes."

I laughed again. "I know."

Jack cleared his throat, getting back to business. "I'll give Bob a yell and get back to you."

"Yep." I hung up, then turned to see Bob standing in the doorway.

"Thought you were practicing." I wondered how much of the conversation he heard.

He frowned slightly. "Jack wants me to help him?"

My eyes strayed to the coffee machine, and I took a second to weigh the option of another cup of coffee. Would the extra caffeine make me have the shakes later if I snuck another cup into the day? Probably, so I decided with a sigh not to gamble with my hormones. I longed for the days I could drink coffee so strong it could walk on its own—thanks to menopause, constant streams of strong coffee were a distant memory.

Bob followed my eyes and read the situation correctly. "Last time you had too much coffee you almost went nuts. I wouldn't chance it if I were you."

My eyes narrowed, and I clamped my lips tight to ensure a snotty remark wouldn't escape through them. Eventually Bob would learn manners. "Does Logan mind if you snoop a bit for Jack?" I didn't need any more remarks regarding caffeine and thought a change of topics was in order.

Bob frowned as he mulled over my question. "It's iffy. As long as I don't accidentally get involved in one of his projects, he ignores my side jobs with Jack."

"There's been another burglary," I said casually.

Bob nodded as he listened. "I'm not surprised."

I raised an eyebrow. "Really? Why not?"

He pointed to Andy's graph on the table. "There's no reason for them to stop. They don't seem to be very worried about getting caught. If they were, they'd spread their operations over the entire township rather than a small neighborhood."

I pulled on my lower lip while I contemplated Bob's remark. I hated to admit it, but he hit on an interesting theory.

I looked at Bob. "Do you think it's time to bring in Sal?" Since Sal had many dubious connections with criminals, I hoped he could give us his unusual perspective on our current problem. He was in the process of becoming a reformed mobster after all.

Bob shrugged. "It couldn't hurt. I'm surprised you haven't called him already."

My eyes drifted toward the window. I wasn't surprised at the amount of activity in the woods. There was enough dead folks roaming around out there to fill a castle. I was a tad surprised Amy hadn't called frantic with the new additions to the gang. She must be spending more time at Sal's place now that they were officially dating. I shook my head at the thought of their relationship. I hated to admit to myself how shocked I was when I discovered there was a brewing romance smack dab into front of my face, especially at their ages. Amy was in her eighties, and Sal probably wasn't far behind. I had to face the sad fact … I was a prude.

The trees finally began their yearly transformation from lush green to vibrant oranges, reds, and yellows. I relished each fall because I enjoyed driving along the country roads that were now shouting with color. The only fly in the ointment was the fact that winter followed close on the heels of such beauty—I'm not a huge fan of snow and ice.

I finally made up my mind. "I'll give Amy a quick call."

Bob nodded. "If you can't reach her on her cellphone, try Sal's."

I sighed. "Yep. I figured it out by myself."

Bob cocked his head. "You still don't like them dating? Gosh, Peg … I thought by now you'd realize how great they are together." His face looked a tad envious.

"I know it's petty, stupid, and wrong. To be honest, it doesn't make sense even to me," I admitted.

Bob shook his head. "I've seen Albert at a few social gatherings. I'll be honest … if he was anything like he is now, Amy has the right to a little happiness. The guy is a royal pain in the butt … talk about pushy!"

This was news. "You know Albert?" Albert was Amy's deceased husband and a real stinker.

Bob nodded. "Only enough to stay out of his way. He causes problems everywhere." He glanced around, then whispered, "There's even talk of barring him from a few of the clubs."

I closed my eyes, shaking my head. "Jeez … at least I'll know to avoid him when I arrive."

Bob looked shocked. "Gosh, Peg … you won't be here for years!"

My eyes flew open. "Really? You know that for a fact?"

Bob's face grew beet red. "Um … no."

I narrowed my eyes, trying to stare him down. "Do you know when I'm going to die?"

"I never said I knew anything!" He moaned. "Logan is gonna kill me for sure."

I waved my hand dismissively. "You're dead now."

"I can't continue this discussion. Call Amy, and I'll check back with you later … Jack's calling me." He faded before I could say another word.

I drummed my fingers on the table. If the dead folks know when we arrive on their side of life, then why is there so much turmoil? Couldn't they just wait out the problems? Bob dropped two huge information bombs on me so far, and I wondered how many more there were. The dead can time travel and they know when we croak.

My eyes strayed toward the woods. I was startled when I realized one of the Indians was waving his arms, trying hard to get my attention. I frowned as I headed out back to see what was so important. I wasn't thrilled when I realized somehow a misty rain began to fall without my knowledge. When did the rain roll in?

I trotted out to the woods, and I was not surprised when I noticed the rain dripped right through my dead gang. They appeared to be nice and dry, which didn't improve my mood—even though it was a light rain, my clothes were already more than damp.

I watched the Indian carefully. "What's up?"

He was not the usual guy I saw, and I wondered if he was new. His short stature was a bit of a surprise, and I noticed the gray streaked throughout his full head of long hair. He wasn't young, but he wasn't an old geezer by any stretch of the imagination. People seemed to age quicker hundreds of years ago, so I was cautious when guessing life spans. It wouldn't surprise me to discover he'd been in his late thirties in spite of the gray hair.

He didn't answer right away, instead he took his time studying my face. I didn't flinch as his eyes bored into mine. I understood his need to satisfy himself that I was fighting on the side of good. After a few more moments he nodded, then turned to the man who wore a kilt.

The man stepped forward and began a long speech which I could not decipher.

I frowned and turned back to the Indian. "I should be able to understand every word he speaks. What's going on?"

I heard a soft chuckle, then looked around for the owner of the noise. I spotted a figure off to the side, head down but standing ramrod straight.

I looked him over. "Do you have any idea why I can't catch his words?"

He raised his head to face me, and I sucked in air. Talk about handsome! I could detect light brown hair beneath the hood, and his gray eyes sparkled with humor. His complexion was smooth but darker than I imagined. Somehow, I expected pale skin, but he had more color than my imagination allowed for. I decided I watched too many movies with Hollywood's ideas of what Druids should look like.

The man finally answered me. "Angus refuses to allow the translation. He is speaking our native Gaelic."

I could feel my frustration grow by the second. "How in the hell am I supposed to know what he's saying?" I stomped my foot much to the Druid's amusement. Angus frowned, but I didn't let it bother me.

"If you prefer, I could translate for you," he offered.

I shook my head. "I don't need word for word. How about just the bottom line?"

His faint smile turned into a full-blown grin and I found myself returning his grin. I could get used to having this guy around the woods. "He wants you to know a descendant of his works for the local law. He asks for you to be kind to him."

I frowned for a second then my mouth dropped open. "Dougal MacMillian?"

My new-found friend turned to the kilt wearing stubborn man who nodded emphatically. As he turned back to me, I held a hand up. "I understood."

I looked at Angus. "Your great-something grandson?"

He nodded, beaming with pride.

"Have you been watching over him?" I asked more out of curiosity than any true need for information.

Angus slammed his hands on his hips, pulled himself as tall as he could manage, which wasn't saying much as he wasn't loads taller than I was, and began another litany of Gaelic.

I sighed, then turned to the Druid. The Druid waited until Angus stopped the flow of words, then he turned back to me. "He informs you that Dougal has no need of having a watch dog. He is quite capable on his own." The twinkle was back in those gorgeous eyes, but he refrained from another grin.

I decided that while he was amused with Angus, he was also showing the man respect by keeping his face controlled. I did the same and nodded slowly. "I agree. Dougal has no need of your aid to succeed, but may I recommend you give him any aid he may require. We are fighting some evil people, both dead and alive. I've needed Logan's help more than I care to mention."

Angus gave my words a few moments of thought, then nodded and began speaking again. I held up my hand. "I respect your position on the translation, but I'd appreciate it if you would consider allowing me to hear you in English." I pointed to my Druid friend. "He may not always be handy to translate."

Angus frowned but didn't answer. Oh well … can't win them all.

The Druid spoke up when Angus wouldn't. "Give him time to think about your request. No one has ever had the nerve to ask him before. Angus tends to intimidate most people."

I nodded. "I hope it doesn't take him too long to decide. I don't have all the time in the world the way people on your side do."

The Druid shook his head. "Time exists even for us, merely a different type."

I cocked my head. "Explain."

His eyes left mine as he studied the view in front of him. I decided he was contemplating how much information to hand over to me. The dead seemed to relish their secrets, and I learned from Logan that they seldom pass along interesting tidbits unless necessary. Bob was an exception but recently, even he began to hand over less news. The fact that he let two huge facts slip in a short span of time showed his personality flaws. Bob reminded me of a sweet puppy dog who was always in trouble due to enthusiasm rather than temperament.

"You have knowledge of Logan's assignment." His eyes were still enjoying the view as he spoke.

"To a point, yes. He isn't what I would call 'chatty' when it comes to details."

The Druid smiled. "Logan is cautious. I understand his motives and agree with his discretion."

There was no surprise there. The folks in Deadsville really loved their little secrets. I took the opportunity to study my new friend. His good looks couldn't hide the level of experience I detected. While his eyes had an ornery twinkle, I noticed the creases of wisdom hidden beneath the surface. Druids lived a long time ago when life was harsher. We have become so accustomed to modern conveniences that I shuddered to imagine day to day life two thousand years ago. The guy must have massive spiritual abilities for Logan to call him to help us.

"Satisfied?" His playful tone caught me off guard.

I blushed, realizing he was aware of my scrutiny. "Sorry … Logan has tons of respect for you, and I'm curious about what you were able to teach him."

He smiled, then turned to face me. "Logan was well on his path before we met. He is capable of more than even he understands."

"Gosh … that's saying a lot. Logan is pretty damn powerful as it is."

The Druid nodded. "Yes. He worries too much which is unnecessary. He has command of the situation."

I frowned slightly. "What situation?"

The Druid became still and didn't answer.

CHAPTER 10

After a few moments, the Druid nodded to himself as though he made a decision. "We do not measure time the same way as the living. Here …" He spread his arms out to indicate my yard. "… you have minutes, hours, days, years, and more."

I nodded. There was nothing new in his words. Why do all the dead guys have to give a dissertation every time they decide to explain anything?

"On our side of life, we measure time by unfolding events."

I frowned. "Events? Such as?"

"Wars, empires rising and falling, religions waxing and waning. Should I continue?"

I shook my head. "Nope … you're talking about historical stuff."

He smiled. "For you it is history. We view those events as markers."

I was even more curious now. "Markers?"

He nodded. "Certain events leading up to the finale."

Oh, Jeez … end of the world talk again.

"So you measure time with world events. Logan said it could be centuries before the end."

"Yes, depending on developments … it could easily be sooner. Evil tries to hasten the end, we try to prolong the final stages."

I raised my eyebrows in surprise. "Why? Does it really matter?"

"Absolutely. Earth isn't the only world involved. The longer this planet thrives the better for other worlds."

Well hell … Andy was going to love this insight about other planets. He devoured shows about aliens, so the last thing I needed was proof he was one hundred percent correct. "So there *is* life on other planets?"

The Druid smiled. "Logan hasn't told you? I'm not surprised."

I snorted. "Logan doesn't give me one ounce of information unless forced." I snapped my fingers as a thought popped in my mind. "What about your ability to time travel?"

Bob would have a heart attack when he found out I mentioned his big secret, but I decided it wouldn't hurt to ask.

The Druid frowned. "How did you come by that knowledge?"

"Heard it in passing. I wondered if it was true." There was no sense getting Bob into any more trouble than he manages on his own.

He shook his head. "We don't discuss it with the living. Too many people would want us to change events in their lives which is not only dangerous, but it is against all rules."

"Then why have the ability? It doesn't make sense to me."

He studied my face for a moment. "I'm sure many matters aren't compatible with your perceptions. Moving through time occasionally allows us a slight edge on our enemies. It is seldom used and never encouraged."

"Does Logan time travel?" I figured I would continue asking questions for as long as he was willing to answer.

The amused glint returned to his eyes. "You need to ask him. I don't pay attention to Logan's schedule."

I laughed. "Okay … I'll stop prying. Logan is pretty tight lipped, so I don't expect answers to many questions."

He nodded. "Logan is cautious for good reason."

I knew I was pushing my luck with my questions, but I was burning to know what those good reasons were. I would have to save it for another day. "Back to the problem at hand … do you know who our culprit is?"

He shook his head. "No, but I am confident you will discover the answers."

I felt my shoulders slump. Thanks for nothing, Mr. Druid. Without another word, I turned and stomped back to the house.

Once inside, I realized my clothes were too wet to continue wearing due to the misting rain, so I headed to the bedroom to change into something dry.

I heard a faint pop before I heard Bob's voice. "Peg, I really think you should call Sal."

I stopped short of the bedroom door and turned. "What's wrong?"

"I've been following Mr. Peters' sister for Logan, along with her husband for Jack. Let me tell you … it's not easy following two people at the same time."

I ignored his complaint. "Great … any info?"

He nodded. "Yeah, I'm not sure about the sister, but her husband is bad news."

I sighed. "How bad?"

"Bad enough to call Sal … I'm not kidding."

I took a moment and really looked at Bob's face. The worry I saw made my stomach knot. He was really scared. "Bob, what's going on?"

He shook his head. "I think the CIA guy wasn't entirely honest with us. His brother-in-law is a piece of work."

I frowned, slightly confused. "Jack has never heard of the guy."

"Yep … there's a good reason. You really need to call Sal."

I sighed. "Let me get into dry clothes, then I'll make the call. You need to tell me what has you so upset."

Bob's face reddened. "I'll wait here." Bob had a huge fear of seeing a stray boob.

I nodded, then made a beeline for warm, dry clothes. Fall is not the time to stand around wet to the skin. I shivered as I peeled off the damp jeans and pulled on a fresh pair. Once I changed the entire mess, I rubbed my arms to get warm. I headed back down the hall.

Bob fell into step beside me. "You gonna call Sal?"

His antsy attitude got on my nerves. "Yes! What's wrong with you?"

"Gosh, Peg … you don't have to be so mean." His hurt tone made me feel a little bad.

I sighed. "Fine." Sometimes, Bob was too much to handle.

I grabbed my phone, then found Sal's number. While I listened to the ringing, I watched Bob pace around the kitchen. He usually spent his time inspecting every nook and cranny for issues but since we remodeled, he couldn't find fault as easily.

Finally, Sal's voice came on the other end of the phone. "Hey, Peg. What's up?"

"Hi, Sal. We may have a problem with a new case." I could hear Amy in the background asking about our next self-defense class. Jeez … the woman wouldn't let up with those classes. It didn't help that our sessions saved our lives more than once. I'd never get her to quit now. "Tell Amy that I'll be at the next class."

Sal chuckled. "She loves those lessons … but back to your problem, what's the case about?"

"What we thought were minor house break-ins may be more, but we're not sure yet. Also, we had a murder in the township."

"Yep. I heard about the murder but not the robberies. What's being stolen?" Sal's expertise in the crime department is one reason he was so valuable to us. The other reason was his connections to that particular world.

"Usual stuff … DVD players, TV's, computers."

He was thoughtful for a moment. "There's nothing suspicious there … must be more to the story."

"The houses are all searched. Jack first thought it was kids, but now we are rethinking his theory."

"Do you think it's mob connected?" I appreciated his straightforward attitude.

I sighed. "Maybe … Bob's worried."

"About?"

"Not sure … he isn't saying much other than it was time to call you in on the situation."

Sal's silence was deafening. "Any idea why Bob didn't contact me himself?"

I raised my eyebrows at his question. "Good question." I turned to Bob, but he was watching the dead folks out back. "Bob! Why didn't you go to Sal yourself?"

"Couldn't." The one word was all he said.

I frowned. "Why not?"

"Um?" He hesitated.

If I learned anything from my friends with no heartbeats, it's that they would rather never answer an uncomfortable question. The trick was realizing when my questions were making them squirm. "Bob! Why couldn't you go to Sal's?"

His eyes never left the woods, but he grew deep red. "Orders."

I felt like banging my head against the table. "From?"

He glanced at me. "Logan."

Jeez … why didn't he tell me before Logan ordered him not to bother Sal? I turned my attention back to my phone conversation. "Logan told him not to contact you."

Silence greeted my statement. After a moment passed Sal spoke. "Any idea why? I talked with Logan yesterday, and he seemed fine with me."

I sighed, turning my attention back to Bob. "Bob, why did Logan order you not to contact Sal?"

Bob finally turned to me, and I was stunned at the sadness in his face. "I talk too much. He doesn't mind me blabbing secrets to you but no one else."

My mouth dropped open. "Why doesn't he care what you say to me?"

Bob shrugged. "I guess he figures you won't use the information I accidentally let slip."

I held up a finger, so Bob would know we weren't finished with our conversation, then I turned my attention back to Sal. "It has nothing to do with you. I'll explain later. When can you meet with me?"

I heard him ask Amy a question before he answered. "How about an hour? Can you come here, or would it be better at your place?"

My laziness wanted Sal to come to the house, but I knew it was easier for them if I went there. "I'll be there in an hour."

"Good. See ya then."

Once I hung up the phone, I turned to Bob. "So Logan finally got mad when you spill the beans? How could someone use the info?"

Bob groaned. "Do we need to have this discussion?"

"No whining! Answer the question."

He sighed. "Somehow, Logan found out I told you about the time travel stuff. If someone less dependable was aware of our capability it could cause a real mess. There's some shady folks that wouldn't mind taking advantage of our abilities."

"I didn't tell Logan about the time travel comment. You know how easily he discovers everything, so you should be careful." No sense in telling him I *had* mentioned the time travel while talking with the Druid. I was pretty sure my new dead friend didn't have time to rat out Bob to Logan with the news that I was privy to the secret.

I did feel a little sorry for Bob. He never meant harm, but he needed to learn how to keep his mouth shut. Even though it probably would mean the flow of information would cease for me, at least he wouldn't be in so much trouble.

Bob nodded. "You're telling me! Logan just about blew a gasket. He almost raised his voice when he was scolding me."

I was shocked. "Wow."

Bob's head dipped again. "Yep. I was freaked out." He sighed. "So my access to certain people is cut off. Sal is one of those people."

I cocked me head. "Logan trusts Sal. Why would he worry if you let any cats out of the bag?"

"Logan trusts Sal. Logan doesn't trust some of the people Sal stills does business with, such as other mobsters."

I nodded understanding. "Ah. Makes sense."

"It's embarrassing," he whispered.

I felt a little bad for the guy. "Maybe Logan is trying to protect you. Remember, Elaine's family is mob."

We discovered during our last case that Bob's wife, Elaine, was part of a mob family. Her family despised both her and her mother, which came as no surprise to anyone associated with Elaine. She was a royal bitch, and it didn't help my attitude that she became friends with my mom once she was in Deadsville. I could understand Logan's concern with the fact that Bob has a problem keeping a secret.

Bob's face cleared, and he looked at me shocked. "I never thought about Elaine's mob connections. I bet Logan *is* trying to protect me in case I accidentally say the wrong thing in front of *them.*"

I shook my head, but I smiled at Bob's enthusiasm for a chance Logan may not hold his big, fat mouth against him.

"I better head over to Sal's. I'm still cold from the wet clothes, but I bet Amy has tea brewing."

Amy was addicted to hot tea. She even had a fancy serving tray with special tea cups. I hated the stuff, but I knew it would warm me up. Too much coffee along with no hormones, wasn't a good combination. Tea didn't seem to bother me, which delighted Amy—I resent menopause.

"I'll come with you," Bob announced.

I turned and looked at Bob. "I thought you weren't allowed to be around Sal."

Bob shook his head. "Not by myself. I can go with you though."

"Ah … well let's hit the road. Are you riding with me, or will you meet me there?"

Bob thought a second. "I'll come with you. At least you won't be alone."

I shot a quick glance toward the woods, and all my guys were still evident. They weren't acting upset, but they were definitely visible. Maybe having Bob with me was a better idea than I originally thought. I nodded. "Let's go."

Once we were settled in the car, Bob took a deep breath. "I love the fall. The colors are great, and there's a nip in the air. It's one of my favorite times of the year."

"Winter is close though," I reminded him.

"Gosh, Peg … all you do is complain about the weather. It's either too hot or too cold. You're only happy about twenty days out of the entire year."

I sat stunned by his words. When did I become so whiny? I despised ice and snow, but doesn't everyone? Ohio summers can be beautiful or hot and humid. I wasn't a fan of hot and humid. Who was? "I don't think I'm that bad."

He snorted. "You complain constantly. To be honest … it gets old."

Oh my gosh! *Bob*, of all people, was slamming me about my attitude. "I enjoy fall weather as much as the next person."

"Yep, but you focus on the fact winter is right around the corner. Enjoy what we have now and worry about winter when it's actually here."

My fingers drummed on the steering wheel as I listened to him. My anger wanted to explode, but my common sense held it at bay. When someone is one hundred percent correct about negative aspects of your personality, you have the responsibility to be honest with yourself—it sucked.

I was saved from further discussion when my cellphone blared. I grabbed it, thankful for the interruption.

Jack's voice came on the line. "Where are you?"

"In my car heading for Sal's. I thought it was about time we brought him into the picture."

"Good. I'll meet you there."

I stared at the phone for a second, realizing Jack hung up before I could respond. I shook my head, wondering why he was so wound up. I started the car and we began the ten-minute trip to Sal's house. Bob sat next to me, enjoying the beautiful scenery as we drove the winding roads to Sal's estate. He took over the house after his son, Anthony, went into an institution for the criminally nuts. I didn't realized until that point that his son didn't actually own the house. Sal moved Anthony here, so he could be treated at a hospital north of us for his mental illness. Sad to say ... the treatments didn't work, and the creep almost killed Amy and me. Our self-defense classes came in handy—Amy and I took him down with his dad lending a hand—it was a big mess.

As we pulled into Sal's driveway, Bob sighed. "I miss the tennis courts."

I glanced at him. "Sal doesn't play, and the area is perfect as a gun range."

"I know but the courts really made this place look luxurious."

I laughed. "Bob, you have no interest at all in luxurious things."

Bob squirmed in his seat. "I didn't want any of that lifestyle, but you have to admit, it looked like a movie set."

I smiled. "Yeah, I agree."

As we made our way to the door, I noticed a few pumpkins scattered throughout the flower beds. Laura, Anthony's ex-wife, was probably sprucing up the gardens and adding a touch of fall to the decor. She had a green thumb and could grow plants no one else would dare try.

The front door opened before we reached it, and I faced Sal's smiling face. He was the happiest mobster in history. I've never met a kinder person from such a dubious background—what a sweetie.

He caught me in a bear hug, and I couldn't breathe for a couple of seconds. He nodded to Bob. "Come on in. Amy's got the tea doing its thing."

I laughed, grateful for the promise of hot liquid to warm me from the damp clothes.

I followed Sal to the kitchen, and I could smell fresh cookies. Amy was going overboard, but I wasn't about to turn down oatmeal raisin delights.

"Made a couple of calls while we were waiting for you." Sal grabbed a warm cookie, then pushed the plate in my direction.

Amy filled the cup in front of me with hot tea which was, thankfully, not the green stuff she loves so much.

I raised an eyebrow. "Did you find out anything useful?"

"Depends." He glanced at a pad of paper on the counter near him. I noticed his frown deepen as he ran an experienced eye over his notes. Sal was tall and maintained his excellent posture even though age was catching up with him. I never had the nerve to ask him exactly how old he was, but I'd bet he was pushing eighty. His gray hair still had a few dark patches of color sprinkled throughout, which allowed him to appear younger. Even though I knew Sal to be a softy in some areas, I also witnessed occasions when he could be cold as steel—he was no pushover.

His eyes met mine. "Does the name Jim Morgan ring a bell?"

I nodded. "Yep. He's our guy."

"To be honest … I would never have given him a second glance." He shrugged. "Small fish in an even smaller pond."

I pursed my lips as I listened to Sal's description. "Well … he's either growing or not as small as you thought."

Sal shook his head. "Or working for someone who is a bigger problem."

My eyes widened. "That's not a good thought."

Sal shook his head. "Nope."

I took a bite of the cookie in my hand and chewed while my mind ran through the bit of information from Sal.

I glanced at him. "Anything else?"

"He owns a landscaping business which could explain the robberies."

I frowned. "How?"

Sal smiled. "Sweetie, anyone who takes care of lawns every week can figure out an owner's schedule. When they are usually home, when they are out of town, how many visitors they have, if dogs are on the property …"

I interrupted him with my hands waving. "Holy moly! I never even gave it a thought. I see lawn services all over the place."

Sal nodded. "Being a crook isn't as hard as you'd think."

"What makes you think there may be someone bigger in the picture?"

Sal glanced at his notes again as he tapped the pad of paper. "No debt … at all."

I frowned slightly. "That's a good thing … it just means he runs the business really well."

Sal shook his head. "He owns very expensive equipment … top of the line. He has hundreds of accounts, which means he has a lot of equipment to service those properties." He thumbed through the notepad. "About half his business is private homes … the rest are major businesses around town … Uh oh."

"What?" I demanded.

Sal looked at me. "He takes care of the mayor's properties … all of them."

I dropped the half-eaten cookie on the plate, then plopped my head in my now empty hands.

"Why don't you call the mayor and ask a few questions?" Amy picked this moment to chime in. "Might as well find out now if he's in the picture."

Even though I agreed with Amy, I resented the fact that the mayor seemed to have his sticky fingers in all of my serious cases—the man kept more dubious balls in the air than a circus clown.

Bennet Hayes has been the mayor of Akron forever, and he has a reputation for rubbing shoulders with many iffy people. Sal was one of those people and as far as the world knew, was a full-fledged mafia guy. Very few were aware of the decision he made years ago to change his ways and become a legit businessman. He worked with Logan, but the idea was to make his connections to the underbelly of society believe he was still one of them. Very few of his former associates were aware of his true goals for his business. So far, the plan had worked, and Sal was still able to access vital information.

"Peg, I know you don't like the man, but he has been helpful in the past," Amy said pointedly. "You should know how important it is to keep him in the fold."

I sighed. "Fine … but you don't have to cope with the man." I narrowed my eyes. "Somehow, it always seems to fall into my lap."

Amy smiled … jeez.

CHAPTER 11

I grabbed my purse, then began the process of searching for my cellphone. Once I snagged it from the depths, I hit a few buttons until I found the mayor's phone number. I sighed again, then made the call.

"Mrs. Shaw?" The second I heard his voice, my stomach churned.

I really didn't like the man but at least I no longer hated him.

"Yep. I have a few questions, but I don't want to take up too much of your time." Silence greeted my statement, so I out waited him.

Finally, he sighed. "I would be honored to help you."

For Pete's sake! Save me from politicians. We both knew he loathed helping, but he knew Logan would pay him a visit if he stalled—Logan scared him spitless.

I gritted my teeth, then took a deep breath. "Do you know Jim Morgan?"

I could feel his frown through the phone. "Sure … his company mows my lawns."

"How many lawns?"

"The house in Bath, my personal property in Akron, and the city properties." He inherited a house in the township, which his son lives in now. I'd never seen his personal home, but I knew the city probably owned enough property to keep Morgan's company busy.

I drummed my fingers on the table while I thought of my next question. "How well do you know the man?"

He hesitated. "Do you suspect him of a crime?"

"You didn't answer my question." I learned the hard way that the mayor could be just as evasive as my dead folks. Even though he could count on my discretion concerning his shady pals, he hated giving me information.

He sighed. "I know him well enough not to cross him."

Oh, Jeez. "If he's a creep why do you employ him?" I snapped. My question was met with silence … uh oh. "Is he blackmailing you?"

Sal's eyebrows climbed north, and I shrugged. The mayor's shenanigans got him in hot water a few times—you'd think the jackass would learn to steer away from shady characters.

"That's not the terminology I would use," he answered slowly.

"I'm not surprised." My tone had a touch of sarcasm.

Amy shook her head, and I knew she didn't approve of my attitude … tough beans.

"So he does have something he's holding over you?" I was treated to another dose of silence. A jab of fear shot through my system. "Does it have anything to do with Alex?"

Alex was the mayor's son and for years, a murder he witnessed caused a great deal of guilt. The mayor covered up Alex's involvement, which led to a big fat mess. The kid had been through enough in my opinion without his dad mucking up his life further.

"Absolutely not!"

I scowled. "Alex better not be involved with your questionable antics. You've done enough damage to his life." I had a soft spot for Alex, and I knew the damage done, due to a friend's insanity, may never improve the outlook for his future. He still worked for his dad's campaigns, but he never carved out a career for himself. I wasn't sure he would ever be able to totally recover from the horror he lived with for so many years.

"I promise you, Alex is not involved." The mayor's firm tone eased my worry to some degree.

"Fine, but you didn't answer my question." I wasn't letting him off the hook.

"Morgan isn't blackmailing me, but I will warn you … he isn't someone I would encourage you to antagonize."

"Do you know his wife?" I decided I would continue to question him for as long as he was willing to answer.

"Cindy?" He sounded surprised at the question. "I've met her at a few fund raisers."

"Did you ever get the feeling she is scared of her husband?"

"Interesting question." He paused. "She's a quiet woman … very pretty and quite well dressed. I don't know much about her."

His use of words intrigued me. "Why did you use the term 'interesting'?"

After a moment of quiet thought, he continued. "I've always felt their relationship was complicated."

"How?" I figured it would keep the ball rolling if I was direct.

"I have no idea. She doesn't have an out-going personality … like I said … she's a quiet woman."

"In other words, you ignored any signs of trouble because of your relationship with her husband?" I could feel my anger mounting.

He sighed. "Mrs. Shaw, I'm the mayor, not the local priest trying to solve marital issues."

Well hell … he had a point, so I changed tactics. "Did you know she has a brother?"

Silence met my question, so I kept my mouth shut, allowing him time to digest my question.

"Why do you know that type of information? I'm not sure I approve of you digging into their backgrounds. Why do you care about a landscaping company?"

The edginess in his voice made me frown. Whenever the mayor wanted me to back off, he tried intimidation. You'd think he would have learned by now that I don't respond well to his tactics. "I'm guessing you can't control this guy if he goes off the rails. I'm also willing to bet he has some type of hold over you, so eventually you'll have to spill the beans. Why not get it over with, and just tell me what the problem is now?"

"I never said there was a problem." His tone was sharp enough to slice air.

I looked over at Sal for guidance. He shook his head. I wasn't sure if he was disappointed with my attitude, or if he merely had no insight into the issue.

"Call me when you're ready to admit the guy is a stinker." I ended the call before the mayor had a chance to reply.

"Peg, when are you going to learn manners?" Amy chastised.

I frowned. "I don't like the guy."

Amy shook her head. "You might consider being nicer to him. He may surprise you and actually tell you what you need to know."

"Ha! Past experience has proven he's a politician through and through … he'll keep secrets till his dying day."

Sal laughed, but Amy wouldn't back down. "I think you should change your approach. At the very least, it would surprise him, and he may actually disclose the information you need."

I opened my mouth to argue, but slammed it shut when I realized she had a point. My fingers drummed on the table while I mulled over her advice. I didn't like to admit that I had an attitude problem at times—well a lot of the time.

Sal saved me from responding. "Peg, why don't we wait until my guys report back to me. I'm sure there's more to be learned about Morgan."

The air suddenly changed causing me to looked around. I spotted Logan standing by the window. It was amazing how often he positioned himself next to windows. I wondered why, but I didn't waste too much brain power solving the mystery. One day, I might discover the reason, but I doubted Logan would be the one to explain—he likes his secrets.

He surveyed the room. "Ah, everyone is present." His eyes stopped once he spotted Bob, but then he gave Bob a small nod.

I spoke up when no one else did. "Jack's not here yet."

He smiled as the doorbell rang.

Damnation … my Indian always knew more than he shared.

Sal chuckled as he left the kitchen to answer the door.

Amy busied herself setting out a plate for Jack's stack of cookies, then she set him out a cup as she waited for the coffee to brew. She was well aware neither of us were big fans of her tea, and she learned the road to Jack's heart was paved with coffee—she didn't worry about paving any roads to my heart.

I could hear the two men making their way down the hall to the kitchen. I shot a quick glance at Logan, he was standing there patiently waiting and looking out the window—no surprise there. The Indian spent most of his time looking out of windows, and I wondered what he saw that was hidden from the rest of us.

The aroma of Sal's special blend of coffee overpowered the sweet smell of fresh cookies. I knew it wouldn't take Jack long to spot the plate by his cup and realize some sort of snack would occupy the plate soon. If he wasn't careful, his waistline would expand more than it already had.

Bob quietly stood next to the cabinets, watching Logan like a hawk. I knew he was waiting for Logan to make some sort of comment regarding his presence at Sal's house. I personally didn't think he needed to worry, but Bob was overly concerned with Logan's opinion. He practically worshipped the Indian, and he knew Logan's powers could easily banish him to parts unknown. I doubted the Indian would ever deal harshly with Bob for one simple reason … he liked the guy.

Jack's eyes scanned the room—must be a cop thing. He nodded to Bob, then smiled at Amy.

"Coffee smells good." He glanced at the table. "Are those cookies for me?" He was pointing to the plate now stacked high.

Amy smiled. "Sit down, Jack. Coffee's almost ready … help yourself to the cookies."

Jack didn't hesitate, he made a beeline for the sweet delights. Amy poured fresh coffee in his cup, then she placed at new cup in front of me, filling it to the brim.

I smiled. "Thanks."

She laughed. "I know you only tolerate tea, and you love Sal's coffee."

I nodded as I took the first sip of heaven. I looked at Sal and gave him a thumbs up.

Sal grinned. "Did you already finished the coffee I gave you?"

Sal's coffee was specially blended, so the cost was well out of our budget.

I shook my head. "I only allow myself to brew it occasionally. I'm trying to make it last as long as possible."

Sal's grin widened. "I'll keep you supplied."

I shook my head. "It's a treat, and I want it to stay that way."

Logan turned from gazing out the window to survey the proceedings. Satisfied we were settled, he spoke. "I am pleased you are all here. We have much to discuss."

I was a little surprised, I didn't know anything changed. "Such as?"

"I have been searching for Mr. Peters' parents. They may have insight into their son-in-law which eludes our efforts. Family has the opportunity to see us not only at our best, but at our worst." He paused as he glanced at Jack. "I mean you no insult ... Mr. Morgan has covered his tracks very well."

Jack nodded as he munched his oatmeal cookie. "No offense taken. The son-of-a-bitch looks clean on paper, but I'm willing to bet he's dirty as hell."

Logan nodded. "I agree."

"You haven't found Peters' parents?" Sal asked.

Logan returned to his window gazing. "No."

I watched Logan carefully. "Do you think they are hiding?"

Logan turned to face me. "Explain your thoughts please."

I scrunched my lips as my brain kicked around an idea. "You're thinking Morgan killed them ... correct?"

Logan nodded.

I could feel my brain forming an idea ... I just wish it would share it with me. I continued my mental gymnastics for a few more seconds. "Well ... what if someone on the other side is protecting them. Maybe they have them in some sort of witness protection. Let's face it ... you can't be the only member of the dead who watches over those of us still living."

Logan frowned, but I could see he was thinking through my statement. After a few moments, he slowly nodded. "You are correct. I am merely one of many whose assignment is to fight evil here."

"Maybe you could put the word out that you are looking for whoever is protecting the Peters." I shrugged. "It would be interesting to know why they are being hidden so well."

Logan looked at Jack. "How would you proceed if you were working through the correct channels to find someone protected?"

Jack choked on the cookie in his mouth. I figured it was the shock of Logan asking for his professional opinion. I glanced down at the once full plate of cookies, and my eyes darted over to Amy.

She grinned, then walked over to the table with a fresh stack of oatmeal goodies to replace the now empty plate. I kept my mouth shut—it wasn't my waistline suffering.

Once he swallowed and took another sip of coffee to wash down any crumbs, Jack looked at Logan. "Well … the first thing would be to determine if they are actually being protected. If that's the case, it could get sticky. I don't know how you dead people operate but from past experience, I can tell you protectors don't usually like giving out any helpful information. The US Marshals run our witness protection program in this country, and I had little luck working with them in similar situations in the past."

Logan nodded. "Yes. I do not enjoy dealing with your FBI, and the US Marshals are not easy to persuade either."

Jack snorted. "I hear ya."

Logan cocked his head, looking mildly confused. "I realize you have the ability to hear me."

Sal and I both burst out laughing.

"Jack means he understands your dilemma," I clarified.

"Ah." Logan nodded understanding as the confusion on his face cleared. Every once in a while, I had to explain verbal expressions used in the twenty-first century.

Jack missed the exchange while he thought through Logan's question. "What type of network do you have on your side? Is there a ranking system?"

Logan nodded. "Of sorts."

Jack looked thoughtful. "So, you'd be a general or something equivalent?"

Logan gave a brief nod. "Your description will suffice."

"How many other generals are there? You can't be the only one."

Logan's face shut down … I knew the look.

"Uh-uh … Logan don't you dare close the doors now. You asked for Jack's opinion, so you'll damn well answer his questions," I snapped.

Bob sucked in a ton of air—I always wondered how the dead folks do that stuff. I thought he was going to faint at my tone of voice. I ignored him, keeping my eyes glued to Logan's face.

Logan narrowed his eyes, but I didn't back down. I understood his concern for security measures when it came to the workings of the other side of life, but there was only so much stonewalling he could do before he impeded the case. He had a bad habit of withholding important information until the last possible second. He and the mayor had this nasty vice in common.

My eyes never wavered, and he knew I wouldn't back off. I could hold my ground with the best of them, but I had to admit … I was sweating bullets.

Finally, he nodded, then turned back to Jack. I looked over at Sal who carefully nodded his head. I knew Sal agreed with my assessment of Logan's security measures.

"Many others of my level of authority exist. I know many of them, but you must remember our system has existed for thousands of years. It would be impossible for me to personally know each one."

Jack nodded, then reached for another cookie. "Who's the head honcho?"

Logan frowned.

"Boss … who's the boss?" I translated.

Logan nodded. "I am not permitted to divulge that information." He held up his hand as soon as my mouth opened. "I have no control concerning certain rules. They exist for a reason, and I respect them."

My mouth slammed shut—I couldn't argue this time. I knew certain rules were hard and fast. Logan could push the boundaries only so far.

Jack waved a hand dismissively. "No problem … just being a little nosey. Back to the main issue … if you're one of many generals, how do you guys communicate with each other? You know … in case you need help."

Logan was thoughtful for a moment. "The situation seldom arises. Our territories do not overlap. It is a very efficient structure."

Jack nodded. "Sure … but it's obvious at points in history you must've needed to work together."

Logan gave Jack an appraising look. "Yes … very astute."

Jack shrugged. "It doesn't take a genius to figure out the need to share burdens. History proves we've come close to destroying ourselves a couple of times."

Logan didn't move an inch, and I knew he was surprised Jack evaluated part of Logan's world so well. I kept my face as neutral as possible, hoping I wouldn't muck up Jack's progress pulling data from Logan.

Jack continued his line of questioning. "So, the long and short is … you've already made high ranking buddies. Can't you just call on them to help you find these people?"

Logan shook his head. "I do not wish to interfere with their work."

"You sure it isn't your ego at work?" I countered.

Bob moaned, and Amy clicked her tongue against the roof of her mouth. I ignored both of their disapproving noises. "Logan, we can't continue without help. Morgan covered his tracks so well that even Sal is having a tough time digging up dirt on the guy."

I glanced at Sal, pleased to see him nod. "She's got a point, Logan."

I looked at Logan, surprised to see his face contained no anger towards me.

"Why do you always assume my ego is involved?"

I shrugged. "Human nature."

He shook his head. "While I still retain my personality traits, ego is seldom involved in my decisions. Those of us in positions of leadership have many responsibilities. Asking for help is seldom encouraged."

I sighed. "Logan, Peters' parents are hidden and hidden well. If *you* can't find them, then no one can. I understand the risk involved if the bad guys discover them due to our questions. What if you merely ask someone to question the parents about their deaths ... at least it could keep them safe."

Logan gave my request a few seconds of thought, then slowly nodded. "You may have found a reasonable solution. I will proceed but with much caution."

Amy poured Jack another cup of coffee, but I shook my head when she offered me some—no need overdoing the caffeine.

Logan looked around the room. "Thank you all for your help." He faded before anyone could comment.

Bob moaned again. "Gosh, Peg ... you really need to reign in your temper. One of these days, Logan is going to lose it."

"Bob, Logan makes a practice of never losing it. He's a master when it comes to controlling himself."

Bob shook his head. "He's not perfect you know."

My mouth dropped open hearing Bob's near criticism of his idol, but before I could speak, Bob faded.

CHAPTER 12

After our dead friends left, the four of us discussed the situation. Amy kept the coffee and cookies flowing, and I kept arguing with myself about eating even one more, sweet treat. My jeans were a little snug the last few days, and I was hard at work convincing myself another cookie was a bad idea. I won the argument with my evil side, but it was a close call.

"Do you think the mayor knows more than he's sharing?" Jack eyed the fresh plate of cookies as he posed the question.

I nodded vigorously. "I'm one hundred percent positive. You'd think he would've learned by now to tell us the truth, so he can move on with his life. He admitted he wouldn't want to cross Morgan, which indicated he was well aware of the fact the guy is shady."

Jack nodded. "It follows his standard pattern ... he's always looking out for number one."

Sal was thoughtful for a moment before speaking. "He's been in office long enough to know everyone's dirty laundry. Maybe he's keeping secrets for himself more than protecting Morgan."

We all were silent as we thought through Sal's idea.

Finally, Jack shook his head. "Nah ... doesn't fit the mayor's psychological profile."

I raised an eyebrow. Amy studied psychology a million years ago, so I considered her the resident expert. Since when did Jack know someone's psychological health?

Amy smiled as I glanced in her direction. "Jack's correct. The mayor has developed a pattern to his behavior. To be honest … each one of us has a pattern which has guided us through life."

Sal cocked his head to one side. "What's my pattern?"

Amy smiled up at him. "To protect the ones you love."

Oh, Jeez.

Sal grabbed her in a bear hug, and they laughed together. I thought I'd puke. Jack, however, enjoyed their romantic moment and grinned.

I kicked him under the table. "Don't encourage them."

His grin grew as he grabbed another cookie.

"You'll explode!" I protested.

He was unphased by my comment. "Yeah … but it'll be a sweet experience."

I shook my head.

Sal turned his attention to me. "What's the deal with Bob not being able to see me if he's alone?"

I waved a hand. "He talks too much, and Logan about had a heart attack when Bob spilled the beans about something."

Jack shook his head. "Baloney. Logan only tells Bob what he wants passed along. How many times has he accidentally told us information that we eventually realized Logan wanted us to have, but for some damn reason, he didn't tell us himself?"

I plopped my head in my hands. "I'm being played again! Damn it!"

Jack chuckled, then looked down at his near empty coffee cup. Amy noticed, then smiled as she reached for the fresh pot of coffee. "Jack, I've never seen anyone drink as much coffee as you. I'm surprised you can handle the volume of caffeine you allow yourself."

I sighed, remembering when I could drink gallons of coffee each day and never experience any backlash. Menopause forced me to slow down on the caffeine—I missed the old days.

I looked over at Sal. "You really can't find any useful information about Jim Morgan?"

Sal shook his head. "Nope. Not yet … but I'm convinced my guys will come through eventually."

My fingers drummed a rhythm on the table as my mind wandered around, trying to determine what direction we should pursue. My brain finally landed on an idea, but I wasn't impressed. "What if we tried contacting Morgan's wife? What was her name?"

Jack pulled a small notebook from his pocket and flipped through a few pages. "Cindy."

I snapped my fingers. "Yep, that's the name the mayor gave me. I wonder how hard it would be to contact her?"

Jack shook his head. "We need to be careful. I don't want to tip Morgan off that we are nosing around his business and personal life."

I waved a hand. "We've got to start somewhere. She may accidentally give us a golden nugget ... you never know."

Amy cut in. "I agree with Jack. She may not realize what a stinker she is married to, or she could be involved with the shady part of his life. Why don't we tread carefully for a change?"

Was her remark a direct hit on my personality? Probably. Along with self-defense classes and gun training, Amy seemed determined to curb my actions. She might have a point but occasionally, someone has to get the ball moving and throw caution to the wind.

Before I could open my mouth with a snappy remark, Sal spoke up. "Why don't we ask your dad to do a little reconnaissance? He would be discreet, so she wouldn't have a clue he was watching her."

Jack frowned. "I usually use Bob. Why bother Dave?"

Sal shook his head. "Bob seems a little out of sorts today. I'd be more comfortable asking Dave."

I had to agree with Sal's assessment of Bob's mindset. He usually loved sneaking around for us and spying, but something was sure bothering him. I had no idea what it could be, but I didn't want to chance him screwing up and mucking up the investigation.

"Dad's been busy lately, but it never hurts to ask." I called for my dad and within seconds, he joined us in Sal's kitchen.

He glanced around the room, then gave everyone present a quick nod. I noticed the harried expression on his face and wondered what caused it. "What's up sweetie?"

"We need a little spying done and Bob seems out of sorts today. Could you fill in for us?"

Dad shook his head. "Can't, babe. I'm busy. Bob's had a rough couple of days with our workload, and I wouldn't advise using him."

My eyes narrowed as I studied my dad's face. He wasn't going to give an inch, and I knew not to push. The dead folks in my life tended to fade or at the very least, lecture. The last thing I needed was a fatherly discourse concerning my needs.

I sighed. "Anyone you can suggest. They have to be dead."

Dad nodded. "Sure ... use Henry. He'd love to help."

Wow ... I forgot all about Henry. He'd been a private investigator during the forties in Atlanta, Georgia. Logan used him as a part of my security team during the last big case we worked. I loved his southern accent and his view of life. "Jeez ... I didn't even think of Henry. Do you know if he's busy?"

Dad shook his head. "He just finished a job for Logan and a little bored. Helping you would probably be welcome."

"Great … thanks for the info." I paused. "What are you guys working on that is so exhausting?"

Dad gave me the 'parent' look, then faded without another word. Well … I tried to pry a clue or two out of him.

"Henry?" Jack was thoughtful for a minute. "A bit out of touch don't you think?"

I snorted. "You honestly believe Logan would use someone not at the top of his game? Henry may look old fashioned, but he knows what he's doing."

Jack shrugged. "Maybe it's the fedora. It dates him in my mind I guess."

"Jeez, Jack … fedoras were the style in the forties. Plus, Henry is *dead*, so he has advantages we don't. Hell … Logan's ancient!"

Jack nodded. "True. Well … give Henry a try."

I called for Henry and within a few seconds, he had joined our little party.

Once he spotted Amy and me, his hand shot up and he whipped his hat off his head. Talk about manners! "Good afternoon, ladies." He nodded to Jack and Sal. "Nice to see everyone."

I smiled always glad to see him. "Hi, Henry … nice to see you too. Could you give us a hand with a case?"

Henry smiled. "Sure thing … fill me in on the details."

I took a deep breath, realizing I was afraid Henry wouldn't help. Logan had our regular helpers working for him, so I was grateful Henry was willing to give us a hand.

He pulled out his little black book to make notes. The notebook was in his pocket when he died and mysteriously stayed with his ghost. He never ran out of paper or ink. Henry didn't understand how the little book worked, but he was grateful it made it to Deadsville with him.

Once I filled him in on what details we had available to us, he nodded. "Don't fret, Miss Peg. I'll scope out the situation and report back." He cocked his head to one side. "Is Logan sittin' this one out?"

I shook my head. "Nope. He's making inquiries on your side of life. I need help here."

Henry frowned. "Are there problems I should know about?"

I scrunched my face as I thought how to answer. I trusted Henry completely, but I wasn't sure how much he needed to know. My stomach flipped when I realized I was doing exactly what Logan always did to me … withholding information … Damnation.

"I don't think so. Logan seems to be comfortable with his inquiries on your side." I shrugged. "You know how he is." I hoped the vague answer covered enough ground to satisfy Henry.

He nodded. "Yep. He's a corker sometimes." With a quick grin and a nod aimed at all of us, he faded.

Sal smiled. "He's a nice guy."

"Yeah, I really like Henry." I sighed. "I felt a little guilty about not telling him the whole story."

Jack drained his coffee cup, then held up a hand to stop Amy from refilling it for him. "No need to feel guilty … Henry will get results with the info you gave him. Too many facts may clog his thinking and take him down dead ends."

I pulled on my bottom lip. "I don't know, Jack … Henry's a pretty smart man. He ran his own business don't forget."

Jack shook his head. "I never said he wasn't smart. The only part you left out was crap on their side. Logan probably doesn't want those details known outside our group." He waved a hand to include Amy and Sal.

Sal nodded. "Jack's got a point, Peg … let Logan decide if and when Henry should know about the problems in their world. The less we muck about in their business over there, the better."

I nodded, but I worried I was becoming too much like Logan. I didn't want the old Indian's habits to rub off on me if I could help it.

Amy smiled. "Peg, it's fine. You aren't keeping vital information from Henry. You gave him exactly what he needs to help *us*. If Logan needs Henry to investigate on their side of things, he knows where to find him."

I sighed. Amy had a point, and I was relieved to hear her opinion. I knew her well enough to know if she thought I was wrong, she would certainly tell me. I looked around the table. "What's next?"

Jack stood. "I'm headed back to the office. This isn't the only case I have, not to mention the mountain of paperwork on my desk." He shook his head, disgusted. "You'd be surprised how much goes into even the smallest incident reported."

Amy looked at him curiously. "Such as?"

Jack scoffed. "A cat stuck in a tree has a paper trail."

Amy laughed and shook her head. "You have to file a report for a cat?"

He nodded. "Sure. If a call comes into the station, it has to be accounted for … paperwork rules the world."

"Cookies for the road?" Amy offered.

Jack hesitated. "I better not. Lori is going to kill me if she finds out I ate a cookie."

"*A* cookie?" I snorted. "How about platefuls of cookies."

Jack blushed. "What she doesn't know won't hurt her."

I smiled. "She'll know as soon as you put on a few pounds instead of losing them."

He shook his head. "Probably." He glanced at his watch. "Gotta go … call if you find out anything useful."

I nodded. "Yep … same goes for you."

Nodding, he started for the door, then hesitated. "Sal, I never thought I'd say this … thanks for everything." Without waiting for Sal's reply, Jack hurried down the hall, then we heard the front door open and close.

I stared after Jack shocked. "Wow."

Sal grinned. "I'll take that as the highest compliment."

I nodded. "You should. Jack has struggled with your involvement since the beginning. The fact that he's come to respect you enough to acknowledge your value to our little group is a big step for him."

Sal nodded. "I appreciate his dilemma."

As police chief, Jack would have a hard time explaining his relationship with a known mobster. So far, it wasn't a problem. That didn't mean it couldn't become a mess in the future.

The phone rang, and Sal nodded. "Probably my guys. Hopefully they've found something useful."

He answered, and I tried to pretend my ears weren't glued to his conversation. I was disappointed. The most I heard was Sal's, 'yep,' 'okay', and some Italian being thrown around—no help at all. He ended the call and looked at me. "My guys have found a few tidbits that might be useful."

I watched him curiously. "Such as?"

Sal smiled slightly. "Morgan has ties to Elaine's family."

My mouth dropped open. Bob's wife, Elaine, was the niece of a mob guy Sal knew from his younger days. Poor Bob had no idea about Elaine's connections until recently. Elaine, along with her mother, were not the favorites of the family and basically had no contact with them since her marriage to Bob.

"What kind of ties?" I asked once I could push my brain back into gear.

"He's the grandson of the old man, Vito Lombardi."

My fingers began their frantic dance on the table while I tried to connect the dots. It never occurred to me that Jim Morgan could be related to Elaine's family—this news came out of left field.

"Jim Morgan is Elaine's cousin." It wasn't a question, but there were a ton of them flying around my head.

Sal nodded.

I looked at him. "Is this a problem for us?"

Sal pursed his lips. "I'm not sure. I haven't had much business to discuss with Vito for quite a few years. I'm surprised Morgan is Vito's grandson … I had no idea."

My fingers slowed their movement, but the tapping hadn't ceased completely. The shock started to wear off, and I worked hard to force my brain to make sense of the mess. "What's this Vito guy like? I mean, is he nasty or someone you can reason with once he has facts."

"Good question. We could be looking at big complications if Vito sanctioned Morgan's enterprise. On the other hand, if Morgan is off doing his own thing without Vito's knowledge, it could work in our favor."

I was thoughtful as all the questions rolled around in my head. "How do we find out which it is, and why didn't Peters know his sister married the grandson of a mobster?"

Sal nodded. "Those are good questions."

"Bob!" I yelled.

The air changed, and I knew he was present. Bob looked a bit surprised I called, but I plunged head first into the matter at hand. "I know you've been nosing around ever since we discovered Elaine's connections to the world of criminals."

His face turned beet red, but he didn't agree or disagree with my statement.

"Jim Morgan is her cousin." I decided I needed to see his reaction to determine if he was holding back on us. I had the answer in a split second.

His mouth dropped open, then after a few moments, he shook his head. "I didn't know." His voice was barely a whisper.

Bob can't lie ... it's against the rules over in Deadsville. More importantly, Bob isn't a natural liar, so I would've known if he was fudging the truth. "You didn't know even though you've been snooping around Elaine's family?"

Bob shook his head. "I've been pretty busy with assignments from Logan. He keeps me hopping."

I tapped my finger against my lips while thoughts whirled around inside my head. "Haven't you been keeping tabs on Elaine?"

"Sure, but not full time. Logan has me checking on her a few times a week. He doesn't really trust Elaine much, you know."

That was an understatement, but I kept the thought to myself. Bob tended to get off track easily, and I learned the hard way how difficult it could be to drag him back to the current situation.

I cleared my throat. "When was the last time you checked on her?"

His face scrunched up as he thought through the question. "Hmm ... let's see, maybe two or three days ago?"

My eyebrow raised. "Is that a question or a statement."

I really had to nail Bob down when it came to details. I decided it must be some sort of virus which infects a person once they arrived in Deadsville. Logan was the master of evasive answers. The problem I faced with Bob was he was never too sure of himself even while living.

Out of the corner of my eye, I saw Amy shake her head. Seldom does she appreciate my tactics. I turned and made a face at her, then turned my attention back to Bob. "You didn't see Elaine with Jim Morgan?"

Bob's eyes widened. "Oh gosh ... no! I would've told you."

I sighed. Bob was telling the whole truth.

"Bob, do you think it would be a problem if you did a little detective work for us?" Amy's sweet tone almost made me gag, but I knew it would work miracles on Bob.

"Sure! No problem." His face shone bright, and I knew he saw himself as Sam Spade in the *Maltese Falcon*. Humphrey Bogart he wasn't.

I eyed Bob, wondering if he was really up to the task. "Henry is doing a little spying for us too. I don't want you surprised if you bump into him."

Bob frowned. "Why didn't you call me?" Sal, Amy, and I exchanged uncomfortable glances. Bob could be dim, but he wasn't stupid ... he saw the looks. "Don't you guys trust me anymore?"

It was my turn to be surprised. "Trust you? Of course we do ... we just asked you to snoop for us!"

"You seemed a bit distracted earlier," Sal added. "We didn't want to bother if it wasn't necessary."

I smiled when I heard Sal speak. He could smooth over almost any situation. I flashed him a grateful glance, then I snapped my focus back to Bob. "Bob, if Logan has you too busy we understand."

Bob frowned. "Busy with worthless errands in my opinion."

My eyebrow rose a fraction, but I kept my mouth shut.

Bob waved his hand dismissively. "Don't get me wrong. I'd do anything for Logan, but he has me running around do busy work."

Amy sighed. "Did it ever occur to you that Logan understands how upsetting it must've been for you to discover Elaine's family secret?"

Bob and I stared at her for a second. Amy's insight into Logan's methods could be unnerving at times.

"Wow ... I never even considered he might be protecting me," Bob whispered.

I rolled my eyes. The last thing Bob needed was another reason to hero worship Logan.

Amy smiled. "Logan cares about your well-being, and I'm sure he realized you needed to keep busy until you had time to digest the news about Elaine."

Amy was laying it on a bit thick in my opinion, but I didn't bother to argue. She was probably one hundred percent correct in her analysis of the situation. Plus, discovering out Elaine didn't marry him for love must've hurt down to his core.

I watched him, mildly surprised. "That's what was bothering you ... thinking Logan didn't trust you anymore?"

Bob nodded. "Sure. When you find out your wife has notorious connections with the bad guys, it seems reasonable the boss may question my dedication to the cause."

I frowned. "What 'cause'?"

He looked shocked. "Fighting evil of course."

I sighed. "Trust me, Logan doesn't believe you could be evil."

He hesitated. "Are you sure?"

"Oh, for Pete's sake! I'm positive. If Logan didn't trust you, he would have told us."

Bob's face cleared. "You have a point."

Jeez Louise.

I returned his attention to the case. "Do you know if Elaine has been in contact with her family?"

"I don't know about this Morgan fellow, but I guarantee she hasn't spoken with any of the others. They won't have a thing to do with her." He shook his head. "They really hate her."

Well hell … I actually had something in common with the Lombardi family—I hated Elaine enough for all of us.

Amy nodded agreement. "She's not an easy person to like."

Sal snorted, but he didn't add a comment of his own.

Bob looked at all of us. "What exactly am I supposed to be detecting? It won't get me into trouble will it?"

I smiled at his questions. As aggravating as Bob is sometimes, he's a kid at heart, and I have a soft spot for him. "We need to know if old man Lombardi knows about Morgan's illegal activities. If so, we need to know if he is helping the creep." I decided to keep it short and simple.

Too bad Sal had to add his two cents. "While you're poking around, find out if Elaine is involved in any way, shape, or form. We need to know who all the players are."

Bob nodded, then began to fade but Amy called him back. "Would it be possible for us to speak with David Peters?"

Bob frowned. "I'm not sure where Logan has him stashed, but I'll ask."

Amy smiled. "Thank you for your help."

Bob's beaming face faded.

I looked over at Sal. "Do you think we asked a little too much?"

Sal grinned. "Maybe."

Jeez.

CHAPTER 13

Once Bob was on his way, we finished a little chit chat, then I decided it was time to head home. After I thanked Amy and Sal for coffee and cookies, I left. As I pulled into the driveway, I spotted a limo parked just ahead. I knew only one man who rode in one of those monstrosities … the mayor—I wasn't a happy camper.

I parked next to the enormous car and immediately after, the back door opened. My stomach turned when I realized it was not the person I expected. Instead a short, pudgy, balding man who was at least seventy years old, if not older, stepped out. I had a sneaking suspicion who my visitor was, and I didn't like it one bit.

"May I help you?" I decided to be polite. Maybe he had the wrong house—a nice dream. I was sure I didn't win the dream lottery this time.

He looked me over carefully. "Mrs. Shaw?"

I had to admit, he didn't appear threatening, but my stomach wouldn't calm down. "Who's asking?" I demanded.

Somewhere in the back of my brain, a teeny thought broke through warning me I might consider better manners at some point in my life. It was too late at this moment, but I made a mental note for future reference.

His eyes narrowed a tad too much for my level of comfort, but I held his gaze defiantly, which shows how stupid I could be at times.

"We need to talk." He turned and gave his driver a quick nod, then started for my front door.

I stood still for a split second, then hurried past him, making it to the door before he did.

"First of all, I didn't invite you. Second ... you haven't introduced yourself, which means you won't be receiving an invitation any time soon. Third ..." I was cut off from further comment.

"Mrs. Shaw, please accept my deepest apologies. My name is Vito Lombardi, and I believe we need to discuss important matters."

I sighed. I was on a roll, and he derailed my rant. Damn ... now I was forced to be nice.

I nodded. "Thank you, but I'm not sure we have anything important to discuss."

He shook his head. "I disagree. Please allow me to join you inside, and I will explain myself."

I looked toward the woods, slightly relieved when I spotted my horde of dead protectors. They seemed interested in my conversation with the old man, but not one of them appeared anxious.

I took a deep breath, then nodded to my unwanted guest. "Fine." I turned to unlock the door as a thought struck home. I did a quick pivot, looking at him. "Are you armed?"

Lombardi frowned as he shook his head. "Mrs. Shaw, this isn't a movie. I am never armed."

I gave the guy a quick nod, then unlocked the door. As we headed toward the kitchen, I felt the air change, so I knew someone without a heartbeat joined us. I glanced around and spotted Dad leaning against the wall near the kitchen entrance.

"The guys ..." He jerked his thumb towards the woods. "... let me know you had company. I thought I'd stick around and make sure all was well."

As much as I hated to admit it ... I was relieved, and my eyes fill with tears. I nodded but kept leading Lombardi as we rounded the doorway.

I pointed to a chair. "Make yourself comfortable. Would you like some coffee?"

He gave me a brief nod. "Yes, please."

I made a quick decision and grabbed Sal's special blend. Silence filled the room as we waited for the coffee to brew. My brain was on overload as I tried to decide how to handle the situation I was in with my newest mob guy.

Once coffee was placed in front of him, I glanced at him. "Milk? Sugar?"

"No, thank you." He took a sip, then nodded his approval. "I see you know Salvatorio." Lombardi grinned and his perfect teeth shone so bright, I knew he had them professionally whitened—those suckers could've beamed messages into outer space.

My eyebrows rose in surprise, but I kept my mouth clamped shut. "What makes you believe I know him?"

He pointed to the coffee cup. "Only Sal imports this blend." He shook his head. "Too expensive for my wallet."

Too expensive for Lombardi? Wow. I looked down at my own cup, suddenly glad Sal gave me the stuff for free.

Lombardi continued when I didn't speak. "Salvatorio has done well for himself. Once he started to go legit, the feds backed off and left him alone."

Again, I found myself surprised at the extent of my guest's knowledge.

He laughed, waving a dismissive hand. "Everyone knows Sal is moving all his business away from the old ways." He shook his head sadly. "It was a sad day for the rest of us. Sal was a good, trustworthy man. Those of us not following his lead, respect his decision and are keeping our distance for his sake."

I frowned slightly. "You don't think he's a good man now?"

"He's probably a better man. He was never comfortable with the old ways and as time marched on, I admit his decision was wise." He shook his head. "Tradition is a hard habit to break."

We took another slurp of the expensive coffee, both of us enjoying the sensation of money pouring down our throats. I'd worry about caffeine overload later.

I looked over at him. "Why are you here?"

He raised an eyebrow. "You are blunt."

I shrugged but held my tongue.

Lombardi took his time looking around the kitchen before his eyes finally settled on the window. "Nice view."

I watched him carefully. "We like it."

He eventually turned his attention back to me. "You work for the local police force."

Since it wasn't a question, I didn't offer a reply.

He continued when I didn't speak. "I know you are trying to solve the recent murder here in the township."

Still not a question, so I continued to remain quiet.

"You think my grandson may be involved," he persisted.

I shrugged, but my mouth stayed shut.

He sighed. "You may be correct."

I looked over at Dad and raised an eyebrow.

Dad joined my surprise with his own eyebrow climbing. "Let's see where he is trying to take this conversation."

I nodded, then turned my attention back to Lombardi. "What do you want from me.”

He shifted his weight in the chair, sighing. “My grandson would like to take my position within the family. He will never be ready to run our operation because he doesn’t have the temperament for leading this family into the future. He will ruin everything we have built for generations.” He shook his head as sadness overcame him. “He’s greedy and dishonest.”

My eyebrow rose again. “Dishonest? Really? You’re the mob for Pete’s sake.”

Lombardi smiled. “The families are honest with each other. If not, wars within the community would frequently occur. My grandson refuses to believe our honor with one another is important.”

I decided to come right out with my question. “Do *you* think he killed his brother-in-law?”

He cocked his head to one side as he thought through my less than subtle question. “The CIA man? It’s possible. Stupid … but possible.”

My mouth dropped open, and Lombardi grinned his high wattage grin again. “I also investigate people. He married a nice girl from a nice family. She looked a little too good to be true, but the fact is, she’s a nice girl.”

I couldn’t say much … my own father researched Adam’s fiancée for me. There’s a lot of nuts out there, so Dad wanted me to know Adam had chosen wisely.

My fingers drummed on the table. “Do you think your grandson killed her parents?”

He shrugged. “That is another incident he is quite capable of committing.”

I frowned. “Why on earth would he kill them?”

“Capital for his company would be my guess. There was a will that favored his wife.”

I was a little surprised by this information. “Do you have any proof for me?”

He shook his head. “No … not yet.”

My fingers continued dancing on the table as thoughts zipped along various pathways in my brain. “None of this explains why you’re here.”

“I wanted you to be aware that James is quite dangerous. He’s not insane like poor Salvatorio’s son … he’s dangerous. Greed will do that to a person. He is also predictable, which is why I may be able to help you.”

I was a little shocked. “You know about Anthony? How?” Sal’s son was totally around the bend, and his insanity created a couple of dicey situations.

Lombardi shrugged. “Word gets around. Plus, I have known the boy since he was born. It didn’t help that Bella also had very serious problems.”

Sal’s wife was worse than Anthony. The thought of her still made my stomach churn. Even residing in Deadsville, Bella caused more than her fair share of problems for the family. Her control over Anthony was just as strong now she was dead as when she was alive.

I studied my coffee companion with interest. He seemed to know a whole lot about Sal's family, which did nothing to ease my stomach. What he wanted from me was the question burning to be asked. "There must be more to this visit than a kind warning. What's in it for you?"

He placed his coffee cup on the table as he carefully considered how to answer me. "I wish I could tell you of the deep love I have for my grandson. However, it is with sadness I tell you I have no love for him. He has disgraced the family on more than a few occasions."

I was still slightly confused. "You're basically throwing him to the dogs. Why me? You could've easily gone to the chief of police."

He shook his head. "It would be best if my visit with you was kept under wraps. The family doesn't need to be aware of our little chat. My presence at the police station would've caused long term problems."

I thought for about a split second. "Bullshit! There's more to your visit than the fact that you don't like your bratty grandson."

He studied my face for what seemed like an eternity. I wasn't frightened of the man, but I felt a hot flash threatening, and it was making me edgy. I held his gaze, taking great satisfaction when Lombardi looked away first. "I heard through the grape vine that you were a tough cookie."

I snorted. "Don't know if I'd describe myself quite in that manner, but I don't like being manipulated."

He held up a hand. "I don't mean to make you uncomfortable. James needs to be stopped before he gets any further out of control."

"I thought you mob guys took care of family situations. I assumed if your grandson was a problem, then you'd have him bumped off."

Lombardi laughed. "You have watched too many movies. Even so, it would upset my wife if James had any type of accident."

I looked at him shocked. "Your wife loves him?"

"Not necessarily, but she did love our daughter, James' mother. James has no siblings, and our sweet girl doted on him his entire life." He paused. "She died a few years ago from breast cancer."

A blast of compassion almost overwhelmed me. "I'm so sorry ... I didn't realize."

He nodded. "Thank you. I don't believe James shed one tear for his mother. I knew then he was worthless."

Family problems seemed to be everywhere, and I was thankful my own family was stable. I was thoughtful for a moment. "So ... this is some sort of revenge against James?"

He sighed. "Revenge is a strong word. I would rather consider my visit here today as a way to contain his greed and vanity."

I watched him carefully. "Who am I allowed to tell about our conversation?"

He pursed his lips. "I would be comfortable if you needed to tell Sal. It could be awkward if your friend, the police chief, was made aware. I will leave the final decisions to you … I trust your instincts."

"You could've gone to Sal yourself. Wouldn't a visit to his house be safer?"

He shook his head. "It could also cause Sal problems he doesn't deserve. You would be surprised how aware all the families are when it comes to our visitors. Sal entertains Chief Monroe often, and we respect their working relationship." He shrugged again. "Plus, there is his lady friend to consider."

I broke out into a full body sweat at the mention of Amy. "Could she be in danger?"

Lombardi held up a hand. "Never from me … but I can think of one or two other families who may see their relationship as a card to hold over Sal."

I sat on my hands once they began to shake. I couldn't tell if the shaking was due to fear or anger. Either way, I didn't want the old man to see my reaction. I glanced at Dad. His eyes had narrowed as he watched the old mob guy carefully.

I cleared my throat, trying to regain my composure. "Should I warn Sal?"

He shook his head. "Sal is a smart man. He understands how things work and will take correct measures to ensure her safety. I wouldn't be surprised if he already put people in place just for that purpose."

I relaxed a bit once my brain reminded me that Sal knew his world a hell of lot better than I did. Lombardi was probably one hundred percent correct about Amy's security, which could explain why she was at Sal's more than her own home. "Am I in danger?"

He shook his head again. "Not to my knowledge. I have certain friends that keep me apprised of your recent plunge into investigative work. I don't believe anyone else is aware."

I frowned. "You keep up to date on my activities? A bit creepy, don't you think?"

He smiled. "Not any creepier than the fact that you see dead people."

Dad stood straight up, and I almost fainted. It took a few moments for me to gather myself together before I could respond. "What makes you think I see dead people?"

"You keep looking over at the guy in the corner. I assume he is someone important to you." Lombardi was matter of fact with his statement. I couldn't detect any menace in his manner, but I wasn't happy he could see Dad or knew about my Deadsville gang.

I nodded. "Yep … he's my dad."

"I also have departed family members who keep me aware of certain activities in my community."

Well hell … I didn't expect this turn of events. I wondered if Logan knew Lombardi was in contact with dead folks.

I decided to find out as much as I could. "Where is your community?"

"South of Akron. Our sphere of influence is mainly farming communities and small towns."

"Farms? The mob controls farms?" I couldn't keep the disbelief out of my tone.

Lombardi smiled. "You'd be amazed at our farming capabilities."

His comment made me wonder what type of *crops* the old guy was growing, but I kept my mouth shut—no sense sticking a toe in water that could be filled with sharks.

Dad spoke up at this point. "Mr. Lombardi, would I know any of your family on this side of life?"

He looked over at Dad. "Doubtful. Do you speak Italian or go to Catholic Mass?"

Dad shook his head as I turned to him. "They have Mass in Deadsville?" Dad glared at me, so I knew my timing irritated him.

Lombardi continued disregarding my question as well. "Then the answer is no. I mean no disrespect, but my contacts from your world are very old school. They tend to stick to familiar surroundings."

Dad's eyes swiveled back to Lombardi, then he nodded. "That's understandable."

I looked at Dad, trying to guess what he was trying to squeeze from Lombardi. I decided he wanted to know if we had a bigger problem on our hands than we realized.

Lombardi continued before Dad could ask any more questions. "They are respectable people. They followed the rules, and they were serious about family ties. If not for their help, I would've never discovered James' illegal enterprises or the extent of his greed."

I frowned slightly. "His business isn't legal?"

"The landscaping is very legal. His antiques business isn't."

My mouth dropped open. "Antiques? What antiques?" Dad and I exchanged glances—this was certainly news.

Lombardi smiled and again, I was almost blinded by the glare from those pearly whites. "You'd only know about the antiques if you were a high roller."

He had my full attention now. "How illegal are we talking?"

"Nazi plunder, stolen art … mostly European stuff." He shrugged. "Objects you'd only read about or see in one of those adventure movies."

"How long has he been operating this little side business?" I needed as much information as he was willing to give.

Lombardi tilted his head back, studying my ceiling. I refused to follow his glance. I didn't want to discover some sort of problem … it's happened before, and I cringe every time a visitor's eyes began roaming. "It's been about ten years by now. I ignored his venture, hoping he would realize the people he was dealing with could cause problems for him." He shook his head. "The boy's greed overwhelms any logic he may have, which isn't much to brag about in the first place."

I was silent for a moment as I did a little thinking of my own. I looked over at Dad, and I could tell he was as stumped as I was. We would probably need our Deadsville gang to enlighten us. I turned my attention back to Lombardi. "People don't just jump into the underbelly of the art world and start making money. Someone must have approached him with a deal he couldn't pass up."

Lombardi hesitated. "I've never been able to discover who he works with."

I snorted. "Bullshit. With your connections? That's hard to believe."

He shook his head. "I'm serious … these types of situations demand extreme caution. Remember … James is angling to take over my position within the organization."

Memories rushed to the forefront of my brain. Anthony's determination to push Sal out of his way and take the mob family back to what he thought were the glory days mirrored what Lombardi was telling me. "Were Anthony and James friends?"

Lombardi opened his mouth to give me a negative answer, then suddenly he slammed his mouth closed.

Slowly, he shook his head. "I never considered Anthony could be involved. James always seemed a bit uncomfortable around him when they were kids. It's an avenue I haven't researched."

I thought back to Anthony's hall crammed full of expensive art. It didn't take a genius to connect the dots. Anthony was probably the person who introduced James to the world of illegal art.

"Do us all a favor and do some digging. I don't want to step into a viper's nest. You have associates who you trust, and I'll talk with Sal."

The old man nodded. "Tell Salvatorio hello for me, will you?"

"Tell him yourself," I countered.

He shook his head, "That's not a wise move … eyes and ears are everywhere."

I studied his face a minute. "Are you afraid of James?"

He shrugged. "Fear is not the word I would choose … I'm suspicious. I don't trust my own grandson."

"You and Sal have a lot more in common than you think … call him."

Lombardi stood. "Thank you for the coffee and your hospitality. I will be in touch." I joined him, and we walked in silence to the door. Before he walked out of the house, he turned. "Be careful. James is quite dangerous."

I watched his driver open the door for him, then without even a small glance back at me, he sat in the car with his eyes straight ahead. As they drove down the drive, I realized he steered the conversation away from his ability to see the dead folks … damn.

CHAPTER 14

I wandered back to the kitchen with my brain in overdrive.

Dad was still leaning against the wall, waiting for my return. "I'll need to inform Logan about Lombardi's abilities."

I nodded. "I agree. He must've seen my pals out in the woods when he was enjoying the view."

"Yep. We should've focused more on exactly who he has contact with on my side of life. I hope to hell Elaine isn't one of his connections."

I shook my head. "She's not liked … remember?"

"That doesn't mean anything. The old man is her uncle, blood ties could be more important to him than we would like."

I dropped my head into my hands. Why did these complications arise with every bloody case?

I could feel Dad's grin, so lifted my head. "What?"

"Twinkle Toes, don't get discouraged. Every investigation you are involved in has unsavory folks tangled up in it. There wouldn't be crime in the first place if everyone played nice."

"How does Peters fit into this mess? How did Lombardi discover he was in the CIA? That information should've been a closely guarded secret. I wouldn't know if I didn't find the hidden panel in his house."

Dad nodded. "Those are all good questions. I'm not sure the old guy has it totally figured out yet. I think he is counting on you to solve his problems with his grandson."

"I don't want to solve anything!" I could feel tears threaten as the hot flash finally arrived in full force. I fanned myself as I kept the tears at bay. I won the battle concerning the tears, but the hot flash lasted longer than usual … jeez. I snuck a glance toward the woods and was slightly relieved when I realized, even though it was filled with my protectors, they seemed to be chatting comfortably with one another as they milled around. I looked over at Dad. "The gangs all here."

"Yep, but they are relaxed, which is a good sign."

I sighed. "I wish they weren't there at all … it would be a better sign."

Dad laughed. "Sweetie, they are *always* there. Their presence isn't the problem. When you can *see* them is when I worry."

"I know." I threw my head back into my hands and sighed. "I'm tired of dead people complicating cases, I'm tired of nasty people trying to kill me, and most of all, I'm tired of being tired!"

"Your reaction is to be expected." Logan's voice came from over by the window.

I lifted my head and faced Logan, narrowing my eyes. "What exactly does that mean?"

"A high percentage of your investigations have been rather troublesome." He was completely calm as he spoke.

I scowled. "Troublesome? That's the best adjective you can come up with?"

Dad laughed, but I didn't think it was funny.

Logan ignored my nasty comment. "I do not believe Mr. Lombardi will be a problem."

I watched Logan, carefully considering his statement. "He has the ability to see the dead … I don't like it."

"You would be amazed at the number of people who have the capability." He was still as cool as a cucumber.

"The last person who had access to dead people tried to kill me!" I countered.

Anthony's mother, Bella, had been whispering in his ear for years, both while alive and dead. She helped push him over the edge mentally—it wasn't a pretty picture.

"I need you to help Mr. Peters." Logan had a bad habit of changing the subject when the conversation became sticky.

"How? Isn't he your problem now?" I'm pretty sure Logan didn't miss the sarcasm in the question, but he chose to ignore it. He does that a lot when I'm in a bad mood.

"We promised to help his sister. After hearing Mr. Lombardi describe his grandson's illegal activity, I fear Mr. Peters' sister may need our assistance."

I stared at Logan shocked. "You were here the whole time?"

Logan ignored my question.

I sighed, knowing he wouldn't budge an inch. "Fine … where is Mr. Peters now?"

"He is completing his orientation classes. I will have Bob bring him to you once he is available."

Orientation classes? I raised an eyebrow. Logan never discussed his side of life in detail before, so I wondered if he knew Bob accidentally let slip another slice of knowledge concerning the weird afterlife routine. I kept my fat mouth shut. I knew the old Indian well enough to realize he would never mention orientation classes if he wasn't already aware I had at least some small insight into their world.

I sighed. "What am I supposed to do with Mr. Peters?"

Logan watched me carefully. "I believe he has information that may prove helpful."

I frowned, slightly confused. "Helpful? I thought he already told us everything he knew."

Logan hesitated before answering—not a good sign. "There may be stray bits of information he is unaware he gathered, so he failed to understand the significance."

My eyes narrowed. I knew deceit when I heard it. The problem was … the dead can't lie. They can confuse and leave out important bits and pieces, but they couldn't out-right lie. At the very least, Logan was fudging, but I'd never manage to force details out of him.

I decided to question him a little more. "What type of information do you think he has hidden in his brain?"

"Ask the correct questions and you may unlock his memories," Logan replied.

I frowned again. "How am I supposed to know which questions are the correct ones? I'm not psychic you know."

Logan smiled. "I have confidence you will succeed."

I watched as the Indian faded, then I turned to Dad. "Did you know Logan was here the whole time listening to our conversation with Lombardi?"

He shook his head. "Nope … I had no idea."

"It's a bit creepy, don't you think?" How many other times had Logan been present during a conversation? It could be why he seems to know every time Bob drops another Deadsville bomb of information.

He smiled. "I would say it's usual for Logan. He's a stickler for rules and manners."

I opened my mouth, but before a snotty reply could fall out, I heard a 'pop'. Bob arrived with Mr. Peters in tow, and they were standing next to Dad.

"Hey Peg ... Logan told me to bring Peters to you." His brow creased. "Sorry ... but I'm not sure why."

I sighed. "I need to ask him a few more questions. Thanks for escorting him. Are you staying around?"

"Gosh, no ... I have a ton of work to do for both Logan and you." Bob began to fade, then stopped. "Be careful Peg ... the situation could get messy."

Before I had a chance to ask him what he meant, he was gone. I looked at Peters. I might as well start asking questions and see what I could drag from his memory banks. "Do you remember any more details?"

He shook his head. "I tried to tell your friend earlier that I don't know anything else."

I studied his face, deciding he was telling the truth. I shot a quick glance at Dad. His nod of agreement confirmed my gut instinct. "Logan seems to believe there is more information ... maybe a teensy memory you don't even realize is important."

Peters frowned as he thought about my statement. I gave him time to sort through his brain cells, watching for a sign of any type. Memories are funny things—they tuck themselves in corners of our brains, and we never know what will shake them loose.

I drummed my fingers on the table for a few moments. "Let's start from the beginning. You are a trained CIA agent, and you know how to retain information, even if it doesn't seem important at the time ... right?"

Peters nodded. "Sure, but I've done quite a bit of thinking since I saw you last." He paused. "Do you realize how boring all these classes are that I've attended?"

I looked at him surprised. "Classes?" Other than orientation, I knew nothing about a person's introduction to Deadsville.

Dad cleared his throat, and I knew he was trying to warn Peters about telling me more than he should.

Peters ignored the signal. "Orientation is bad enough, and I used the time to go over every scrap of info I could remember." He looked around the kitchen, finally settling for looking out the window. His eyes grew huge as he spotted my gang in the woods. "Are you aware you have a crowd out back?" He jerked his thumb in the direction of the trees.

I nodded. "Yep. They are my guards."

He turned to look at me, astonished. "Guards?"

"It's a long story. We really are the good guys."

Peters stared at me for a few moments before continuing. "I'm beginning to grasp that there is more going on than I ever imagined." He shook his head in disgust. "You'd think the living would've caught on to the fact that there are beings influencing them."

I snorted. "Why would you think the majority of the population would ever believe that? Even if you were told, would you have believed ghosts walk around interfering in our lives?" I heard the front door open and voices drifted down the hall. I glanced at Dad.

He smiled. "Andy and Floyd."

A quick glance at the clock informed me I should've started dinner hours ago ... damn—grilled cheese again.

My sweet hubby turned the corner, stopping short when he spotted Mr. Peters. His eyes darted to dad, then met my eyes. "Peg, is there anything I should know?"

Floyd was standing behind Andy, and Mr. Peters spotted him immediately. "I know you!"

Floyd nodded as he stepped around Andy. "Yes, sir."

"You were at my house when ..." He abruptly halted mid-sentence.

"Yes, sir ... it's my job." Floyd's voice was calm and quiet.

I looked at Andy, deciding an introduction was in order. "This is Mr. Peters. We are working on his murder case."

Andy gave Peters a nod, then turned back to me. "How bad is it?"

I knew he wanted to know how messy the investigation was but to be honest, I had no idea what direction we were headed. I just shrugged my shoulders.

Andy sighed. "That bad, huh?"

"Well ... Peters brother-in-law has mob connections. The head mobster has the ability to see ghosts, and he doesn't like his grandson who happens to be Peters' brother-in-law. Peters was CIA before someone killed him, and Logan thinks Peters knows more than he realizes. Plus, as an added bonus, the mayor is involved somehow." I decided it would be easier, in the long run, to give Andy the sticky news first, which would allow his brain time to digest the information.

He sighed. "Peg ..."

I cut him off. "Andy, we have to roll with the punches. There's no sense in getting upset until we see how bad gets."

He opened his mouth to reply, but Peters spoke first. "Mob? Did you say mob? As in mafia?"

I nodded. "You looked into Morgan ... why are you surprised?"

Peters shook his head. "I just ran a quick check. I wasn't about to ruin my career using official resources for personal business. I told you before, it's frowned on."

"Yep ... but I have a hard time believing you wouldn't do a little digging."

He shook his head again. "I had no reason to think Cindy was involved with anyone bad. She was such a good kid, and she never hung around losers."

I turned my attention to Floyd. "Do you have anything to add?"

He nodded. "Yes, ma'am. I cleaned a crime scene in south Akron this morning, and I think there may be a tie-in with Mr. Peters' case."

I felt sweat begin to form on my upper lip. "How so?"

"Same mess, same time frame, only difference was no dead body involved."

"Did you call Jack?"

He nodded. "First thing. I have a feeling that somehow the two cases are linked." He shook his head. "I'm not sure how though."

I nodded as my brain kicked into overdrive. "Did you have cleanup duty on the other houses involved here in the township."

He shook his head yet again. "My friend Dean had a couple of those houses. He never mentioned anything odd though." He paused, watching me carefully. "Do you want me to call him?"

I thought over his question, then finally shook my head. "We aren't even sure what we are looking for, so I wouldn't bother him yet."

Floyd nodded.

I turned my attention back to Peters. "Mr. Peters, there must be something you know or suspect that will lead us to the path we need to be on. Are you sure you can't think of anything at all?"

He sighed. "Call me David … it will be easier for both of us."

I nodded my thanks, then waited for some sort of illumination from the guy.

He shook his head. "I'm sorry."

I looked at Floyd. "Did you only come by to tell me about the place in south Akron, or is there more?"

Floyd nodded. "I'm positive the cases are connected. I've called a few of my friends who also work in crime scene cleanup. I had to leave voicemails, but I'm pretty sure they'll have stories that will match my own."

I grabbed a pen and pad of paper, then I started writing.

Andy walked over, so I knew his curiosity was getting the best of him. After a few minutes of writing, I sat back satisfied.

Dad leaned forward to read what I wrote and grinned.

I looked at Floyd. "I'm going to call Jack once you've heard back from your buddies. I'll need addresses from them for any scenes they thought matched with evidence you feel connects the crimes."

Floyd nodded. "Do you think this Morgan guy is hitting only his landscaping customers."

I nodded. "Yep. His employees certainly have the advantage of knowing when their customers are at work or out of town … it makes sense."

Floyd tugged his ear as he thought through my theory. "You may be right. Once my buddies call me, we'll be able to sift through the addresses and hopefully discover if they use Morgan's lawn service."

I opened my mouth to ask a question but before I could, a loud noise filled my kitchen, making me jump.

Floyd turned beet red. "Sorry." He fumbled for his phone. "I had to turn up the volume so I can hear a call over the noise of the equipment I have to use sometimes."

As he answered his phone, I turned to Andy. "Well … what do you think?"

"Explain your list." He nodded his head in the direction of the pad of paper.

I took a deep breath. "They are questions to ask Jack. Once Floyd gets off the phone, we may have enough info to see a pattern." I glanced at Floyd who was nodding his head but saying little.

Andy frowned, thoughtfully. "Okay … but are all those questions for Jack?"

I shook my head. "A couple are for Logan. We need to talk with the parents. If they were murdered by Morgan and can tell us how, when, and where, we may have enough for Jack to start an official investigation."

Andy's frown deepened. "You sure that's the best way to go? It would alert Morgan to the fact that you have him in your sights."

I shrugged. "We have to start somewhere. Sal was the one who brought my attention to the possibility of landscapers knowing a family's schedule."

Floyd turned back to us. "Great … my buddy, Frank, told me he was able to ask the homeowners a few questions while he was cleaning up the mess. They've been using Morgan's landscaping company for about two years, and they have been quite happy with the work. They even had a patio added to the back of the house with electricity running through for outdoor lighting."

I tapped my lips with the pen I was holding. "Electrical work means someone entered the house in order to have access to the fuse box."

"Yep." Floyd grinned. "The work crew was given a set of keys, so they could add fuses and run the line."

I thought over everything Floyd was saying. "That explains who? But why? That's the question. Anything taken of value?"

Floyd shook his head. "Not that Frank is aware of … mostly electronics. The homeowners didn't mention anything expensive … they mainly made a mess."

"What are these people after? If Lombardi is correct, his grandson has a legit business and also a black market art business. How could robbing his own customers help his shady art dealings?"

We all looked at another, stumped.

David Peters cleared his throat. "I'm pretty new at being dead but not at dealing with criminals. What if the robberies are meant to throw a shadow on Morgan's legitimate business causing people to mistrust him?"

I watched him suspiciously. "I thought the CIA doesn't deal with common criminals. Aren't you guys supposed to deal with foreign problems?"

He shook his head. "Most of the foreign problems I personally deal with are nothing but crooks in high places." He shrugged. "It's the same principle."

I snorted. I knew someone in a local high place that Peters' description fit very well—the mayor.

"Peg, be nice," Andy chided.

I threw him a dirty look but kept my mouth shut. Peters' gave me a quizzical look. I sighed. "The mayor of Akron has iffy friends."

Peters nodded. "Yeah … but mostly small potatoes. I know about his shenanigans."

My eyebrow shot to epic heights. "Really?"

Peters grinned. "He isn't as important as he thinks. He's a big fish in a little pond."

I laughed. "Did you know your brother-in-law's company takes care of not only the mayor's personal properties, but also all of the city property?"

Peters looked shocked. "I had no idea."

I cocked my head watching him carefully. "You must be a lousy investigator."

Peters surprised me with a grin. "My specialty isn't petty crime. I deal with …" he paused. "I *used* to investigate terrorist cells. They are still thugs, just thugs with a cause."

I thought his explanation of the threat of terrorist activity was a little on the over simplified side, but I decided to change the direction of our conversation. "Do you know Vito Lombardi?"

He shook his head. "Nope."

"He's Morgan's grandfather?" I pushed the issue. It was hard for me to believe he hadn't found out about the mob connection before his sister married into the family.

"I told you earlier … I wasn't about to ruin my career. I trusted her to marry into a good family. Even though my parents weren't thrilled, I chalked it up to not wanting their little girl to marry so young."

"How young was she?"

"Right out of college. My parents were very protective of her. By the time she started college, I was already in the agency and not home much." There was a wistfulness to his voice that surprised me. He saw my expression and gave me a wry grin. "Those were the days before life became so crazy. Young, ambitious, and full of myself. It was a time of innocence."

I grinned. "No longer pie in the sky thinking?"

He shook his head. "Nope. The world is becoming more dangerous every day, and now I find out the dead can influence world events." He sighed. "I wish I had known while I was alive … it would've explained a lot."

I snorted. "Ha! I'm alive and well aware of how dangerous the dead can be to those of us still living. Trust me … it doesn't help knowing."

There was a faint 'pop' in the air, and I looked up to see Henry's face. His expression brought no sense of relief since it was too serious and concerned to invoke warm and fuzzy feelings … damn.

CHAPTER 15

"Henry, what's wrong?" I asked even though I wasn't sure I wanted to hear his answer. My stomach started growling, so I snuck a quick look at the clock.

Andy saw my movement and grinned. "Peg, we'll eat leftovers."

I flashed him a small smile, wonder if he realized there were no leftovers worth eating—a dab of this and tad of that isn't what I call a meal. No, he'd have to live with grilled cheese. There was a small chance a nice salad could be on the side, but I doubted it—grocery shopping had taken a backseat the last few days. I forced myself to ignore my noisy stomach and instead, I turned my attention back to Henry.

Henry cleared his throat, twisting his fedora with his thick fingers as he looked around the room. His eyes finally rested on Mr. Peters. "I believe the woman I was sent to investigate is your sister."

Peters' mouth dropped open, then he glared at me. "You sent someone to spy on my sister?"

I shrugged. "I've learned the hard way that you don't leave any stone unturned."

Peters slowly shook his head. "I can't believe you think my baby sister could be dangerous."

I opened my mouth to comment, but Henry beat me to the punch. "Miss Peg didn't necessarily suspect your sister of wrong doing. Her husband is another matter. He's up to his neck in dirty dealings. He jumped whole hog into a mess … but that's my opinion."

"What mess?" I asked before Peters could argue.

"He wants his grandfather's position in their … um … family business."

"It's fine, Henry. We've met the old man, and we know he's mob."

Henry gave me a surprised look, but he was too much of a gentleman to reprimand me for my acquaintances. "The grandfather runs a successful farming empire. I've never seen anything like it, to be honest with you. Talk about a well-oiled operation." His grudging admiration astonished me. Who knew the old gumshoe could have even a little respect for a mobster.

I was a little surprised to hear this new bit of information. "How well-oiled?"

"I was raised on a farm, and believe you me, he's got the business so tightly organized that even my old man would've been impressed."

My eyebrows raised slightly. "How so?"

Henry scratched his face as he thought how to answer. "Farming's not an easy way of life … too much rain, not enough rain, too much sun, not enough sun, insects, animals eating your crops before you can harvest. The list of everything that can go wrong each season is long. Farming isn't for the faint of heart."

I nodded. "Okay, but what's so special about Lombardi's farm?"

"Everything. To begin with … the old man employs hundreds of Mexicans, all working legally. He brings them up from Mexico each year at the beginning of the planting season. You have to figure the cost of hiring legal, foreign workers must be sky high. Those work visas don't cost peanuts, you know … but every single Mexican's paperwork is above board. That alone is impressive."

"You checked the paperwork?" I was surprised he took the time to examine the nitty gritty.

He nodded vigorously. "Oh, yes ma'am. Paperwork gives me an idea on how the man runs his businesses."

"He has more than one business?" This was another piece of new information.

"Yep." He glanced down at his notebook. "If you separate each piece of his enterprise, there are at least five that I've uncovered so far … two of which the feds have no idea exist."

My mouth dropped open for a second, then snapped shut. "Lombardi told me he had a farm, but he didn't give any details about his business."

Henry nodded. "Sounds about right. His property includes organic farming, which is a pricey enterprise. No pesticides allowed, and the soil has to be fertilized without chemicals … it's expensive."

Andy decided to ask a question of his own when I didn't immediately ask anything else. "How much property does he own?"

"Whooee ... thousands of acres. I'm talking more than two counties worth of land. The man was smart ... he bought up land as the owners died because their kids didn't want to run the farms. He paid top dollar to ensure real estate developers didn't get their greedy hands on open land."

I still wasn't certain how any of this was important to the case. "Fine ... but why farming?"

Henry's hand rubbed his chin as he considered what he was about to say. "When I was a kid, farms were handed down through the generations. I was born thirty years after the Civil War ended, so the south was still trying to recover from the destruction. It was a real mess, but people need to eat, and farms produced food. A man could carve out a decent living on a farm ... at least he could feed his family." He looked at me. "There are three things people need to survive." He held up a finger. "Air ..." Another finger went up. "Water ..." The third finger rose. "Food. There doesn't seem to be many family owned farms anymore, which is a shame in my opinion, but people need to eat. Where do you think food comes from?"

Even though we live in what is consider a semi-rural area, no one in Bath *farms* anymore. My measly garden didn't compare to an actual farm ... not by a long shot. I realized I never really gave it much thought until Henry asked the question. "The grocery store?"

Henry burst out laughing. "That's what I figured. A while back, I got nosey and went to one of those grocery stores to see what they were like ... it had food from all over the world." He shook his head. "Damn shame, in my opinion. There is no oversight on how other countries raise their crops. Hell ... they could be spraying anything on their fields, but no one gives it a thought. If people realized what was on their veggies, they'd holler like a stuck pig."

I made a mental note to scrub any raw vegetables I bought from now on.

Andy turned the conversation back to the case with his next question. "What is shady about his businesses?"

Henry snorted. "His organic produce is about as pure as yellow snow."

I have to admit, it took me a hot second to understand he meant snow someone peed on, but Andy grinned, knowing immediately what Henry was talking about.

I frowned, slightly confused. "I thought organic farms had to pass some sort of test."

"You'd think so, but even people who work for the government can be bought," Henry replied.

My eyes narrowed. "Lombardi is paying off officials to look the other way?"

Henry nodded. "It's the only way he can claim his produce is organic … but that's the least of the situation. He's selling black market organic."

My frown deepened. "There's a black market for organic vegetables?"

Henry nodded. "Yep. He undersells a few of the local organic farms by half, then if those farms go out of business he buys them."

Andy shook his head. "Underselling isn't black market."

Henry grinned. "Not only is the old scalawag selling his phony organic produce to stores, he sells the stuff to *other organic farmers* at a cut rate price. Those other farmers then turn around and sell it for top dollar."

I sighed, trying to understand the point of Lombardi's business. "That doesn't make sense."

"I bet they have legitimate organic farms which pass vigorous inspections. Lombardi has to be careful who he sells his bogus crops to, just in case someone gets righteous about the term *organic*. The farmers who buy produce from him grow enough crops to maintain their reputation, but they save money by purchasing inferior crops. Lombardi is making money every direction he turns." Andy's explanation helped make sense of everything Henry was saying.

Henry nodded. "As long as no one gets their feathers ruffled, everyone's ahead of the game."

I scoffed. "I bet Lombardi makes damn sure no one gets upset along the way."

Henry nodded again. "Everyone wins, and he ensures they all profit."

"Godfather of the farming community." I may not understand the ins and outs of Lombardi's little agricultural endeavor, but I did realize he was making money … lots of it.

"So how does my sister fit into this?" Peters asked when no one else had anything to add.

Henry studied Peters' face a moment. "She's not entirely ignorant of her husband's desire to advance his standing in the family business. I'm not sure if she realizes his illegal activity could get them both into trouble." He shrugged. "He's a sneaky bastard."

I saw the fire in Peters' eyes, and I knew he was fuming. "Now look here! She's not the type of girl who gets involved in illegal business dealings."

"She married him," Henry reminded Peters.

I intervened just in the nick of time, before Peters exploded. "Do you think she is in danger from her husband? We promised to help her."

Henry thought a moment before answering. "He's a pig for sure. He treats her terribly, in my opinion." He glanced at Peters. "Nothing physical, if you get my meaning, but he's not nice. Maybe she's waiting for the perfect moment to leave, but I wouldn't bet the farm on it."

Henry's analysis of the situation put a wrinkle in the situation that I wasn't prepared for, so I started to wonder how to deal with the sister. I assumed she was innocent … probably an abuse victim. Now I had to admit, she may be part of the problem. I turned my attention back to Henry. "You seemed concerned when you arrived. Are you worried Cindy is more entrenched in the enterprise than we thought?"

Henry nodded. "Yep. Along with the fact Lombardi may be blowing smoke up your …" Henry paused, and his face grew beet red. "Sorry … he may be sliding around the fact that he's no angel."

Andy grinned at Henry's embarrassment, but it warmed my heart—he was such a gentleman.

Dad stayed quiet while Henry explained the situation but interrupted now. "How much should we trust Lombardi?"

Henry looked over at Dad. "That's the question of the year. I would be cautious, but in the long run, he wants to block Morgan from taking over the family business. I hate to admit it, but I think the old man is absolutely correct … Morgan is bad news. Lombardi may be making money illegally, but he hasn't been involved in murdering people since way back. Morgan has the ambition to step over as many dead bodies as necessary."

"Lombardi used to murder people," I squeaked. I could feel sweat beginning to form in places I'd rather not mention.

Henry shook his head, slightly disgusted with me. "Miss Peg, this is a mafia family." He held up a hand. "Don't get me wrong … I like Sal, but he's cut from a different clothe than Lombardi."

Henry had no idea how correct he was regarding Sal … he wasn't even a natural born mafia guy. His parents secretly adopted him, hoping to, literally, bring new blood into the family.

I glanced at Dad and Andy, and they shook their heads. I had no intention of informing Henry of Sal's secret, but it was nice to know they agreed with me about the information being 'need to know'. I sighed, knowing it was another peg in the board showing how close I was to following in Logan's footsteps—withholding information because *I* decided someone didn't need it. I made a split-second decision regarding another issue Henry did have the right to know.

"Lombardi can see ghosts."

Henry looked surprised for a split-second, then he nodded his head. "Good to know … explains a few things for sure."

I cocked my head. "What things?"

Henry's face squished as he gathered his thoughts. "I decided to poke around his office and listen to a few conversations. I noticed his posture change as soon as I arrived."

My eyebrows shot up in surprise. "His posture?"

"Yep. Body movements give a person away nine times out of ten." He stopped as he relived the scene in his mind. "I wondered at the time why he seemed so cautious while he was talking with his buddies. I have to admit … the old guy is good … very good. He kept himself in check pretty well once he knew I was there. He never looked around the room to find me … he didn't let on at all." He nodded again. "Impressive."

"My sister is innocent!" Peters declared.

I glared at him, then pointed my finger in his direction. "I'm going to be as clear as possible. If she's involved at all, I'm not protecting her from the law. I promised you we would help her when we all assumed she was an innocent bystander. You were away from home, so you have no idea what type of person she has become. You need to back off for the time being … understand?"

You could've heard a pin drop as Peters' eyes bored into mine. I held my ground and didn't blink first. Peters crossed his arms and sat back, but I knew he was still fuming.

I turned my attention back to Henry. "Henry, did you have a chance to follow Morgan's wife?"

"Yep." He consulted his notebook again. I watched as he flipped through a few pages until he reached the notes in question. "She had her hair done this morning at a swanky place here in the township." He looked up. "I couldn't believe the prices they charged. I used to earn that amount in a week!" He shook his head, then continued going through his notes. "She drove up to Cleveland to a butcher for meat. I don't know why the local store wasn't good enough, but they must not like the meat around here." He shrugged, then continued. "Once she dropped the meat off at home, she headed to the elementary school where she read to the first grade class for thirty minutes. I have to admit, she was really good with those kids."

I looked over at Peters who nodded. "Cindy can't have kids, and Morgan refused to adopt."

I sighed. I knew another mob kid who rejected any ideas of adoption … Anthony. Some people are really odd about bloodline heritage.

"She loves kids," Peters added.

Henry agreed. "You could tell by the way she handled those little stinkers." He returned to his notes.

"Wait a minute." I held up a hand. An idea was forming, and I didn't want Henry to derail my already overloaded brain. I needed absolute quiet while the gears turned. I sat stock still, hoping the silence would allow the brain cells to connect the dots. Finally, I sighed and relaxed as the idea appeared. "Cindy loves kids, but she can't have any of her own. Henry, was there any indication that Morgan has a gal on the side?" I looked over at Peters. "We've been here before with another case. These mob people take blood pedigrees seriously."

Peters nodded but remained quiet as he waited for further information.

"No ma'am … no evidence so far."

I nodded, then turned back to Peters. "Did Cindy ever go through fertility testing?"

His eyes grew large at my question "How on earth did you know?"

I plopped my head in one hand. "I think Anthony and Morgan were closer than the old man ever realized." I turned to Dad. "Remember all the artwork in Anthony's house? It was top notch stuff, and I'd bet dollars to donuts he bought it all from Morgan."

Dad nodded. "Sounds about right … some of his paintings were pricey. The Nazi's plundered Europe during the war, and it was well known that they had mountains of stolen art."

"Do you think Morgan's as nuts as Anthony?" I asked Dad.

He shook his head. "No. I do believe Lombardi would've warned you if his grandson was crazy. Remember, he doesn't like the kid, and he doesn't care what happens to him in the long run."

"Sal may have insight into this new wrinkle." I glanced at the clock again, deciding it might be time to call it a night. The dead don't need to eat or sleep, but Andy and I sure as hell did.

"I'll call him in the morning. David, I know you are confused and angry that we would suspect your sister of anything sinister, but I need you to be available at a moment's notice, just in case we have to ask you questions."

"I'm not going anywhere," he snapped.

I laughed. "You'd be surprised how preoccupied you could become in your new life."

He gave me a confused look, but I decided he would be better off discovering the social side of death on his own.

"Bob!" I yelled. Everyone jumped at the sound of my voice, but there was no way I was allowing David Peters to melt away without knowing where he would end up if he was left on his own.

There was a pop in the air, and Bob stood in front of us. His hair was wilder than usual, and dirt covered his clothes. He had a black eye, and his shirt was torn. I saw Dad straighten at the sight in front of us, and I was relieved I wasn't the only one worried. Bob is usually disheveled, but this was a new look entirely.

"Has it started?" Dad asked.

"Oh, yeah! But we're winning. You should see …"

Bob was cut off from explaining the situation by Dad holding up his hand. "Too much information."

Bob turned red. "Sorry Dave … I didn't think."

Dad nodded. "We need to get back there."

"You wait a damn minute! What is going on?" I demanded.

Dad shook his head and pointed to the woods. "They are here to protect you. No matter what happens on our side, you'll be safe."

Before I could utter another sound, they were both gone. Andy and I looked at one another in shock.

Peters frowned. "What's going on?"

I shook my head. "I have no idea … but it looks bad." I glanced out back, but dusk was settling. I knew the guys were there, but I had no idea what their mood was. I stood, then headed for the back door.

Andy watched me with a slightly worried expression. "Whoa there, sweetie … where are you going?"

"Out back to talk to the guys. Are you coming?" I snapped.

Andy nodded, and we trotted ourselves to the edge of the woods.

The closer I got to my protectors, the more confused I became when I realized they were calm and steady.

Frowning, I approached the main Indian. "Anything I should know about?"

He shook his head. "We are here, and you are safe." He spread an arm in a wide arc to include the entire entourage who were gathered in my woods.

I scowled. "Bob just showed up and he's a mess. What's going on?"

The Indian shook his head again. "Do not allow Bob's appearance to upset you. We are here to guard and protect."

"You aren't really answering the question." The Indian's evasive answers were starting to annoy me.

His face grew serious. "We will not leave you, no matter what is happening in the other realm."

"That's nice to know, but you still aren't giving me any information."

He nodded. "It is not my job to inform you of the struggles in the afterlife. They have occurred for centuries, and they will continue to develop." He shrugged. "The battle is not yours to fight."

My eyebrows rose as I looked at Andy.

"There is a battle over there?" Andy sounded intrigued. "Should we try to help?"

The Indian smiled. "You have battles of your own here that are your responsibility. Logan would not be happy if you withdrew from one field of battle only to enter another you are ill prepared to fight."

The Druid stepped forward. "Peg, let the dead fight the dead. Your job is to fight the living."

"Ha! Shows how much you know. I fight the living *and* the dead."

His smile grew. "You can't help Bob. These battles have existed for a long time. We try to keep them in the spiritual realm but as you know firsthand, these fights spill over into your world."

For some reason that I couldn't put my finger on, I trusted the Druid completely. I wouldn't put it past him to be doing some type of magical Druid mojo on me, but I couldn't detect anything underhanded in his face.

I sighed. "I don't want Bob hurt. He's a pain in the butt, but he's *my* pain in the butt. You understand?"

The Druid grinned as he nodded. "Completely. Bob is unique, and he very helpful in his own way."

"As long as we understand one another ... no harm comes to Bob, right?"

"I have no control, but I can assure you the battle being fought is minor compared to previous encounters. You may want to ask yourself why a battle is being waged now and if your investigation part of the picture." He turned, then made his way to the back of the herd of dead folks.

Andy grabbed my hand. "Somehow, we always end up in the middle of the struggle between good and evil."

I nodded. "Yep. I'll bet Logan was well aware, from the beginning, of our involvement and how much we would be dragged along concerning Deadsville."

Jeez.

CHAPTER 16

After a nice meal of toasted cheese sandwiches with tomato soup on the side, we settled down for the evening. Andy caught up on the world's weather courtesy of a foreign cable weather channel. I ignored our situation as much as possible, which wasn't easy considering my brain's refusal to obey any orders I sent its way. On the bright side, we had no further visits from Deadsville, so I had to wait to find out the final score of the battle. I slept poorly, which didn't surprise me. In the middle of a sticky case, I have a difficult time turning off the thought processes.

The next morning, I forced myself out of bed and started my day before Andy could take command of the bathroom. As I stood waiting for my first energy-in-a-cup to brew, my mind began sorting through the current crisis. So far, we had mafia in spades, new dead guys out back, Nazi plunder, screwy farming practices, one mafia member who has access to the dead, a dead CIA guy whose sister may or may not be up to her pretty little neck in crime, and her worthless husband whose number one goal in life is to take over the family business. It was a mess, and I fought hard to find a reason not to go back to bed and forget the entire kit and kaboodle.

By the time I finished my second cup of coffee and was waiting on the third to brew, I was in a better frame of mind. At least my desire to head back to my warm, cozy bed was gone. I was still combatting the idea of throwing in the towel where the dead folks and crime was concerned. I was definitely leaning in the direction of quitting when I noticed the aroma of men's cologne. I quickly glanced around the kitchen, finally spotting Bob standing in the corner.

"Cologne?" I frowned in slight confusion. "Since when?"

Bob smiled nervously. "Your dad mentioned that my appearance yesterday freaked you out, so I decided you needed to see me spiffed up a bit."

I gave Bob a once over. I was astonished to see his hair slicked back with some sort of hair gel, cleanish clothes with only a few wrinkles, and brand-new sneakers. Since the dead have the ability to appear dressed however they choose, I wasn't surprised Bob considered this his best—he's rumpled at the best of times. I thought his hair was a little on the slimy side but, out of kindness, I decided not to mention it. "I appreciate the effort. Who won the battle?"

"Oh, we did ... we always win you know. If we ever lost, it's all over." He shrugged. "This wasn't the first battle I've fought. If you didn't call me when you did, you would've never seen me so messy."

I've seen Bob pretty damn messy before, but I didn't comment. He is usually oblivious to how sloppy he can be, and I didn't think now was the time for a heart to heart on the matter.

I raised my eyebrows in surprise. "These battles have happened before? It's the first I've heard of them."

Bob waved a hand. "We aren't supposed to talk about them ... it upsets people."

My eyes narrowed. "You aren't supposed to talk about a lot of things, but you do."

His face turned the color of a perfect apple. "Well ... I don't *mean* to spill the beans. The battles are ongoing, and Logan decided centuries ago it was better if the living were unaware of them." He shrugged. "If you are jumpy about them, just think about how the general public would feel ... it would be a catastrophe."

As much as I hated to admit it, Bob was one hundred percent correct. I had to deal with Deadsville, but most of the population wasn't even sure an afterlife existed. Learning they continually fought some sort of battles would freak out people and cause panic.

He watched me carefully. "What did you call me for?"

I shrugged. "I wasn't sure what to do with Mr. Peters, but he decided he could find his way back without help."

Bob nodded. "He made it back safe and sound. You'd think he's been at it a lot longer than he has ... it's pretty impressive." Bob made a face, and I knew he was remembering how long it took him to handle even the basics when we first met—he'd come a long way since then.

"Maybe his CIA training gave him an edge." I mentioned it hoping to soften the memories.

"Maybe." He shrugged, looking doubtful.

"From the little I know about the agency, their agents go through tough training. You didn't have the same advantage."

Bob's face cleared. "You really think that's why he was able to make it back so easily?"

I nodded. "Yep." Why not toss him a bone?

He moved a little closer to me. "How's the case coming along?"

I was relieved to see him exit the shadows of the corner. Bob is sensitive, so he tends to hide when feeling a little down about himself.

I frowned at the question. "I'm not sure. Lombardi seems to be nice enough, but he's a little too happy for us to nail his grandson."

"I don't blame him … Morgan is a jerk."

I raised an eyebrow. "You seem pretty sure about his jerkiness."

He shrugged. "I hear things on my side. Even his family isn't fond of the guy. His mother is disgusted with him, but he doesn't listen to her at all."

I cocked my head to one side. "Does he hear anyone from your side?" The last thing I needed was for another creep hearing from Deadsville.

"Nope. They refuse to contact him. I'm not even sure he could hear us through his arrogance."

I shook my head. "Anthony was arrogant as hell, but he sure could hear his mother."

"That was different. Bella had total control of Anthony even when she was alive. She merely continued her hold over him after she died."

I thought about Bob's analysis, deciding he was probably correct. I couldn't image Morgan being swayed by anyone. He wasn't crazy, just greedy and power hungry. "I agree with you … the boy is greedy. Has Logan had any luck locating Cindy's parents?"

"If he has, I haven't heard about it. If they're being protected, it will be tough to find them."

I decided to ask a few more questions to find out what he knew. "Do you have any ideas why these homes keep being robbed?"

He shook his head. "Nope. Has Andy seen a pattern yet? He's pretty good at that stuff you know."

I held back my irritation—I was pretty good at finding patterns myself. "There was a pattern before Floyd told us there have also been numerous burglaries in surrounding communities. That revelation blew it to smithereens. The only connection is Morgan's lawn business."

Bob leaned against the wall, and I realized he was beginning to have more abilities every time we met. Physical contact, as simple as resting against a solid structure, was difficult. "Have you checked back with the mayor?"

I made a face and shook my head.

Bob smiled slightly. "He may be able to help."

"Ha! He's part of the problem. His involvement with the underside of the population is causing me headaches. Why can't he just play it straight and stay away from crooks?"

Bob laughed. "He'd never get elected."

I shot Bob a nasty glare, but he waved it away.

"Peg, every city needs contracts for projects. Those projects cost the city money, but they also bring in money. Labor gets paid, and they eat at the local diners and restaurants. A smart mayor will hire companies within his own city limits because they pay taxes. Sal has numerous businesses, and he does a ton of work for Akron." He shrugged. "It makes economic sense. It's a shame some of those businesses happen to be on the shady side, but they provide jobs, and people need jobs."

Even through his goofball personality, Bob could occasionally utter insightful analysis. I sighed. Bob's logic was surprisingly depressing. I wished everyone could play nice and be honest—it probably wouldn't happen in my lifetime.

"Do you think Morgan's illegal art business is at the root of the robberies?"

Bob's face crinkled as he focused on my questions. "Maybe … maybe not."

"Oh, for Pete's sake! That's not an answer," I snapped.

He waved away my irritation, then continued analyzing the problem. "I do think Morgan is involved with selling stolen art pieces … but that doesn't mean he's robbing homes. I guess a good question would be … why rob homes if your side business is selling hot art?"

Every once in while Bob could really stun me with his ability to cut to the core of a situation—sorta made me proud. I glanced out back as the sun began to shine through the trees. As much as I hated dragging my butt out of bed every morning, I loved watching the sun make its appearance— made me feel as though the day was a fresh start. The feeling was usually short lived, but I enjoyed it while I had the chance.

Sure enough, the phone rang as Andy rounded the corner to grab his breakfast. He raised an eyebrow as I reached for the phone.

I was greeted by Jack's voice on the other end of the line. "Peg, has your coffee count been met?"

I had to smile … everyone knew my morning rule of three cups of coffee before I was civil. "You're safe."

He sighed. "There's been another break-in."

My stomach knotted, and I shot my eyes to the woods. I frowned when

I noticed my guards where quiet and watchful—no agitated pacing or worried looks. Someone was waving their arms, and I realized my guy in the kilt was yelling at the Druid. Other than their argument, everything was quiet.

I turned my attention back to Jack. "Where?"

Jack cleared his throat. "Hudson."

Ah ... not our township. Hudson was an upscale community that was fourteen miles northeast of Bath. It's known for quaint shops meant for those who love shopping—I'm not in that group since I detest shopping of any type. Hudson has more than twice the population of Bath on roughly the same amount of land, so they aren't what I consider 'semi-rural' in any way.

I was thoughtful for a moment. "Are the Hudson police asking for help?"

"They've got a couple of dead bodies, and the crime scene has been ransacked. They thought we'd be interested, so they called us in for a joint investigation."

I frowned slightly. "Do you know anything about the people murdered?"

I could hear Jack shuffling papers around his desk. "Here we go ... older couple, they immigrated from Germany sometime after World War II. According to the local PD, they've lived in the same house for over sixty years."

My mouth fell open in shock. "Holy cow! They must be near a hundred years old!"

"Just about, he was ninety-eight and she was ninety-three. I'm not sure if they had kids or not, but I'll find out later today. You want to see the crime scene?"

I was thoughtful for a moment. "Who's cleaning it?"

"No idea."

I glanced at the clock, then snuck a quick peak at the woods. Other than the Scotsman, everyone was quiet. I realized Andy was standing at the counter with the milk carton still in his hand, staring at me. The word 'murder' must've caught his attention.

I turned my attention back to Jack. "Do you have the names of the dead couple?"

"Not yet."

I sighed. "Give me the address, and I'll meet you there in an hour."

After writing down the address, I started digging in my pile of junk stacked by the kitchen table.

Andy finally broke the silence. "What are you searching for?" Bless his heart, he didn't bother peppering me with questions about the robbery.

I glanced at him. "I bought a GPS, so I wouldn't have to worry about always asking Jack for directions."

"Do you know how to use one?" I caught the hint of laughter in his voice, but I ignored it completely.

"Sort of."

He put the milk carton on the counter, then helped me dig through the mess. "You need to organize this pile," he advised.

"Someday I will. Got it!" I grabbed the box and handed it my hubby. While he read the instructions, I turned to Bob. "Do you think you could nose around ... maybe figure out who this couple was and where they came from?"

Bob nodded. "Sure ... no problem. I'll meet you there." Rather than his usual fading, he disappeared in a flash, which worked for me.

I turned back to Andy. "Here's the address to program into the GPS. I'd better get dressed."

He nodded, but he was so engrossed studying the pamphlet, I wasn't sure he really heard me.

I headed down the hall. As I reached the bedroom, there was a 'pop' in the air, and the hairs on my arms stood at attention ... damn.

"Thought you were rid of me, didn't you?" Elaine sneered.

I kept moving and ignored her. I didn't want to waste time confronting her—if she wanted to talk she'd have to follow.

She did follow. "Your mother should be free soon. She isn't very happy with you."

I continued to ignore the bitch as I dug through a drawer for a clean blouse.

Her eyes narrowed. "What's your hurry?"

I glanced at her. "None of your business."

"My uncle won't help you ... he's using you."

Her statement almost made me vomit but, blouse in hand, I headed for the bathroom for my own morning ritual—teeth, hair, and makeup—no sense in going out in public looking like a wreck.

"Uncle Vito never helps anyone." Her sneer was still firmly in place.

I swung around the face her. "You mean, he wouldn't help *you*. You and your mother must've been a real pain in his ass considering *your entire family* hates you."

Her eyes narrowed ... never a good sign. "My family dynamics is none of your business. You won't be able to solve this crime spree, and you'll regret being involved."

I sighed. "I regret ever meeting you, that's for sure." I closed the bathroom door in her face. "Leave!" I yelled for good measure.

The air changed, and I knew Elaine left the building—good riddance. My saving grace while dealing with creepy, dead folks was the fact that they had to leave if I told them to—saved me from additional headaches.

Once I brushed my teeth, and I checked my roots for tell-tale signs of gray sneaking through, I quickly dressed. Once that was done, I threw on enough makeup to pass muster. Basically, a hit of mascara and splash of blush. I shrugged at my image in the mirror, the face looking back at me wasn't going to get any younger no matter how much effort I took … oh well.

Andy was beaming when I reached the kitchen. "All set and ready to go. Do you want to take the back roads or highway?"

I gave his question a split-second thought. "Back roads."

He nodded. "That's best way this time of the morning. You should miss the clog on the highway."

"Yep." I hate traffic, and morning rush hour around here is a nightmare.

He watched me hesitantly. "Anyone … you know … dead going with you?"

I shook my head. "Not that I know of … why?"

He shrugged nonchalantly. "Just wondering."

I stood on my tiptoes and kissed his cheek. "I'll be fine. There's no reason to worry."

He kissed my forehead. "I always worry."

Flashing him a grin, I peeked at the woods. My Scotsman was still ranting and raving, and my curiosity finally got the best of me. I turned and headed for the door. Three steps outside and I wished I took the time to grab a sweater. Somehow, I missed the warning about the cold front now firmly in place. I shivered as I made my way to the woods. The entire gang turned to watch me approach … all except the man in a kilt. He was too busy yelling to notice my arrival.

I looked at the Druid. "What's the problem?"

He grinned down at me. "He's worried his bloodline is being disrespected. It seems he snuck over to the building where Dougal is employed and realized the boy isn't in a position of authority."

"He's brand new to the department. He has to build his career and advance according to department protocol."

The Druid nodded. "Yes, I explained the procedures to him. I don't believe he agrees with the rules." His grinned widened.

The kilted man turned and glared at me. "Listen here, lassie. Tis a black mark on our family name."

I stepped back in shock. "You're allowing me to hear English!"

He turned red, then stomped his foot. "See how upset I am?"

I burst out laughing, which did nothing to calm the old Scotsman down, but I couldn't help myself.

His glare intensified, and I struggled to control my giggles. "What if I spoke with his boss and asked how soon Dougal can be promoted? Would that make you feel better?"

He considered my proposition, then gave me a quick nod. "Keep me apprised of the status." He turned and stomped to the back of the crowd.

I looked up at the Druid. "How long has he been complaining?"

The Druid laughed out loud. "All night. Angus is serious about family."

I shook my head, then looked over the gang. Everyone seemed calm. "Do you guys have anything to tell me?"

The Druid turned, surveying the group. "All seems under control."

I turned to leave, but the Druid called me back. "You promised Angus you would discuss Dougal's situation. Don't forget … he isn't someone you want mad at you."

I nodded. "I figured that out for myself, but thanks for the warning."

I hurried back to the house, silently scolding myself for not dressing warmer. I'd have to add a sweatshirt to my ensemble before heading to Hudson. There wasn't a cloud in the sky, but the air was crisp with a slight breeze which intensified the cold, so I found myself shivering.

When I entered the kitchen, I looked around a little surprised Andy wasn't waiting for me. I grabbed the milk carton and stuck it back in the refrigerator, just in case he forgot—the last thing I needed was to come home to spoiled milk smelling up the house. The kitchen door opened, and Andy walked in with an air of a knight in shining armor. "All set. The GPS is ready to go in the car, which I've warmed up for you. It should take you about half an hour to make it to Hudson. You're not the only one partial to back roads during morning traffic." He grinned at me.

I stood on my tip toes and planted a kiss on his cold lips. "Jeez!" I said as I stepped back.

Andy laughed. "Coldest day so far this year."

I nodded. "I believe it. I need to grab a sweatshirt before I leave." I turned to head back to the bedroom, but I stopped when I saw my dad.

He smiled. "I thought I'd tag along, Twinkle Toes."

I frowned. "Do you know something I don't?"

He shook his head. "Nope … I've just been busy lately, so I haven't been able to spend much time with you."

I narrowed my eyes but nodded. "Let me add a layer to my wardrobe, then I'll be ready to roll." I didn't believe for a second this was merely father-daughter time. He was going with me for protection. Thoughts swirled around my head as I pulled the sweatshirt on, making my stomach begin to knot.

CHAPTER 17

I was thankful Andy warmed up the car as I slid into a toasty seat, smiling.

Dad watched me curiously. "What's the grin about?"

"Andy warmed up the car for me. It was sweet."

Dad grinned. "I never warmed up the car for your mother. Does that make me a bad husband?"

I laughed. "The fact that you didn't murder her proves you were a good husband."

Dad shook his head. "She wasn't always bad. The rot was certainly there, but at the beginning your mother was fun as well as beautiful."

This was news to me. I turned to face him. "You really did love her, didn't you?"

His eyes got a faraway look as he nodded. "She had such a love of life and a great sense of humor. I came to realize how selfish she truly was, but her beauty and exuberance captured my heart." He shrugged. "Even after you were born, she was still fun. I'm not sure what happened ... I believe she was bored, which led to her wild side rearing."

I frowned, slightly confused. "Bored with being a wife and mother?"

"Possibly. Maybe she was bored once she figured out life wasn't one thrilling adventure after the next. As the years passed, she hardened. Before I died, I knew she was bad news … it is one of the reasons I kept such a close eye on you throughout the years. I didn't trust Nell, so I encouraged your grandmother to take you under her wing."

I felt tears threaten. No one ever shared this much information about my mother, so it was sad to hear that, at one time, she wasn't such a bitch. My memories had no good times to recall … it was all bad. I decided it was time to pull myself back to the current problems. "Do you know anything about the couple in Hudson?"

Dad shook his head. "Sorry, but I stay focused on Bath unless Logan asks me to check out another area. It happens, but seldom … he knows my interests are centered around your safety."

My throat constricted, and I knew tears would make an appearance if I didn't stay zeroed in on the newest murder.

"They came over from Germany after the war. They were both in their late nineties. Crime scene is a little too similar to David Peters' place, so I'll bet money they are connected.

Dad nodded. "Yep … sounds too close to ignore as coincidence."

I sighed. "Hudson is a long drive."

Dad burst out laughing. "Sweetie, anything over a couple of miles is too far for you."

I grinned. "Horrible … isn't it?"

He shook his head, but I knew he thought my hatred of traveling outside my immediate area was hilarious.

He cleared his throat. "I heard Bob hint at the fact that you may need to call the mayor."

The grin left my face and turned into a scowl. "I don't like him."

"It doesn't matter if you like him, but it makes a difference if you allow your personal feelings to interfere with a case."

Jeez … why did he have to nail my butt with parental wisdom.

He sighed when I didn't respond. "Give it some thought. He may know an important piece of the puzzle."

My teeth gritted. "Maybe … I'll think about it."

I could feel Dad's grin, but I didn't give him the satisfaction of glancing over at him. "You're going the back way?"

I nodded. "I don't like the highway … too much traffic."

We rode in comfortable silence until we came into Hudson city limits. I glanced at the GPS, realizing I would have to make more than a few turns to arrive at the address. I stay focused on my task, finally finding the house in question.

Dad and I sat surveying the property for a few minutes—nice house, flower garden ready for winter, a long driveway that snaked around the back to what I assumed was the garage, and two large oaks trees right in the front. The property was more than the usual city lot. I took a stab at the size. "Do you think it's an acre?"

Dad shrugged. "Depends on how deep the backyard is, but you may be right."

I nodded as I decided sitting in the car wasn't going to give me any additional help. I looked over at Dad. "Are you coming with me?"

He gave me a firm nod. "Yep … right by your side."

I flashed him a smile. "Let's go."

I spotted Jack's car as we headed up the driveway. I knew he was probably frothing at the mouth waiting for me. I kept looking for signs of a break-in but so far, I hadn't spotted anything promising.

The front door opened, and Jack's face appeared. "Took you long enough."

I shrugged. "I took the back way … the roads wind around enough to make a person car sick."

He frowned. "Hells bells, Peg … why didn't you take the highway?"

"I don't like the traffic." I pushed past him to enter the house. "Wow." The scene in front of me was impressive if total destruction was the new wave of interior design—every chair was overturned, sofa cushions were slit open on the floor, lamps were smashed against the walls, and even the carpet was torn up in places.

I glanced at Jack. "Am I allowed to walk through the room?"

Jack nodded. "Yea, they've already taken pictures and dusted for prints."

I looked around, trying to decide where to start. "Is the whole house in this condition or only this room?"

Jack watched me carefully. "Oh, the entire house … even pulled up the tile on the bathroom floor."

"They had enough time to really search." I looked around. "Where were the bodies?"

Jack nodded towards a hallway. "Back bedroom. They must've been sleeping."

I looked at him surprised. "So it happened at night. Could you tell if they put up a fight?"

He shook his head. "Doesn't appear as though they even woke up."

I frowned. "Surely one of them must've woken up when the other was attacked."

Jack shook his head again. "They were shot in the head … probably weren't even aware and died instantly."

I turned to Dad. "Where's Peters?"

Dad gave me a quick nod, then faded.

Jack frowned. "Why Peters?"

I studied the chaos while tapping a finger against my lips. "I want his opinion."

Jack's frown deepened. "Why?"

I shrugged. "Gut feeling."

Dad suddenly appeared, and he wasn't alone.

"That was a quick trip," I observed.

He shrugged nonchalantly. "I knew exactly where Logan had him."

My eyes narrowed, but I kept my mouth closed and turned my attention to David Peters. "Does anything look familiar?"

He looked around the room, then back at me. "No … should it?"

I turned to Jack. "Are the bodies still back there?"

He nodded. "Yep."

I glanced at Peters before starting down the hall. "Come on David."

As we trooped to the bedroom, I had a quick discussion with my stomach to stay put no matter how bad the scene appeared. We rounded the corner, and I took a deep breath. We stepped into the room, and I avoided looking at the bodies until I took a survey of the scene—absolutely no destruction here. When I couldn't avoid the obvious another moment, I stepped closer to the bed and reminded my stomach of the deal we had made. Looking down at the bodies, I was slightly surprised how peaceful they both appeared. Out of the corner of my eye, I noticed Peters joined me.

After a moment of silence, I glanced at him. "Do you know them?"

He shook his head. "I don't have a clue who they are. Should I?"

I sighed. "A gut feeling … sorry to bother you." I kept my voice low since Jack was the only officer present who knew about David.

Peters was thoughtful for a moment. "Can you pull the blanket back a little?"

I glanced at Jack and he nodded. I carefully pulled the comforter down a few inches. Both were in pjs, so I felt comfortable moving it a bit farther. We all leaned forward, studying the couple. I forced my eyes to take their time—I was glad I did. I pointed to the wife's arm. "She has numbers tattooed on her arm."

Jack grimaced. "Shit … she was a camp survivor."

I nodded. "Yep. I wonder which Nazi camp she survived."

Jack sighed. "There's a story here I'm not looking forward to discovering."

I was thoughtful for a moment. "How old did you say she was?"

Jack dug in his pocket for his notebook. After thumbing through a few pages, he looked at me. "Ninety-three."

David cut in when I didn't immediately speak. "That would have put her in her early twenties at the end of the war."

Jack nodded. "Yep."

I looked at Jack. "Any children?"

I watched Jack flip through a few more pages before he spoke. "None. I wonder why?"

David was thoughtful for a moment. "Probably couldn't have kids."

I turned to face him. "Why not?"

He shrugged. "Starvation, torture, rape … could have been a number of reasons."

My stomach lurched, but I fought it and won. The thought of a young woman being tortured by the Nazis made my stomach turn and my blood boil. I looked around the room again, this time with more care. Pictures of their life together were scattered around the room—on both dressers, on a vanity table, on the wall, and on the bedside tables. The furniture hadn't been destroyed nor the pictures.

Jack watched me carefully. "What is it?"

I continued to examine the room. "Nothing in here was disturbed."

Jack frowned. "So?"

I walked slowly around the room, taking in details as I went and filing them away for later. I stopped at a large painting which hung on the wall of our two newly deceased, then I carefully looked for clues it may have hidden from the world. Finally, the emerald ring the wife wore caught my eye. I leaned closer for a better view.

I looked at Jack. "Does the wife have a ring on her finger?"

Jack nodded. "Sure … her wedding ring."

"What about on her other hand?" I pressed.

I waited while he looked. He shook his head. "Nope."

I walked over to her dresser, then opened the jewelry case and with one finger moved the pieces around—no emerald to be seen. "Is there a ring on her nightstand?"

Jack looked, then shook his head. "Nope … why?"

I stood stock still, hoping my brain would give up the idea which was floating around but after a few minutes, I gave up. I was pretty sure the ring was stolen, but it still didn't explain the mess throughout the house. I continued walking around the bedroom, but my eyes were drawn back to the picture hanging on the wall.

"What was their last name?" I asked, grasping for clues.

More rifling of pages then Jack looked at me. "Wilson."

I frowned. "Wilson doesn't sound German."

He nodded. "Good point."

"Do you know their first names?"

Jack looked over at one of the Hudson police officers who answered. "Bob Wilson and his wife, Edith."

I nodded my thanks. I reached out to touch the painting, and I could feel it move a tad. Ah … so that's what my brain was trying to tell me. I grabbed the edge and swung it open. Grinning, I turned to Jack. "Wall safe."

His eyebrows shot up. "I'll be damned."

"Anyone know the date of their marriage?" I waited as the police officers conferred.

Finally, Jack turned to me. "No idea, but we should be able to find out easily enough."

"When?" I could feel excitement at the pit of my stomach. I wanted to know what was inside the safe—there may be an actual clue to our recent crime spree.

Jack shrugged. "Hell, Peg … it could take days to track down their records."

I scoffed. "Baloney. Did anyone bring a computer with them?"

Each officer raised a hand. I nodded, then held out my hand for a computer. To my surprise, Dougal MacMillian stepped forward and handed me his. I didn't even notice him as we were searching the room.

He grinned. "I'm ahead of you, I think. I opened my genealogy subscription and was in the process of typing in their names."

I laughed. "Go ahead."

We waited while he punched in what little information we possessed, but it didn't take long for him to look up at me with a huge smile. "Robert Wilson was an Army sergeant during the war. He was one of the American military men who helped liberate Dachau prison camp in April 1945. His job was to help process the prisoners, and he helped the medical officers classify their condition." Dougal looked up from his computer with tears in his eyes. "It must've been horrible."

I nodded but waved a hand for him to continue. I needed a date!

"There isn't a reference to how they met but they were married the following year on April 11, 1946."

Jack looked at the computer curiously. "You found out all that information on a genealogy site?"

Dougal nodded. "Sure. They have military records online, I've even accessed my grandfather's." Dougal smiled proudly. If he only knew his ancestor was roaming around my woods as he watched over not only me, but him too.

I smiled, then turned to the wall safe. Rubbing my fingers together I took a deep breath, then begin spinning the dial. I decided I had two dates to work with—the combination was either the day she was liberated or the marriage. I chose their wedding date first and manipulated the dial. When I reached the last number, there was no satisfying click of success. I sighed, then twirled the dial a few times to clear the numbers and began again. When the last number was spun into place, I was relieved to hear the tumbler fall into place. I excitedly turned the handle … eureka!

I turned to the room full of men and smiled. They surged forward, moving closer to the safe. We peered in to see what secrets it held. I began to carefully pull out paperwork, which we could go through later. There was a box that held jewelry, there was cash totaling well over five thousand dollars, and finally there was a key. We looked at the key, then at each other.

Jack threw out an idea first. "Safety deposit box?"

"Maybe …" I hesitated. "What else could it go to?"

The police officers looked at each other and shrugged. David stepped in for a closer look. Jack and I glanced at one another, but we kept our mouths shut. There was no sense in the Hudson police department believing we were nuttier than fruitcakes.

David finally spoke up. "Uh oh."

"What?" I whispered.

David looked at me. "I'm damn sure it's a key to a Swiss bank deposit box."

"Shit," Jack muttered.

I snuck a quick glance at our friends from the HPD, and was met with questioning stares. How on earth could I explain our guarded conversation?

A flash of insight hit me. "Is there a passport?"

One of the Hudson officers quickly searched the stack of paperwork retrieved from the safe. As we all held our breath, he finally held up two passports.

I continued watching him. "What's the last stamp in them?"

We waited as he thumbed through the passport, and it was all I could do to keep from snatching the damn thing out of his hand and looking for myself.

He frowned. "Switzerland." He looked up perplexed. "Why would two old people go there? It's cold as hell in Switzerland."

I sighed. "It gets cold here too."

"Ha!" He replied. "My in-laws went there a few years ago with a tour group, and it was eleven below zero." He shook his head as though they must've been out of their minds to visit a country whose temperatures reached below zero. Hadn't the man noticed the last four Januarys right here in northeastern Ohio? We hit two weeks of subzero weather each of those Januarys, so I threatened to move south for the winters. Andy laughed, but I didn't think it was funny when my car battery died because of the ridiculous cold.

I turned my attention back to the matter at hand. "When was the last time they visited Switzerland?"

He glanced down at the passport. "Two years ago."

I looked at David and Jack. "What do you think?"

Jack shrugged. "No damn idea. They obviously have something precious stashed in a bank over there."

I looked at Dougal. "Any idea what her maiden name was?"

He pushed a few buttons on his computer then looked up. "Peters."

Jack looked up startled. "What?"

My mouth hung open, and I turned to look at David.

David looked uncertain. "It must be a coincidence."

I scoffed. "I don't believe in coincidences."

Jack looked mildly confused. "Peters isn't a Jewish name."

David nodded. "Exactly my point … we aren't Jewish."

"Wilson isn't a German name, but Edith Wilson was from Germany," I retorted.

To keep from looking like a lunatic, I addressed Jack rather than David. No sense in the Hudson PD believing we were completely bonkers as we talked to air. I glanced around at the others. "We'll have to do a little research into the murder victim in Bath."

David began to argue, but I shot him a dirty look and he snapped his mouth shut.

Jack nodded. "Yep. Might as well get started." He nodded to Dougal. "Son, I'd appreciate it if you took the lead concerning the research. You seem to know your way around the genealogy site."

Dougal grinned. "Yes sir. I'll start immediately."

Jack turned to me. "Have you seen enough?"

I shook my head. "Nope. I want to see their will. If they had a stash of cash in a Swiss bank account, someone must be named to inherit."

Jack looked over to the Hudson officer still holding the passports. "Do you see a will in those papers?"

He shook his head. "Not yet … but give me a second to look." We waited while he thumbed through the stack. Finally, he looked up at Jack. "No will, but there is a list of important numbers."

Jack watched him confused. "How do you know they're important?"

The officer turned the paper, so we could see the writing. Sure enough, at the top of the page in large block writing it said 'IMPORTANT NUMBERS'.

Jack whistled in surprise. "Well, I'll be damned."

I held out my hand, and he passed over the paper. I quickly scanned the page, stopping when I reached a familiar name. I looked up at Jack. "John Abrahams … doesn't he live off of Bath Road?"

Jack nodded. "Sure. He's our lawyer."

I tapped the paper with my finger. "Well … he's their lawyer also."

Jack looked at the floor for a few moments. When he raised his head and met my eyes, he didn't look happy. "Peg, I'm too old for this crap."

One of the Hudson officers spoke up. "Gosh, Chief … seems as though it would make it easier since you already know the man."

Jack threw the man a look that would melt ice. "Not necessarily."

The Hudson man grew red, but he wisely kept his mouth closed.

David began to add to the conversation, but I stopped him with another look. He glared at me, but I didn't care. I felt a hot flash starting, and I needed the cool, crisp air waiting for me outside. I looked around the room one last time, spotting Dad in the corner watching the proceedings. I cocked my head at him, sending him a silent question. He shook his head and pointed outside. I nodded understanding. I walked over to the bed and forced myself to look at the bodies. Tears stung my eyes as I studied their faces one last time. Edith had been through so much when she was young, and her murder broke my heart. I reached out to pull the covers back up, but David stopped me.

"Leave it. I want everyone to realize the woman was branded by the Nazis. I don't want one person to be able to say they never noticed."

I nodded, letting my hand drop to my side … he was right.

CHAPTER 18

Once outside, Jack grabbed my arm. "What's on your mind? Do you really think she could be related to Peters?"

I opened my mouth to answer but David interrupted. "There is no way Edith and I are related. She's Jewish and I'm Methodist … or at least I was when I was a kid. I haven't been to church since I graduated from high school."

I looked at him considering what I wanted to ask next. "How long has your family been here in the states?"

He was thoughtful for a moment. "My great-grandparents came over after the war."

"Ha! See … there could be a connection."

He shook his head impatiently. "Not world war two … the first world war. It ended in 1918, and as soon as they could leave Europe, they came over."

His information deflated me, but I knew there was some type of connection. "You're related." I was standing by my assessment as we headed to my car.

David sighed. "You're too stubborn to listen to reason."

Jack laughed. "Welcome to my world."

I shot him a glare, but he just grinned. Jeez.

David cleared his throat after a few moments of silence. "What makes you so damn sure?"

I opened my mouth, but nothing came out that would make sense to either Jack or David. I slammed it shut and shrugged. "Just a gut feeling."

"Oh hell … Peg and her gut instinct." Jack turned to David. "I hate to tell you mister, but Peg's gut is usually as good as radar."

As I reached my car, I turned to David. "Which grandparents came over? Your mother's or father's?"

He frowned as he thought about it. "I'm not sure. My parents just told us the story about how they came over and how they were grateful to be here."

My eyebrows raised slightly. "You don't know your heritage?"

David shrugged. "We weren't the type of family that bothered with the past much. I don't remember many stories other than how my parents met."

"Which was?" There's nothing wrong with being a little nosey every once in a while.

"They met in college. My dad's roommate set them up on a blind date … nothing unusual."

I nodded. He had a point. "It sounds as though they were avoiding conversations dealing with heritage. Don't you find that a little weird?"

He sighed. I knew my questions were exasperating to the point of irritation. If I wasn't careful he'd disappear, and I had no idea if he knew how to hide over in Deadsville. Hell … I wasn't even sure if it was *possible* to hide—Logan seemed to know where everyone was most of the time.

I snapped my fingers as a thought struck me. "I wonder if Logan was able to locate your parents yet?"

David shook his head. "I have no idea. If he found them, he hasn't bothered to contact me."

I leaned against my car to support my brain efforts—deep thinking can take a lot out of a gal. All eyes were on me as the gears in my head spun a few cycles trying to make the connection.

Finally, I looked at the others. "I don't think Logan would necessarily alert you if he contacted your parents. There's no telling who's spying for the bad guys." The gears continued to whirl as I pulled my bottom lip. "To be honest David, this isn't really about you."

He sputtered the start of a nasty comment, but I held up a hand. "Even if Logan knew where your parents were being hidden, he would keep the information to himself. His goal isn't to have a big family reunion. He wants answers and so do I." I looked David square in the eye. "If we don't figure this mess out soon, don't be surprised if you end up in the dead's version of a witness protection program."

"Hell, no!" He shouted as his head vigorously shook from side to side. "There's no need to protect me."

I sighed. "David, you aren't in the CIA any longer. You're *dead*, and in your realm the evil is very real. The political games we play here on earth are no match for the real wars taking place on the other side. We only see the results of those battles here on earth." I scrunched my face. "We are basically pawns on a chessboard."

Logan's voice interrupted before David could speak. "That is not entirely true."

"Jeez Louise, Logan! Give a gal some warning once in a while!" I snapped. Startled by his appearance, I almost peed my pants—there was no way I was sharing that newsflash with anyone.

Logan ignored my irritation and nodded a greeting in Jack's direction. Jack returned the gesture.

Logan's eyes settled on David. "Mr. Peters, we have located your parents." He inclined his head in my direction. "Peg is correct ... your family is involved in the present circumstances."

David frowned. "I don't know how the hell that's possible! I've never heard of the dead couple."

A new thought smacked me upside the head. I held up a hand. "Why couldn't we see the Wilsons' spirits? Don't the newly dead hang around during crime scene cleanup?"

Logan smiled. "That's an excellent question."

I glared up at the Indian. "What's the damn answer?"

He turned his head, staring toward the woods. I didn't bother to follow his gaze since I had a sneaking suspicion he was trying to evade answering. I refused to back down. "Logan? What's going on?"

Instead of answering me, Logan turned to Jack. "I advise you to research the family history of Mrs. Wilson. I believe Dougal will be capable of the task."

Jack nodded. "I'm already on it."

Logan smiled, and I knew the sneaky bastard was aware of Dougal's participation. His advice was a backhanded way of letting us know we were on the right track. Why couldn't he just tell us the details? My partners with no heartbeats must have rules I still couldn't piece together. Even Bob seemed able to keep certain secrets, and it was driving me nuts.

David watched Logan carefully. "Are you going to allow me to see my parents?"

Logan studied him for a few moments, then he slowly nodded his head. "Eventually ... now is not the time for them to make contact with anyone who knew them while they were alive." He gave David a wry smile. "Eventually, I believe you will appreciate the need for secrecy. Their involvement with our present circumstances makes it necessary to protect them."

David shook his head vigorously. "There's no way they are mixed up in this mess." He pointed to the house we had vacated minutes ago as he spoke.

Logan continued watching David. "Mr. Peters, please trust my judgement in this matter. Your parents have been kind enough to explain their relationship with certain parties. They were not willing participants but rather, they found themselves tangled in unpleasant conditions." Logan shrugged. "They maneuvered to the best of their ability under very questionable circumstances, so they could protect both you and your sister from the consequences of their past." He sighed. "We have little say over the family we are born into, so we either make the best of it or struggle with circumstances outside our ability to control."

I frowned. "Explain please."

Logan turned to me and smiled. "You will be led down certain paths, and I refuse to interfere with the process."

I stomped my foot. "Damn it, Logan! You need to tell me which direction to go. My mind is spinning in a million different directions."

His smile broadened as he slowly began to fade.

"Logan!" My protests fell on deaf ears.

He continued fading, and I could feel my blood pressure rising. I took a deep breath, hoping it would help. One of these days, I'd have a heart attack over these damn investigations.

Jack spoke up after a couple minutes. "He was not much help."

"When is ever helpful?" I snapped.

"He has his reasons," Dad's quiet voice caught my attention.

I shot Dad a look, but I didn't receive the explanation I wanted.

He sighed. "Twinkle Toes, Logan sees the long view ... remember?"

I scowled. "I'm sick and tired of Logan's 'long view'!"

Dad shook his head, and I knew he was disappointed with my attitude.

Jack cleared his throat. "I agree with Logan's decision not to give up too much information."

I spun around to face him. "What the hell! You're *constantly* complaining about how closed mouth the old Indian is during a case."

Jack nodded. "Yep ... but this time he's right."

I opened my mouth to give him a piece of my mind, but he held up a hand, cutting me off. "Hear me out. Every single case we've worked on comes down to your gut instinct."

I shrugged. "So?"

"If Logan shares too much, your brain will try to make the evidence fit his analysis. What if *Logan* was wrong, and he gave us his conclusions rather than us finding the truth." He shook his head. "He can't take the chance that his influence would override your instinct."

"Baloney! What if my gut is wrong due to salami before bedtime?" I snapped.

Dad laughed. "Even if your instinct takes you down a wrong road, you have the possibility of changing course. Jack's correct ... if Logan reads the situation inaccurately, you would have no way of knowing."

I knew deep down I *needed* Logan to always be one hundred percent correct. I could feel tears threaten at the thought of my Indian ever being wrong—I needed to be able to trust him each and every time.

Dad could read me like a book. "Sweetie, why do you think Logan takes such pains never to tell you too much? Remember ... we only have partial sight when it comes to human events. That is why Logan's army of followers is so vast ... he's flying blind in many areas, so he needs the living to unearth evidence."

Oh ... Jeez Louise. I felt my body sag against the car.

Jack frowned, slightly worried. "Peg, are you okay?"

I could hear the concern in his voice, so I knew I had to pull myself together. I took a deep breath. "Yep."

He watched me for a moment longer. "What's next?"

I shook my head. "I think we have to wait on Dougal in order for the connection to make sense. I'm sure his genealogy search will reveal the relationship lurking beneath the surface."

Jack nodded. "I agree."

I rubbed my head as I thought through my next move. "We need to focus on Morgan for the time being ... I think."

Jack smiled. "Works for me." He looked back toward the house. "I feel sorry for the old couple."

I turned to get in the car but stopped short. "Jack, why wasn't Floyd here for crime scene cleanup?"

"He's working on another scene, but he should be here in a couple of hours. Hudson PD will post a man outside until the scene is secured and cleaned."

Maybe Floyd's absence was the reason the couple vacated the area—no one to talk to while they processed their new circumstances. Maybe Bob would be able to explain the procedures but somehow, I doubted it.

There was a pop in the air as I grabbed the door handle, and I froze my movements. Even Jack's expression was surprised. I glanced quickly around until I spotted Henry. He grabbed his hat off his head the second he saw me. "You'd better get to Sal's ... there's been an incident."

My throat closed, and my stomach turned so knotty I thought I'd puke.

Jack spoke before I could. "What type of damn incident?"

"Bad enough that I came for you," Henry snapped. "I don't go off half-cocked Chief. I'd only tell you if it was serious."

Jack turned red at the rebuke but nodded. "We're on our way."

I looked at Henry and Dad. "Are you coming with me?"

Dad shook his head. "You'll be fine without me. I'm headed back with Henry to see how serious this is."

I watched them fade, then I tried to calm myself with a few deep breathes. The trick didn't work, but I really wasn't expecting miracles. I buckled my seatbelt, then turned the car towards home.

A gazillion thoughts were flying around my brain. Why didn't Sal send Bob instead of Henry? If either Sal or Amy was injured, how bad was it? Who was the culprit? What exactly happened at Sal's? The questions were swirling so fast, I was nauseous and frightened.

"You're allowing your imagination to run ahead of the facts. Slow down and wait till you have the whole story ... it's not as bad as you think."

I looked over and saw my Druid sitting in the passenger seat.

I raised my eyebrows in surprise. "You've left my woods," I informed him in case he wasn't aware of the fact. You never know ... he might have gotten lost somehow.

He gave me a small smile. "Yes. I'm weary of Angus."

I laughed in spite of the worry. "Is he on another rampage?"

The Druid shrugged. "He's always wildly upset about something or other. It's his personality."

I nodded and grinned, then grew serious. "Do you have any idea what happened at Sal's?"

The Druid nodded. "There was a break-in, which is surprising considering his security system is vast and impressive."

I cocked my head, keeping my eyes on the winding road ahead. "You know about Sal's security?"

"I have become acquainted with as many of the people involved in your life as possible. I have yet to meet your sons, but I'm sure it will occur eventually."

This information was probably meant to make me feel safer, but in all honesty, it scared me spitless. If my guards felt it was essential to meet everyone important to me, it could only mean everyone in my life was at risk.

The Druid was taking in the sights as I wove around the curving roads.

Every so often, he would nod his approval as we drove past a grove of trees.

My curiosity started to get the best of me. "Do you like trees?"

He nodded. "I feel very at home among the trees, especially oaks. There are few oaks here, but those that do exist are magnificent."

"Do oaks trees have some sort of religious significance?" I knew very little true facts concerning the life of a Druid.

"Oak is a very useful wood. It is not the only tree important to people of my time."

I nodded agreement. "They are fabulous, and they live for decades."

"Centuries in some cases," he corrected.

"Wow … I had no idea." I could see him nod out of the corner of my eye. "What other trees do you consider important?"

After our first encounter, I spent a couple of hours on the internet researching everything about Druids. I discovered there wasn't much actual knowledge. Everything I found was more along the lines of guessing and flat out inventing 'facts' about the ancient people. What insight there was came from early writers and would-be conquerors but even then, that was in short supply. The vast majority of information was essentially made up during the nineteenth century when there was a resurgence of interest in Druids. It wouldn't hurt to be a tad nosey and be able to add actual facts to the abundant fiction roaming freely around the world.

He smiled slightly. "Trees are seen as the connection between earth and sky. I'm sure to your modern mind we seem quite primitive."

I thought about his explanation, then I shook my head. "Not entirely … I remember science class from school explaining photosynthesis, which is when the plants change carbon dioxide to oxygen. Plants need carbon dioxide and animals and people need oxygen. It makes perfect sense that ancient people would understand the importance of healthy trees, even if they didn't know the science."

I swung into Sal's driveway, then turned to my friend.

His smile widened. "You give us a great compliment." I could see the twinkle in his eyes, so I knew he was teasing.

I grinned. "People aren't stupid. I'd bet money their instinct kicked in, and they knew plants were vital to their survival somehow."

He nodded, then his eyes darted to the house. "Do you need me to assist you?"

I shook my head. "Nope … Jack's here." I pointed to his car. "He probably has everything in order."

The Druid shook his head but smiled. "I will return to the woods and endure the Scotsman."

I burst out laughing as he faded. Once I faced the house again, my mood changed. I took a deep breath as I hauled my butt out of the car, glad the sun was warming the air. I could no longer see my breath, but I knew the reprieve was short lived—winter was right around the corner.

As I approached the front door, it swung open to reveal Laura waiting for me. Laura was a pretty woman. She was slim … at least five inches taller than me, and the stress was completely gone from her face now that her ex-husband was in the loony bin. I noticed her blonde hair was longer than the last time I saw her, but she still pulled it back in a ponytail. It was simple but on her, it gave the appearance of elegance.

Once look at her face and I knew there was trouble. "How bad?"

"Bad enough. Everyone's alive, but Amy was smacked around while Sal was tied in a chair and forced to witness the brutality. He is livid."

She held the door wide, so I could pass by her, then we headed to the kitchen.

I heard Jack's anger as I approached. "Damn it Sal … you need to let the police handle this mess. I can't have you acting like a mafia king and offing people in the township!"

"Jack, I appreciate you wanting to help, but this is between me and that sneaky little bastard. Plus, I don't 'off' people … at least not anymore."

"What sneaky little bastard?" I asked as we rounded the corner.

Relief flashed across Jack's face when he saw me. "Thank God you're here, Peg. Talk some sense into this idiot."

I walked over to Amy, eyeing the bandages, the sling around her arm, and fresh black eye. "Are you okay?"

She gave me a weak smile. "Oh, yes. I'll be fine in a few days. Just a few bumps and bruises."

I shook my head. "Amy, you aren't getting any younger. Maybe you should stay with us for a few days."

"Oh, no … I couldn't leave Sal alone! What if they come back? He'll need backup."

I raised an eyebrow. "Backup? Are you kidding?"

She smiled, then pulled a small gun from the sling holding her injured arm.

"Shit," Jack muttered. "That's just what I need."

I had to laugh. "Amy, you aren't in any condition to have a shoot-out with the culprits."

Sal looked at me. "Don't worry, I've called the guys."

Jack snorted, but I felt relieved. The 'guys' were three highly trained men who protected me on more than one occasion, and they saved my life a couple of times. They secretly worked for Logan until Bob let the cat out of the bag. Now, they worked openly for my Indian. Sal was their boss, and they were totally devoted to him.

I looked from Amy to Sal. "How did this happen? Amy's taken enough self-defense classes to clean everyone's clock … and Sal, you're an old pro."

Sal shook his head, disgusted. "The sons-of-bitches snuck in while we were outside finishing up winterizing the garden. When we came back inside, they jumped us."

I frowned. "What about the alarms? You have this house wired to the hilt."

"The bastards cut the wires. Trust me … I've already been on the phone with the security company, and they're on their way. I told them years ago to put the damn wires underground, but they argued it wasn't necessary." The veins in his throat were pulsating at an alarming rate, and I feared if he didn't calm down soon he'd have a stroke.

I decided to change the turn his attention away from the alarm system. "When is my favorite trio arriving?"

He glanced at his watch. "They should be here any minute."

I nodded, then looked around the room searching for Dad and Henry. They were nowhere to be seen. "Anyone else here?"

Sal grinned. "You mean our dead friends?"

I nodded. "Yep."

He threw a thumb in the direction of the backyard. "They're out back checking the bushes. I told them it was unnecessary, but Henry insisted, and your Dad didn't argue."

"Why don't I check on their progress?" I headed for the back door.

Laura caught up with me. "I'll join you."

We firmly closed the door behind us, and neither of us said a word until we were positive we were out of earshot.

I looked at her. "What's wrong?"

"There's more going on than Sal told you." Her face was grim, and my stomach began a circus act of flips.

CHAPTER 19

I looked back at the house, ensuring no one stepped outside. I didn't want anyone overhearing our conversation—all was clear. Once we made it to the far end of the patio, I felt better.

As we trudged towards the bushes, Laura spoke. "Sal called me as soon as he could. I'm still not sure how he was able to untie himself since Amy was on the floor when I arrived. I've learned not to ask too many questions."

I nodded. I wouldn't have the guts to push Sal too far. He may be a reformed mobster, but I had a sneaking suspicion he could get mean if he felt the need.

"Why call you and not an ambulance?" I decided it was a fair question, considering the circumstances.

Laura smiled. "I've helped in the past. There were a couple of times I dug bullets out of Antonio and taped broken ribs for Santino. Bill seems to escape serious injury for some reason."

I grinned. "He probably ducks quicker." Even though I joked with her, I was surprised she was so deeply involved with the iffy side of Sal's business. I guess I shouldn't be surprised—Sal trusted her completely.

Laura smiled, and we continued our march across the vast lawn. I had never been this deep into the property, so I was surprised at how large the estate was. "How many acres does Sal own?"

Laura shrugged. "Tons. He bought almost the entire farm when it was up for sale years ago. The house wasn't built immediately, but he loved tromping through the woods."

I looked at her mildly surprised. "I didn't realize he owned the property for so long."

She nodded. "Yep ... about forty years."

"Wow. Was he still living in Youngstown at the time?"

Youngstown was the mafia hotspot in Ohio for a long time. The last twenty years or so, their influence faded, but the old timers hung onto their legacy for as long as possible. Some, such as Vito Lombardi, stretched their empires to other arenas, but there were a few die-hards that wanted their glory days to return.

"Oh, yes ... this house was built before I married Anthony, but I believe Sal misses the open land."

I gave her a surprised look. "He doesn't think this is enough open land?" I swept my arm to indicate the open field around us. "This is bigger than a football field."

Laura nodded. "When you hear Sal talk about this place you'd think it was Shangri-La. He probably felt freer here than anywhere else on earth. Bella hated nature, so she never set foot on the property until the house was built."

I snorted. "I'm not surprised ... the old bat hated anything beautiful. She was destructive while alive, and she hasn't improved since she joined her ancestors."

Laura nodded in agreement. "She was horrible."

We walked in silence, moving closer to the wooded area. I wanted to give Laura time to gather her thoughts, but after a few minutes of silence, I couldn't stand the suspense another moment. "What is Sal keeping from me?"

She took a deep breath. "He knows who's behind the attack. I'm worried he'll take the law into his own hands before Jack has it under control."

I wasn't surprised. Sal's anger alerted me to the fact that he may know more than what he was sharing. "Who does he suspect?"

"Oh, it's more than a suspicion. He's positive it's Lombardi." She shook her head. "I think he's wrong."

I nodded. "I agree with you. The old man came for a visit the other day. He spoke very highly of Sal. He respects his decision to leave the old ways."

Laura turned to me, surprised. "Vito Lombardi dropped by your house?"

"Yep. Scared the crap out of me, but he was very kind."

Her eyes glazed over, so I knew her mind was hard at work. I kept my mouth shut—figured she could connect the dots quicker without my help. After a few moments, she sighed. I looked over at her, startled to see tears in her eyes. My mom mode kicked in, and I placed a hand on her arm. "Laura? What's wrong?"

She shuddered. "Sal is going to overreact. His love for Amy is blinding him."

I glanced back to the house—all quiet. Maybe Jack would be able to talk some sense into Sal, but I highly doubted it. I sighed. "Maybe we should head back."

Laura nodded. "Where is Henry and your father?"

I shrugged. "They'll let us know if there is a problem ... let's go."

We made quick time crossing the massive lawn. Raised voices greeted us as we approached the patio. Laura gave me a worried glance, but I smiled reassuringly. Through the window, I could see Jack's arms waving around, so I knew he was in full anger mode.

As we walked in the door, Sal was speaking. "Jack, I respect your position." He pointed a finger at Amy. "The love of my life was beaten! I will not tolerate her being used against me."

Amy's face glowed as she listened to Sal, but she interrupted him. "Sal, I'm fine ... really ... please calm down."

Seated at the table, Amy didn't look fine to me. Pale, tired, and tiny ... she wasn't the picture of health in my opinion. Her naturally curly hair was as wild as I'd ever seen it, and I detected a tad of shakiness that she was trying to hide from Sal.

He crossed the kitchen, then knelt down beside her. "Amy, the thought of losing you is driving me crazy. I was going out of my mind watching those bastards hurt you."

Amy put her uninjured hand on his face, "Sweetheart, this is the price we pay to fight evil. I'll mend ... I promise."

Sal's eyes filled with tears. "The price is too high."

Amy's eyes widened with shock. "Sal! You know better than to be so foolish. There are many who gave their lives before us, and they'll be many after we're gone. They were using me to upset you. Have you considered that they were trying to goad you into irresponsible action?"

Sal looked as though he'd been slapped across the face. His shock could be felt throughout the room. "What?"

Amy smiled as she shook her head. "Think. Whoever they represent must know you very well. You protect people ... it's what you do." She tried to shrug, but the pain made her wince. Sal reacted to her obvious discomfort, but she waved away his concern. "I'll heal."

"I can't stand the thought of anyone hurting you again." The agony in Sal's voice brought tears to my eyes.

I glanced at Jack, and his shocked expression was priceless. His uneasiness with the fact that Sal was a reforming mafia guy made their relationship rocky at times. Witnessing the obvious love between two people, almost old enough to be our parents, was unsettling for him. However, it didn't take long for his law and order instinct to kick in. "Sal, you need to listen to Amy. I think she hit the nail on the head. Whoever is behind this mess wants you to overreact for some reason." Jack shook his head. "I'm at a loss as to what they hope to gain, but they are pushing you for a reason."

Sal scowled at Jack. "I'm happy to push right back!"

Jack looked at me for help. I sighed. "Sal, knock it off. You know damn good and well any action you take could have dire consequences. What would Logan advise?"

Sal's eyes narrowed, so I knew he was irritated that I pulled Logan into the mix ... tough beans. The last thing we needed was for Sal to go 'godfather' on the situation.

I ignored his expression and plowed ahead. "Plus, there's fact that you are blaming the wrong person."

Sal shook his head. "Nope ... it's Lombardi."

"I disagree. Mr. Lombardi visited a few days ago. He seems to have a great deal of respect for you *and* your decision to go legit." I shrugged. "I'm not saying he's interested in making all of his own business interests legal, but he's proud of your choice."

Sal looked at me shocked. "Vito was at your house?" The impact of this news almost made Sal lose his balance. He stood, then walked to the window. I knew Sal considered himself above the other mafia men, and the fact that Lombardi respected him came as a surprise.

I nodded. "Yep. He spoke very highly of you."

"What else did he have to say?" He continued to stare out of the window as he spoke.

"He thinks his grandson is a little turd, and he wouldn't be surprised if he is behind our newest crime spree."

Sal turned to face me. "So even Vito believes Morgan is the culprit?"

"Yep."

Sal hesitated. "Vito is a shrewd and a cunning man. Don't believe everything he says."

I nodded. "I agree. Even Elaine thinks he's using me, and I hate her." The room exploded with exclamations. I held up a hand for quiet. "Elaine showed up earlier, gloating about how her uncle was using me. I'm not the idiot she believes me to be, but I did find it fascinating that she couldn't wait to tattle on the old guy."

Dad spoke before anyone else could. "When did Elaine visit?"

I searched the room for Dad ... when had he arrived? Jeez ... I didn't even sense him when he joined the group meeting. Was I losing my abilities to detect the dead's presence? Or was the emotion in the room so high that I ignored his entrance?

Henry's face turned bright red. "I had no idea she was there!" He turned to Dad. "Dave, I'm so sorry."

"Henry, it's fine … no harm done," I assured him.

He shook his head. "Miss Peg, it's my job."

I hated that he felt so bad for missing her appearance. "I was dressing in my room. No one … not even Dad, is allowed to watch me change clothes!"

He continued to shake his head, his face full of worry. "Logan will skin me alive for missing Elaine's appearance."

I sighed. "She wasn't at the house for more than a few minutes. How were you to know?"

"It doesn't matter. My job is to protect you inside the house, and Elaine's capability to sneak in undetected is a big problem," Henry said firmly.

I shook my head but didn't argue. Henry is old school, so I knew he took his assignment seriously.

Dad's eyes never left my face. I tried to reassure everyone again. "She left when I told her to go. Other than irritating me, no damage was done."

"What else did she say?" Dad's voice was so quiet, I knew he was fuming.

I thought back to my brief conversation with Elaine. "She said Mom was going to be free soon, and that Mom isn't happy with me." I shrugged. "Nothing new there … Mom has never been happy with me."

Dad's stance changed when he heard Mom would be released soon. "Nell shouldn't be expecting freedom yet. There is still a big debate concerning her imprisonment. A few want her banned from ever gaining freedom." His frown deepened. "I think Logan needs to be informed." He was gone before anyone could say a word.

The knots in my stomach increased and I could feel sweat forming between my boobs … jeez.

Those of us remaining in Sal's kitchen looked at one another, dismayed.

"If your dad is worried, it's serious." Jack wasn't any happier than I was that Mom may be free soon.

Amy looked at me. "Do you believe Elaine?"

I scrunched my face while I thought about her question. "Maybe."

"Peg, that's not an answer," she chided.

I sighed. "The dead can't lie. They can veil the truth, skirt around the truth, and ignore the truth … but they can't outright lie." Some tidbit was scampering through my brain cells, and I was having a difficult time grabbing hold of it.

Finally, light dawned and I snapped my fingers. Every eye was on my face as I spoke. "Mom learned how to send her *essence* to a certain place, which is usually somewhere designed to freak me out of my mind." I gave everyone a small smile. "It would work if I actually saw her form standing in front of me. So far, I've been lucky, and it hasn't happened. If Mom was able to convince Elaine that she was gaining freedom any minute, then suggested Elaine announce her pending release, wouldn't it upset all of us?" I didn't wait for input, instead I continued my theory. Ideas had a nasty way of vacating my thought process if I wasn't careful—aging has plenty of drawbacks. "Elaine would believe Mom … she would have no reason not to trust her. Of course, Elaine's an idiot, but that's beside the point. Mom is using Elaine to terrorize me or try to."

There wasn't a sound made as everyone looked for holes in my theory. I waited while their brain gears went through the motions of deep analysis.

Finally, Amy nodded. "You may have discovered Nell's plot. I believe Elaine does hero worship your mother. Nell could easily deceive the foolish woman." She looked at Sal. "Any thoughts?"

Sal shrugged. "It's as good a theory as any. If your mother has enough power to project her essence, it is cause for concern."

I nodded. "I agree. It's bad enough when she actually appears. The last thing we need is a fake version of her showing up."

Jack visibly shuddered. "Hells bells … the havoc that she could cause from jail could be as serious as the mess she makes already."

I sighed, hoping Logan had her under control. "Logan promised to perform some sort of magic stuff to thicken whatever holds her, but I'm not sure how powerful Mom has become."

Sal cleared his throat. "I'm still not convinced Lombardi isn't behind what happened today."

I could feel his stubbornness and shook my head. "My gut tells me Lombardi isn't involved. However, his jackass grandson might be."

Sal nodded begrudgingly. "You could be right. Morgan is a problem, and he could be trying to throw suspicion on his grandfather."

Amy drew in a breath. "Sal, what if that is exactly what Morgan wants! For you to believe Vito was involved in the attack on us! Everyone knows your personality, and it would be normal to expect you to plan revenge. You would be responsible for removing his grandfather from power, then Morgan could easily step in his grandfather's shoes."

Sal's face paled. "Oh my god."

Amy patted his hand. "Now do you understand why we all agreed that you shouldn't react? Even before Peg came up with her theory, we wondered if this was a setup of some kind."

Sal nodded, but the color didn't return to his face. I glanced at Laura, slightly worried. She seemed so calm, so I decided he wasn't having a heart attack. She knew him better than the rest of us, and I trusted her judgment.

Jack sighed his relief at the outcome of the discussion. "Thank God," he whispered to himself. I nudged his shoulder and smiled. "It was a close call," he whispered to me.

I nodded, still smiling. "Yep."

The doorbell rang twice, then we heard the front door open. I looked at Sal.

He straightened. "It's the guys."

Ah … about damn time the trio showed up. We could hear their voices as they walked down the hall. When they turned the corner into the kitchen, they stopped and stared at us.

Santino was the first to speak. "Uncle Sal, what the hell happened?" Santino is a big guy, but he is the most fun-loving of the trio. He was also Sal's nephew. His dark hair and eyes, along with his muscular build, made him stand out in a crowd. The usual twinkle in his eyes was gone as he surveyed Amy and his uncle.

As Sal explained what happened, I grabbed Jack and headed to the patio. Once safely outside, I pointed to a chair. "Sit."

Jack hesitated. "I'm not going to like this … am I?"

I smiled slightly. "You need to sit and calm down a little. Your argument with Sal was stressful, and the last thing I need is for you to have a breakdown or heart attack."

He snorted. "I'm fine. Sal is so damn hard headed. I thought for a minute he was going to start a mafia war."

I nodded. "Amy's injuries have shaken him, and he was lashing out."

Jack sighed. "I understand his anger, but he really needs to cool his jets. The last thing I need is for a statewide mafia war."

A grim expression crossed my face. "A mafia war is peanuts next to the possibility of my mom getting out of Deadsville prison."

Jack sighed again. "You have a point … neither one is good news."

I watched him carefully. "I believe we are being manipulated, so we need to be careful."

He nodded in agreement, then we headed back inside. Antonio was on his phone, Bill was on the computer, and Santino was inspecting Amy's injuries.

"Tomorrow will not suffice. I expect your crew to be here within the hour." Antonio hung up his phone, then he looked at Sal. "They'll show. We do entirely too much business with them for them to take the chance and cause us to switch to their competitor."

Antonio was the biggest of my mob trio. I never had the guts to ask him exactly how tall he is, but I wouldn't be surprised to find out he was more than a couple of inches north of six feet. While he also had dark eyes and hair, his physical appearance was secondary to his demeanor. Antonio is a born leader, so he is all business, all the time—he doesn't suffer fools easily.

I was guessing Antonio chewed someone's butt at the security company … the ones who installed the alarm system. I was glad I didn't hear the entire conversation—Antonio could be scary sometimes.

Sal nodded but stayed silent. I eyed him, and I wasn't thrilled by what I saw. He looked defeated, and we needed him to be firing with all barrels.

Santino smiled down at Amy. "You'll be fine in a few days. No broken bones, and Laura did a great job patching you up. You should take something for the pain for the next day or two."

Amy shook her head. "No need … I don't really feel as bad as I look. As long as I don't move around too much, there isn't much pain."

"Think about a few aspirins," Santino insisted. "Just to make you more comfortable."

Amy smiled slightly. "Maybe."

Bill closed his laptop. "Lombardi wasn't involved as far as I can tell."

I frowned. "How can you be so sure?" Even though I agreed with Bill, it would nice to know how he came to the same conclusion.

He shrugged. "I have a tracking device on his limo, and I bugged his phones."

"What?" Jack was nearly yelling. "It's damn illegal to bug someone's phone!"

Bill grinned. "It's standard operating procedures. We have all the big family bosses bugged. It saves time and trouble when we need to decide who's doing what."

Santino was my favorite, but Bill ran a close second. He was the opposite of Santino and Antonio in appearance. His dirty blonde hair and blue eyes were a sharp contrast to his partners. His presence was the least menacing of the three, but if I was a bad guy, I wouldn't want to meet him in a dark alley. His skill level was equal to his friends. They trusted one another completely, which allowed them to work harmoniously.

Jack opened his mouth to argue, but I jabbed his ribs. "Forget you heard that. We need the information, and you know damn good and well that we don't have enough for a warrant. No judge in his right mind would give us squat on the word of dead people and a mobster." I nodded toward Sal.

Jack's mouth snapped shut. While he knew what I said was true, he didn't have to like it. His position as chief of police could sure cause headaches sometimes. He glared at me but gave me a quick nod.

"Sorry, Jack … we need to be damn careful, which means we have to step around the law every now and then." Sal still didn't looked too great, so I glanced at Laura.

She smiled. "He's fine … just angry as hell, and he has no place to release the emotions."

I looked at Sal. "Why don't you go out to the firing range and shoot the hell out of a target."

Sal thought a moment, then smiled. "That's not a bad idea." He looked down at Amy. "You'll be safe with the boys. They aren't leaving until we discover who's behind today's break-in."

Amy gave him a huge smile, then pulled him toward her for a big kiss … jeez.

CHAPTER 20

As soon as I possibly could, I made my exit and headed for the grocery store. There was no way was I serving Andy grilled cheese again for dinner. I needed meat and potatoes for energy—to balance out the meal, I'd make a salad on the side.

I was hitting the store at an off hour, so the parking lot was almost empty, and I was able to breeze through the store in record time. I hated grocery shopping as much as I hated every other type of shopping. I sailed past the bakery, determined to ignore the call of the sweet treats staring me in the face—I won the battle. I decided a fruit salad would work, so I drove the cart toward the produce section. Grabbing what few selections of fruit were available this time of year, salad ingredients, a couple of pork chops, and a bottle of white wine … I made my way to the self-checkout aisle.

I was bursting with glee as I loaded the car with the groceries. I managed to make it out of the store in less than twenty minutes. My mood while driving home was dampened at the sight of Lombardi's limo parked in the driveway. I shook my head in annoyance when I saw the old man nod to his driver as he exited the comfort of the backseat.

He approached me as I was pulling the groceries out of the backseat of my car. I waited for him to get closer before speaking. "I hope you have information for me." I figured I might as well cut to the chase instead of prolonging his visit.

He nodded, then pointed to the house. "I would feel more comfortable if we talked inside."

I sighed but nodded. We entered the house and found Dad waiting for us in the kitchen. I wasn't surprised, but I *was* relieved. It was always nice to have a little backup, even if the backup didn't have a heartbeat.

I glanced at Lombardi. "Coffee?" It always pays to display a sense of manners.

Lombardi shook his head. "No, thank you. If you don't mind, I'll make this visit short. I have a business meeting at one of my farms." He made a point to nod toward Dad, acknowledging his presence. Dad returned the favor but remained silent.

I raised an eyebrow, but I didn't want the old coot to know I was aware of his shady farming practices.

"I have information concerning James' businesses. It appears his lawn service is completely legit, but the art business is one hundred percent illegal. It is all black market art from Europe, mostly before and during the war." He shook his head. "The boy doesn't seem to care what happened to the original owners."

I nodded. "That's pretty much how I had it figured."

The old man seemed lost in thought for a few moments. "He isn't a good person. He has no respect for anyone."

I thought his analysis of his grandson was a little hypocritical since he was running his own scam with organic produce, but I kept my thoughts to myself. "Did you find out anything unusual concerning his friendship with Anthony?"

He shook his head. "Nothing more than I shared the other day. They were friends, but James doesn't seem disturbed by his absence."

I glanced at the clock and decided it was time to start dinner whether the old guy was here or not. I began the process of gathering pots, pans, a cutting board, and knife. Lombardi watched my actions, but he didn't take the hint that it may be time for his butt to leave.

His eyes roamed the kitchen. "You have recently redecorated."

I nodded. "Yep. A snotty teenager running drugs decided shooting the place to pieces was a good idea."

His well-trimmed eyebrows shot up. "I heard there was a problem with the Mendoza fools, but I had no idea your home was involved."

I frowned. "I thought you were kept apprised of any crime in the township … it was big news."

"I was out of the country at the time. My men must have decided it was old news by the time I returned."

I watched him curiously. "Out of the country?"

He continued to look around. "I have business interests in various places around the world. A businessman must diversify in today's world."

I narrowed my eyes. "What type of diverse businesses do you have?"

He waved a hand. "Nothing that bleeds over into our current situation."

"Are you absolutely sure?" The last thing we needed was for a foreign complication to arise.

He nodded firmly. "Yes."

I looked over at Dad who slowly nodded. "I believe he's telling the truth."

Lombardi looked at Dad. "Thank you."

I drummed my fingers on the counter for a few seconds while I thought about the little information Lombardi shared. "Either James wasn't a partner with Anthony concerning the illegal art, or he's relieved he's out of the picture. Do you think Anthony was the one who guided him and provided contacts for the paintings?"

His pudgy shoulders raised an inch. "Possible ... Anthony knew many shady characters."

I burst out laughing. "You might be considered 'shady' by a lot of people."

He grinned his million-watt smile. "Yes ... your point is taken."

My cell phone rang, and Lombardi took the hint I was way too busy to be entertaining the mob. I grabbed my phone, raising an eyebrow once I saw the caller ID ... Santino.

"Is the old guy with you?" His blunt question greeted me as soon as I answered. Jeez ... not even a 'hello' for Pete's sake.

I glanced at Vito. "Yep."

"How much longer do you think he'll be there?"

"Hopefully, not long." I eyed the aging mobster as I spoke.

"I will see myself out." Lombardi turned to leave, and Dad joined him.

"I'll call you back." I hung up before Santino could argue.

I walked with Lombardi to the front door. "I appreciate you taking time to update me. Any more news is welcome." I paused as I studied the man in front of me. "I hope you haven't jeopardized your standing in the mafia community by visiting me."

Lombardi grinned. "I am careful. I only ride in the cars Sal has a tracker on, just in case of an emergency. I feel confident he would send a man immediately if trouble arose."

My mouth dropped open. "You know about the tracker?" I asked before my brain warned me that I shouldn't admit Sal spied on his former business associates.

"Of course. The cars are swept each day to search for these attachments. I recognize Sal's handywork ... he always uses the same brand of electronics." He shrugged. "I feel better knowing Sal has my back."

I was damn sure having Lombardi's back wasn't even close to why Sal tracked his old buddy, but since my brain now had control of my mouth, it stayed firmly closed.

Lombardi nodded to my dad, bowed to me, then turned and headed for his car. I waited until his driver made it to the road before I closed the door.

"Better call Santino back," Dad advised. "Tell him Vito is on to them."

"Yep." I made the call, then waited for Santino to answer.

He answered after several rings. "Is Lombardi gone?"

"Yep … he knows you have a gizmo on his car to track him."

My comment was met by complete silence. I frowned slightly.

"Did you hear me?" I prodded.

Santino sighed. "Yes. I thought I hid the damn thing well. How'd they find it?"

"He told me they sweep the cars every day. He thinks Sal is keeping tabs on him for his safety."

Santino hesitated. "He has to know better … Sal has to be careful with the old ties. Lombardi must be out of his mind."

"I'm merely passing along the info. Talk to Sal and see what his take is on the old guy's idea."

Santino was thoughtful for a moment. "He could change cars and we'd never know. I only bugged a few of them."

"Nope. He said he'll only ride in cars he knows Sal has a device on."

"Hells bells … the guy is nuts." Santino's shocked tone made me smile a little.

"I told you, he respects and trusts Sal."

He sighed. "This could complicate Sal's position. The last thing he needs is Lombardi asking for help at some point."

"Don't tell Jack … he has enough problems," I warned.

"Oh hell no." He scoffed. "I regret saying anything in front of him earlier. I didn't think fast enough."

I smiled slightly. "That's unusual for you."

He sighed again. "I've become too comfortable working with Jack. It's not a mistake I'll make again."

My curiosity started to get the best of me. "Did Sal hit the roof once we were gone?"

"Nope … he was too upset about Amy to worry about my screw-up." The relief in his tone was evident.

"I'm in the middle of cooking dinner. Call if anything new pops … otherwise, I'm off the radar tonight."

"Yep. You need a night crime free … I understand," he agreed.

I smiled, relieved. "Thanks."

Once off the phone, I returned to the task at hand—broiled chops, salad, boiled potatoes with a little butter and parsley, along with chilled wine. I also threw a fruit salad together for dessert. What could be better?

Andy opened the door at the same time the phone started to ring. I shook my head in disgust. I wanted some time away from the investigation, so I hoped the call wasn't work related—no such luck.

Jack's voice came on the line. "Peg, I'm convinced the Hudson murders are tied to our case. I'm positive the Swiss bank account is the key to the entire mess."

"Hello to you too," I snapped.

He hesitated. "Sorry … a lot on my mind."

Andy looked at the stove, then smiled. "Smells great."

I nodded, then pointed to the phone. "Let me get Jack off the phone, then we can enjoy our meal."

"Call me after you've eaten." Jack cut in. "I need to run a few things past you."

I sighed. "Fine … I will if I remember."

"I'll call back." He hung up before I could snap a snotty remark.

Andy wrapped me in his big arms. "Let's eat. You'll feel better. You can call Jack back once you have your belly full."

"I wanted the night off," I pouted.

Andy laughed. "Sweetie, you're in the middle of a case … we always take it as it comes."

I pulled my head back to look up at Andy. "You seem like you've made peace with our circumstances. Did something new happen that I'm not aware of?"

Andy rested his chin on the top of my head. "Babe, I've done a lot of thinking recently. You were one hundred percent correct … we know too much now to ignore the dead's influence over the living. I'd rather be aware instead of pretending it isn't real." He sighed. "I'm not happy that you could get hurt, but I understand the need to be active and maybe, just maybe, you'll make a difference."

"Well said." Logan's voice came from over by the window.

I plopped my head against Andy's chest. "Hi, Logan."

"Andy, I believe you have given your present situation much thought. I admire a person who honestly views their current circumstances and realizes careful involvement is necessary." Logan never turned from the window, so I knew he was worried.

Knots formed in my stomach, making dinner no longer appealing. I pulled away from Andy and walked over to the window. "Logan, is there anything I should know?"

He turned to face me. "Your mother is a great concern. She is gathering strength rapidly." He shook his head. "We have not been able to determine how or who she is gaining the power from … it is troubling.

I stared at Logan. No words formed but sweat sure did—the damn stuff was pouring down between my boobs … ick! I couldn't think of a single word to say. Mom gaining strength was one of my biggest nightmares.

"I realize this is causing you a great deal of stress. It is unfortunate that Nell has managed to evade our security measures concerning her abilities." He held up a hand as I started to argue. "She is well guarded, and she is the main topic at our meetings."

My eyes narrowed as I listened to the old Indian. He truly believed he was assuaging my fears, but in reality … he was only increasing the anxiety.

I stomped my foot out of sheer frustration. "How positive are you that Mom is locked down good and tight?"

He looked surprised by my question. "Completely."

I shook my head. "Logan, I know you think she's under your control for the most part, but she's obviously gained some damn dangerous friends. Friends who are able to pierce whatever armor you have surrounding her."

I looked over at Dad. He knew her better than anyone. "Do you have any ideas?"

His lips tightened in a thin line. "She was always sneaky. I wouldn't trust her as far as I could throw the woman. Plus, she has Elaine running around doing errands for her … not good. How on earth is she capable of contacting Elaine?"

Logan frowned. "You do not trust our security?"

"Ha! If your security was so airtight, then Mom wouldn't have the ability to throw her essence around."

Before another fight between Logan and I became a reality, Andy stepped in. "Logan, Nell is a problem. We are all aware of that fact. You do the best you can on your side. Here …" he swept his arm around. "… we will work the case. Somehow, Nell is involved the same as she was with the Mendoza family."

I drew a deep breath at the memory. Mom was whispering to the Mendoza idiots for years. She was able to talk them into a pile of trouble, not only for them, but anyone in their path—it was a mess.

Logan studied Andy for a moment, then his face broke into a smile. He turned to me. "This is why Andy's involvement is crucial. He points us in the right direction."

I frowned, slightly confused. "What direction?"

"Sadly, I dismissed Nell's interference with the Mendoza's as a fluke. They are not very intelligent, and we decided she was fortunate to be able to encourage them due to their greed." He inclined his head in Andy's direction. "However, Andy has opened my mind to the possibility of her meddling in some person's life involved in the present investigation. It deserves great consideration. We will discuss this potential issue at the next meeting."

I sighed. "When is the next meeting?"

Logan ignored me. I expected that response, but it never hurt to try and dig a little information out of the old stinker. You never know, one of these times … it might work. Logan watched me carefully. "What contact have you recently had with the mayor?"

I dropped my head. I hated dealing with Akron's crooked politician, and Logan was well aware of my feelings—he didn't care one bit. "I'm pretty sure he's told me everything he knows."

Logan's eyes bored into mine, and I glared right back at him. "Peg, it would be helpful for you to keep in touch more regularly with him while we are trying to solve a dilemma. He has contacts we do not."

I scoffed. "Oh for Pete's sake, Logan! *You* have contacts no one else has, so why should we bother the mayor?"

He shook his head. "You are well aware that we have limitations on our side. Many situations are …" he stopped as he searched for an appropriate word. "Murky."

I threw my head back and stared at the ceiling for a moment. "Fine. It seems a bit wonky that you know so much … except for vital details we need."

He gave a brief nod. "Yes, it does seem unfair. However, I do not control what has been true throughout human history."

I narrowed my eyes, but he turned back toward the window. He is a master when it comes to ignoring my temper. I was aware that the dead are not all knowing, but it sure seemed strange that vital info was always 'murky'. Just goes to show … being dead ain't all it's cracked up to be.

Logan turned and looked at the table. "You and Andy enjoy your meal. Please do not forget to call Jack … I am positive it is important."

Before I could ask how he was so damn sure, he quickly faded … jeez.

Andy moved toward the table. "Peg, let's eat. I'm starving."

"Yep … everything's ready."

"You two enjoy your meal," Dad said as he began to fade.

"Dad!" I called before he could completely disappear.

He stopped fading, watching me carefully. "Yes?"

I smiled slightly. "Thanks for everything."

He smiled, then disappeared.

Andy and I looked each other for a second. Without a word, we began filling our plates, then Andy poured wine. After a few satisfying bites of food, he turned to me. "You have to admit that our lives are different than anyone else we know."

In spite of my irritation, I burst out laughing. "Yep … but it's more complicated than I like at times."

He nodded as he took another bite of pork chop. His eyes drifted toward the window, but before he could ask what was on his mind, I spoke. "Don't you dare ask me if I can see the dead gang out back! I want to eat my meal in peace and quiet. I can see them, and they aren't upset."

He smiled and nodded. "I was just wondering ... sorta like having radar."

I stuck my tongue out at him, then looked down at my plate. How did I finish already? I was still hungry, so I headed back to the stove for more potatoes. Just as I got there, the phone rang.

Andy grabbed it before I could. He listened for a second before handing it over to me. "The mayor."

What a way to ruin a perfectly nice meal.

While I wanted to start the conversation with a snotty remark, I refrained. "How can I help you?" I thought my question was pretty reasonable, but Andy shook his head at me.

"Tone of voice, Peg ... tone of voice," he whispered.

I glared at him as I put my hand over the mouthpiece. "It could've been worse!"

His head shook again, but he kept any further remarks to himself.

The mayor cleared his throat. "I realize I'm calling at a bad time. I apologize for the inconvenience, but there is a development you should be aware of."

I frowned. "Sure ... what's up?" My tone changed. The old coot caught my attention. The fact that he was calling me with information was intriguing.

The mayor cleared his throat nervously. "Morgan called earlier to inform me that he is relocating his business."

I sat straight up in my chair. "What!"

"I have to admit, his call shocked me. Now, I have to find another lawn service company and keep the costs down. These people also do most of the snow removal during the winter ... that's a pretty penny in itself."

I shook my head in disbelief. It was just like the jerk to think about his own problems rather than how this news impacted the case. My mouth opened for a snarky reply when I remember his explanation of how city budgets work. A thought suddenly came to mind. "What type of deal did you have with Morgan? Fair prices or better than fair?"

There was a pause, but thankfully, I didn't have the feeling he was trying to decide which lie to tell. "The prices weren't bad overall. A little pricey on a few of the city owned areas, but they are in dicey areas. Landscaping companies usually do charge a little more because the risk to their equipment is higher ... theft, damage, harassment ... all drive prices up."

"You wouldn't say the deal you had with Morgan was better than what you could get with another company, would you?" I wasn't backing down on the point.

Another pause, but this time I *knew* he was going to fudge. "Well, depends on what you call a good deal."

I dropped my head as frustration began to build.

"Peg, calm down," Andy advised.

I nodded and took a deep breath. "What do *you* call a good deal?"

Another pause—this couldn't be good.

The silence continued, so I knew his honor, the crooked mayor, was fighting a battle within himself.

Finally, he spoke. "I might as well tell you the truth."

Jeez … it would be one of the few times the guy actually offered the truth without Logan dragging it out of him.

CHAPTER 21

I decided to keep calm and see where this conversation went. "So what's the scoop?"

He sighed, and I could picture his large bulk leaning back in his super comfy office chair. "Morgan's company is located in Akron."

"That's the big news?" I frowned. "So what?"

Another pause before he continued. "He doesn't have to pay company taxes to the city. His employees pay taxes but the company doesn't."

I wanted to laugh. Compared to his many other iffy schemes, this one was cake. "You've basically given him a tax break?"

He hesitated. "In a manner of speaking."

I frowned. "Explain."

"It's sorta off the books." The mayor no longer sounded very comfortable with the course the conversation was taking.

"How 'off the books' are we talking?" I didn't give a fig if the city decided to give Morgan a tax break but obviously, it was a dicey situation.

"Everything is computerized, so we have to be careful when we negotiate deals under the table," he explained.

I was starting to understand. "If the city is ever audited your ass will be in a world of hurt."

He cleared his throat. "Not as long as the books balance."

I scowled, starting to feel my annoyance rise. "How in the hell can you balance the books if you cut deals with crooks?"

My question was met with brief silence. "It's complicated. We have an excellent accountant."

I shook my head, trying to calm my irritation. "The accounting mess is yours to handle. What else did Morgan tell you?"

"Not much. I was shocked to be honest, so I didn't think fast enough to ask many questions."

"Did you at least ask why he was relocating?" I snapped.

"Yes, I did. He said it was a personal matter."

"Where's he relocating to?"

"I have no idea. I did ask, hoping his move would still make it possible for our contract to stand, but he told me out of state ... but he didn't give specifics."

I sighed in annoyance.

The mayor heard the frustration in my voice and quickly spoke. "Mrs. Shaw, I asked where he was planning on moving, and he avoided the question. That alone told me something was fishy, so I knew you would want a heads up."

As much as I hated to admit it, the mayor actually thought about the investigation. This may be the first time since we've been forced to work with him that he actually thought of someone other than himself and his career—maybe he was finally understanding Logan's point of view.

I turned my attention back to the mayor. "I appreciate the call. If you hear anymore from him, please let one of us know."

"No problem. Thanks for your time." He immediately hung up.

Andy cocked an eyebrow at me. "You were nicer than expected toward the end of the conversation."

I shrugged. "The mayor had the courage to call me with the news that Morgan is moving his company out of state. He only hedged on the fact that, somehow, the city doesn't make Morgan's company pay Akron taxes." I shook my head. "I don't know how, and I don't care ... taxes are his problem. *Our* next issue is the fact that Morgan is moving and why."

"Well ... one nice thing is ... the mayor called you, so now you're off the hook with Logan about calling the mayor."

I grinned. "One problem solved."

Andy was thoughtful for a moment. "Do you think we could find out where Morgan is moving to?"

"Sure ... Bob!" I yelled.

There was a 'pop' in the air, and Bob stood in front of us. "Hey, guys. What's up?"

I quickly took inventory of him—hair decent, clothes rumpled but that wasn't unusual, and facial expression normal. Good … the last time he showed up, he was a mess. "No battles today?"

He shook his head. "Nope … they don't happen all the time."

I nodded. "Good to know. I need a favor."

"Sure thing!" Sometimes, I worried Bob was too eager to help. I didn't want anyone thinking we were taking advantage of the goof ball.

I hesitated, watching him carefully. "Are you doing okay? Is everything going good?"

Bob frowned. "Yep. Why? Do you know something I don't?" I could hear the immediate worry in his voice.

For Pete's sake … my concern poked his self-doubt. When would I learn to keep my mouth shut? I shook my head. "Nope. I need you to find where Morgan is moving. He called the mayor today and informed his highness of the impending move."

Bob's mouth fell open. "You've got to be kidding … Logan needs to know!"

I nodded. "Yep. I figured you could handle it for us, but we need to know *why* the move is happening and *where* he's going." A thought hit my brain. "Also, does his wife know, and is she going with him?"

Bob's head bounced up and down. "Wow … this is big, really big."

I sighed tiredly. "I agree. I don't like surprises, and this one is from left field."

"I'll nose around, but I have to tell Logan first. He won't mind me helping as long as he's kept in the loop."

"Fine, but try not to take too long. Find out what you can, then get back to me in the morning," I instructed.

Bob tilted his head. "I'm not sure I can dig up the info so fast, but I'll try."

I nodded. "Check in with me whether you discover anything or not … sound good?"

"Yep. Later." He smiled as he faded.

I looked at Andy, and he grinned. "You almost started a mess with Bob. You know how insecure he is … you can't say certain things to him."

I sighed. "I didn't realize he would overreact."

"Peg, you've worked with Bob enough to understand his lack of confidence. Logan is very self-assured … even Henry understands his strengths and weaknesses. Bob lived with Elaine for a lot of years, and she bashed him every chance she got."

"I'll try to remember." I was thoughtful for a moment. "I guess I was so focused on why Morgan is moving it never dawned on me that Bob would take my questions so personal. I was honestly worried we were taking advantage of his faithfulness and willingness to help."

Andy squeezed my hand. "Next time ask him if we are over-stepping any boundaries. I'm sure the question will surprise him, but it will also make him aware of your concern ... that alone will make him feel like a million bucks."

I smiled. "You're probably right. I don't want to overwork him. I had no idea they were fighting battles in Deadsville. Neither Bob or Logan ever mentioned it before now."

Andy nodded. "The news was disconcerting, but it explains a lot. No wonder Logan is always worried."

My mind wandered back to times when I knew Logan was upset, but he refused to explain why. Now, I knew part of the reason. Knowing didn't make me feel any better, but knowing is better than ignorance.

I stood up, then started to gather our dishes. Andy helped and in no time, we had the kitchen in ship-shape. I glanced around the newly refurbished kitchen and smiled. My eyes landed on the bullet sunk in the wood from the last investigation we worked. They were still noticeable in the cabinets. Andy fought to have them dug out, but I stood my ground. We would never be able to match the aging woodwork, plus ... having a reminder of the danger never hurt.

Andy's eyes followed mine, then he shook his head. "I still wish you let me have those bullets removed."

I patted his back. "I know, but I like them." An eyebrow rose, but he remained quiet. I shrugged. "They're a testament to our work ... sorta."

He grinned. "You have an odd way of looking at things sometimes."

I stood on my tiptoes to give his cheek a quick kiss. "It makes life interesting."

"Oh, gosh ... sorry guys. I didn't realize you were having a private moment." Bob's voice startled both of us.

I swung around, surprised to see him so soon. "I thought you were checking in tomorrow morning."

"Well ... I found out where the Morgan's are moving." The excitement in his voice was evident.

My eyebrows shot up in surprise. "Where?"

He beamed at us. "South America! Argentina to be exact!"

I couldn't believe my ears. "Argentina? What the hell is down there?"

Bob shook his head. "I have no idea ... but I heard him talking with one of his crew chiefs. It seems they are trying to skedaddle pretty quickly."

I watched him carefully. "How quickly?"

"Six or seven weeks." Satisfaction was written all over Bob's face. He knew he discovered a juicy piece of news quickly.

I smiled. "Good work, Bob. Thanks."

His face lit up like a roman candle. "No problem, Peg."

"Have you told Logan?"

He shook his head. "Nope. I wanted you to be the first to know. I'd better head over and let him know."

I nodded. "Thanks again." He began to fade, and his grin was all I needed to see to know he was thrilled with his find.

Andy and I looked at one another.

Andy spoke first. "Argentina? A bit far … don't you think?"

I didn't answer Andy because my brain was on fire, but it wasn't giving me much direct information. Argentina lit my memory like a firework. Now, I just needed to figure out why my brain was in overdrive. I stood stock still, hoping everything would fall into place if I was immobile. After a few seconds, I decided to give up. As I opened my mouth to reply to Andy, the idea slipped into place, stunning me. I turned to Andy. "Remember the special we watched on TV? The one about some Nazis escaping to South America?"

Andy nodded.

I smiled, exited with my sudden thought. "A lot of them ended up in Argentina."

Andy's mouth fell open. "I forgot about that. Do you believe the stolen artwork Morgan's selling is stored in Argentina?"

I considered the possibility. "Maybe, but it's more likely that it's his contacts."

Andy frowned. "There can't be any Nazis still alive … the war was over seventy years ago."

"No, but their children could still be there. If you were sitting on millions in illegal art, you'd want to start selling it. The mission would be to deplete inventory before there could be any change in attitudes within the local government. Seventy years is a long time for local people to protect war criminals."

Andy frowned. "Do you believe the local citizens were protecting them because they agreed with the Nazi propaganda?"

I shook my head. "Some yes … but most were probably scared to death to say anything against their newest members of society."

Andy nodded. "You're probably right … fear is a good motivator. The locals were frightened that there would be retaliation against their families if they didn't cooperate."

"Yep. Plus, the program we watched mentioned that it was well known that stolen art had been removed from Germany toward the end of the war … much of it was sent to South America. Some was sent to Switzerland in bank vaults, and the rest was hidden throughout Europe."

"Do you think Morgan has contacts in South America and now that he feels pressure he's decided to move?"

I nodded. "Seems reasonable. The question is … why kill David Peters, the old couple in Hudson, and rob a bunch of homes in the area?"

Andy shook his head. "It doesn't make sense. Murder is a guarantee to bring the local authorities into the equation. If stolen art is proven to be a source of income, the feds get involved."

"Someone made a mistake." I squished my face in thought. My brain hadn't calmed down, and I needed it to inform me what piece I was missing.

Andy stayed silent as I tried to pull the threads together, but my mind wasn't in the mood to cooperate. I sighed.

"Sleep on it ... you might wake up and have it figured out," Andy advised.

I made a face. "I don't like trying to sleep when the questions are flying around my head."

He grinned. "Maybe you'll have a dream that lays out the entire operation."

I gave him a dirty look, but his grin only widened.

While Andy watched one of his TV shows, I searched the internet for any information concerning Argentina and Nazi plunder. While there was a ton of articles surmising, actual facts and proof were few and far between. I was exhausted, so after a couple of hours I decided to call it a day and head for bed. Maybe Andy's idea of sleep wasn't so bad after all.

Surprisingly, I was able to sleep. However, I dreamed so much that I woke up exhausted. The dreams weren't cohesive, and I didn't wake up with anything close to a eureka moment of clarity.

I dragged myself to the kitchen, ready to start my morning caffeine intake. As I stood waiting for the first cup of elixir to brew, I felt a presence. With a bid of dread, I slowly turned to face whoever joined me.

My mouth dropped open when I spotted the intruder. "Angus! What are you doing in my kitchen?"

"Morning, lassie. I've come to discuss a *very* serious situation."

My head dropped for a moment, then I looked at my Scotsman. I shook a finger at him. "You better stay absolutely silent until I've had at least two cups of coffee. If that proves too difficult for you, then you should return to the woods until I call for you."

His eyes narrowed as he listened to my demands, and he must've heard something in my voice which convinced him I was serious. He finally nodded, but he planted his feet firmly and crossed his arms. "Deal."

I pointed to a corner, and he moved to the indicated spot. At least he would be out of my line of vision. I glanced toward the woods, but it was still too dark for me to observe any nervousness among the gang out there. I focused on my coffee, ignoring Angus. I could feel his eyes boring into me, but I was successful at avoiding his eyes through the first cup of coffee. Finally, I turned to face him with feelings of total exasperation. "What do you want?"

He rubbed his hands together. "Well ... it's like this ... my grandson does not receive the level of recognition he deserves. He is a good lad, and he works *very* hard."

I noticed his accent came and went as he pleased. I narrowed my eyes as I watched him lecture me. I grabbed my second cup of coffee, then headed to the table and plopped down in my chair. Might as well let him get it over with, so I could enjoy my time-honored ritual.

"You promised to take care of this injustice," he reminded me.

I held up a hand. "Angus, there is little I can do at the moment. We are in the middle of an important police investigation, and Dougal is helping us enormously. I fully expect him to receive some type of commendation in his file for his work on this case."

Angus shook his head. "What good is a piece of paper in a folder? No one will remember it in a week."

I agreed with his assessment, but there was no way I was in the mood for this conversation. "I will talk with Jack as soon as the case is solved. You have to realize the more Dougal helps us with the vital research, the easier it will be to convince not only Jack, but the trustees, that he deserves recognition of some sort."

Angus listened to my words carefully, then he nodded. "Aye … I do agree with your analysis … but the MacMillian name is at stake!"

I refused to argue any further, I merely pointed toward the woods. The old Scotsman nodded and disappeared.

A few seconds later, Andy rounded the corner. "Did I hear voices? Already?" He looked from me to my coffee cup.

"God … yes. Angus was campaigning for Dougal to receive some sort of medal for his work."

Andy's eyebrow shot up. "Do you agree with him?"

"Dougal is a solid cop with good instincts. He knows his way around a computer and genealogy sites." I glanced around the kitchen. "Plus, he fixed the worn-out wallpaper for me." I shook my head. "Doing your job well isn't necessarily a reason to get recognition. He's good, but I might have a hard time convincing Jack that he deserves a promotion."

Andy nodded, then started his breakfast routine. I turned back to my coffee, enjoying the comfort of hearing the normal sounds of Andy pouring his cereal and making his cup of coffee. He kept to himself as he ate, respecting my need for peace and quiet. It was short lived.

"Peg! Do I have news for you!" Bob's bouncy voice echoed throughout the kitchen.

I groaned, seeing Andy smile out of the corner of my eye. I looked at Bob. "Hey, Bob."

He glanced down at my cup. "Where are we?"

I held up two fingers.

"Whoops … sorry." He moved to the window, trying to keep to

himself.

He was fidgeting so much I finally snapped. "What?"

He turned to face me, his face glowing. "The reason Morgan is going to Argentina is stolen art!"

I heard Andy choke back a laugh, but I ignored the noise. "What makes you think it's stolen?"

"I heard Morgan talking to one of his guys about the need to move the paintings and sculptures as soon as possible."

I was surprised by this new piece of information. "Sculptures? Not just paintings?"

Bob's head bounced. "Yep! Along with china, crystal, and silver. You wouldn't believe how much stuff was stolen!"

"Wow ... I did a little research last night about how much the Nazis plundered, but I didn't realize it included items other than art. I read there were sculptures also."

Bob's smile widened. "Oh, yeah ... tons of stuff. It's amazing."

I sat in thought as Bob continued to bounce in excitement. The energy leaping off the guy was enough to cause whiplash.

I turned my attention back to Bob. "Is all the stolen art in Argentina?"

Bob shook his head. "Gosh, no ... some of it is actually in museums around the world."

I raised an eyebrow. "Museums?"

"Yep. They can't prove ownership, especially for things which disappeared during the war years. So the museums display it."

I wasn't quite sure how any of that worked. "Is that legal?"

Bob shrugged. "I have no idea, but they've done it for decades."

I grabbed a pen and pad of paper. I decided to jot notes to myself since I couldn't rely on my memory if a new idea cropped up along the way—it didn't take much at this point in life to dislodge a thought.

Bob peered over my shoulder as I wrote, which irritated me, but I kept my mouth shut. Finally, I sat back, relieved that my ideas were now on paper. Now, I had to ensure I didn't lose the damn paper.

Andy pointed to the pad. "What's that for?"

"So I wouldn't forget to ask Jack and Sal a few questions. Anthony had an awful lot of paintings scattered around his house. I know for a fact Sal is trying to handle them carefully and if stolen, he wants to get them back to their rightful owners."

Bob spoke up with a curious expression. "What questions?"

"I want to know if either one of them can remember the paintings, and I want to know if Sal still has any. Could Anthony have been one of Morgan's customers? If so, who else in the township may be on his customer list."

Andy whistled. "That alone could open a can of worms."

I sighed as I looked over my list one more time. "Yep."

CHAPTER 22

Eventually, I was allowed to finish my third cup of coffee and get ready for the day. I had a lot on my mind, so I was relieved when I heard from Jack. I spoke before he had a chance. "I have a few questions for you."

"Same here," he agreed. "You first."

I consulted my pad. "Do you remember any of the paintings at Anthony's house?"

"Nope. I'm not an art guy … but it's interesting that you bring up this subject. I just got off the phone with Sal because I had the same thought. He's been secretly trying to find the rightful owners. It's been tough because they were stolen during the war, and everyone is a bit touchy about the situation."

I nodded. "It's good to know we are on the same wave length regarding Anthony's art. To add to the mess, paintings aren't the only art stolen … sculptures, silver, china, and crystal have also been stolen."

Jack whistled in surprise. "Damn … Sal didn't mention those items."

"Anthony probably didn't own them. He was more into the flashy, recognizable items. However, it's a good bet that Morgan has been moving stuff through dubious means."

Jack snorted. "Of course, he's moving items through the black market."

"Anyway, can we catch him in the act?"

Jack was silent for a moment. "I want someone watching him at all times … maybe Bob?"

"You could always ask. I'm not sure what Logan has him doing, but I'm sure spying on Morgan would meet Logan's approval."

Jack paused. "Do you want to ask him for me?"

I frowned. "What's wrong with you contacting Bob? You've done it before."

I could feel his hesitation growing by the second. "Do you think I've been using him too often?"

"Who knows? If Logan hasn't blown a gasket by now, I'd say you're fine." I was pretty sure Logan would let Jack know when he crossed a line.

Jack sighed. "I don't want to push him to the blowing up point. I'm trying to avoid a problem."

"You could always talk to Logan and work out a system. If he doesn't want you using Bob, it's better to find out the easy way."

"Damn," Jack muttered.

I grinned but kept quiet. At least on the phone, he couldn't see how much I enjoyed his dilemma. For once, it was someone else worrying about Bob and Logan.

I snapped my fingers as I eyed the pad with my questions. "Do you think anyone else in the township has been buying stolen art from Morgan?"

"Oh hell … the last thing I need is for the feds to swoop down on us. Stolen Nazi art is right up their alley." Jack sounded disgusted at the thought.

"Yep … but it's worth investigating."

"You want me to go door to door asking people if they've been breaking the law?" Jack snapped.

I laughed. "I'm not sure that would be effective. They'll lie till they're blue in the face."

"Probably. If we could have access to Morgan's office there might be something in his files." Jack went silent as he contemplated the possibility.

It was a good idea, but I wasn't sure it was possible at this point. "You'd need a warrant, and we have nothing at this point for a judge to agree to one."

Jack sighed. "I know." He was silent for a minute, then he spoke. "Bob could nose around and with any luck, he may actually overhear shop talk between Morgan and one of his goons."

"He's been snooping, and there's nothing new," I reminded Jack.

Jack was so quiet, I thought one of our phones stopped working until I heard papers shuffling. "I've had Dougal do background checks on Morgan's employees. Not much help so far, but it is interesting that he only hires guys recently released from prison."

I was shocked at this bit of news. "Prison … all of them?"

"Yep. Petty stuff though … nothing serious. Six months for having a little too much pot, drunk driving, bar fights … not one has a major felony."

I realized my fingers were dancing on the table. I decided my brain knew a nugget of information I was clueless about—too bad the brain cells weren't apprising me of anything important. I would have to wait until all the neurons agreed it was time to enlighten me. "I wonder if he has a deal with probation officers?"

I could hear Jack shuffling more papers. "You could be right. They all have the same probation officer. I'll have Dougal interview him immediately."

"Well …" I started. "… maybe hold off for a few days."

"What? Why?" Jack demanded.

I took a deep breath. "Gut feeling."

Jack sighed, almost in defeat. "Hell."

"Yeah, I know how you feel. Maybe Morgan hires these guys because he believes he can control them, or he has promised them a big pay out."

Jack was silent before questioning me more. "Concerning the art or the break-ins?"

I sighed. "I'm not convinced the two have as much in common as we believe."

Jack made an annoyed noise. "You honestly expect me to believe the same guy is running two different scams?"

"Why not? His grandfather easily runs more than a few businesses … some overlap in areas, but not all of them."

Jack snorted. "Morgan is not in the same league as Lombardi. He's small potatoes compared to the old guy."

"Baloney. If Morgan is trying to muscle into his grandfather's position, he would need to be able to balance an awful lot of deals at the same time. Lombardi's been at this his whole life, and Morgan is a mere babe in arms, but he has to sharpen his skills somehow."

After a few moments of silence, Jack spoke up. "Yeah … you're right … damn."

"Why did Elaine marry Bob?" I wondered out loud.

"What the hell? Who cares?" Jack demanded. "Don't get tangled up in their lousy marriage issues."

"I think it's important," I insisted. "She married a sweet guy, and I'll bet she thought she could keep him under her thumb."

Jack scoffed. "She succeeded."

"Yes and no … if she steered him one hundred percent the way she wanted, I don't think she would be so angry at him. She really hates Bob."

"I never thought of it in those terms." Jack's tone was thoughtful. I could almost hear the gears turning in his mind. "Do you think she was working with Morgan in some capacity?"

"I wouldn't be surprised. It's worth a look." I really wouldn't be surprised—the woman was evil.

Jack cleared his throat. "Are we going to need Bob?"

I shook my head. "Nope. He's too close to the situation. I'm thinking either Dad or Henry."

"Both solid choices. Your call," Jack agreed.

I thought about it for a moment. "Let me think about it, and I'll let you know."

"Yep," he agreed.

After the call ended, I roamed around the house hoping the activity would trigger a plan. I decided to have Dad and Henry hear my theory and see what ideas they may have concerning Elaine and Morgan.

"Dad! Henry!" I called, and within seconds they appeared.

Dad looked me over, seeming slightly worried. "Are you okay?"

I nodded. "Yep … I have a theory, and I need your help." Once I outlined my ideas and Elaine's possible involvement, they both nodded.

Henry pulled his notebook out of his pocket. "I don't know why we didn't see this before." He jotted a few things in his little, black book, then he looked at me. "What do you think we should do?"

I looked at them both. "How hard would it be to nose around in her life?"

Dad shook his head. "It would not be easy. She's been on our side for quite a few years, so any evidence of her involvement would be long gone."

I tapped my finger against my lips, trying to make a decision about an idea that hit me out of the blue. I made the leap. "Could your ability to travel back through her timeline help?"

Both of their expressions registered shock as they looked at me, then one another.

Henry cleared his throat. "What makes you think we have the ability to go back in time?"

I shook my head. "I'm not telling how I know, but I know you *do* have the capability. We need to step outside the rules a little."

Dad shook his head. "Twinkle Toes, we need to go slow here."

I waved a dismissive hand. "Not necessarily … you would have to be careful, but I'm sure you could manage."

They exchanged looks again.

I sighed. "What?"

Dad watched me carefully. "Have you, by any chance, run this plan by Logan?"

Dad and Henry both knew my answer before I even opened my mouth.

"Ha! He'd have a fit!"

Dad grinned, and Henry looked worried. "He'll have more than a fit."

I waved my hand again. "Tough beans."

Dad shook his head with a hesitant look on his face. "You're asking us to break a big rule."

I shrugged. "Maybe, but I think the knowledge would help us deal with Elaine better, and there's a chance we would gain useful information concerning Morgan … they are cousins."

"The family hates her," Dad reminded me.

I knew he was right, but there was still a small chance. "Maybe not the *entire* family."

He sighed. "You're opening a can of worms."

"The worms need to be squashed." I was standing firm by my suggestion. I had a feeling it could give us some answers.

Dad and Henry continued to stare at me, and I wondered if they were going to continue arguing or agree with my idea—it didn't take long for my answer.

"We need to discuss this between ourselves." Dad gave me a firm look, keeping me from arguing. "Give us a few moments and we'll make a decision."

I nodded, watching as they faded. I knew my request put them on edge, but I was convinced Elaine's marriage to Bob was not a coincidence. She may have cooked up the scheme with her creepy cousin, and we needed to know what they planned. My theory could be dead wrong, but I'd rather be dead wrong than *dead dead*. Not knowing pieces of the puzzles was dangerous to my health.

As I sat drumming my fingers on the table, waiting for the guys to return, I focused my attention on the woods. The guys were milling around, looking bored to tears. I decided to go out for a visit. It couldn't hurt, and I might find out a nugget or two of info.

Once they noticed my arrival, they began exchanging glances and I even noticed a few frowns. "What's up fellows?" They nodded a hello but remained quiet. "Anything I should know?"

The Druid smiled but instead of answering, he turned to the main Indian who stepped forward. "Is there a problem?"

I shook my head. "Nope. I just wanted to check and make sure all was well."

He nodded. "Nothing to report."

I studied his face, but I couldn't find anything to indicate he was fudging.

"Fine. Anything exciting happening for you?" I realized it probably wasn't a good sign I was so bored that I resorted to conversing with dead folks.

The Druid stepped closer. "Everything is in order. Do you have a problem?"

I shrugged. "I'm waiting on Dad and Henry to make a decision. I guess I was too antsy to sit any longer."

He studied my face for a moment. "You asked them to cross a line and have created a dilemma for them."

I raised my eyebrows, surprised he was aware of my idea. "You can hear our conversations?"

He shook his head. "It was only a matter of time until you used the information you received … human nature."

Oh jeez … psychology from a dead person? I narrowed my eyes. "Are you saying I can't be trusted with sensitive information?"

He smiled. "Peg, your desire to solve a case overrides your common sense. You must be aware your request has the possibility of upsetting Logan. We are not encouraged to jump back into the past … it is dangerous for all."

I frowned. "Dangerous how?"

"Even a small bump could alter the future, for that reason only experienced spirits should indulge in the activity."

I stood my ground. "I need to know if Elaine married Bob for reasons which impact the current investigation. Morgan is trouble, and if he and Elaine worked together at one time to take Lombardi down, it would be nice to know."

"I agree. You should've asked me, and I would've been able to supply the answers."

My mouth dropped open. "Why haven't you shared this before now?"

He shrugged. "My hope was that you wouldn't travel this path. Having delicate information concerning our abilities doesn't mean you should ask us to cross lines. Rules exist for good reasons."

I sighed feeling a little chastised. "I'll tell Dad and Henry to forget my request, but I need answers."

The Druid nodded. "I will supply the necessary information. Elaine and her cousin plotted to overtake the family business. Her untimely death halted his plans … he needed her help. It took him time to find another person who could aide him in overthrowing Lombardi."

"Who?" I was shocked by how much he knew.

The Druid shook his head. "You must discover the person on your own. I have faith you will be successful."

Gritting my teeth, I stomped a foot. "I don't have time for games."

He shook his head again but remained silent. I knew I would never drag the person's name out of him, so I turned to head back to the house. I was furious but at least, I knew for sure Elaine had been Morgan's partner.

Dad and Henry were waiting for me but before they could say a word, I held up a hand. "I take back my request."

They looked at each other, surprised. Dad watched me carefully. "Why the change of heart?"

I jerked my thumb toward the woods. "The Druid told me I was crossing a line with the request. He also informed me Elaine *had* been working with Morgan to overthrow Lombardi."

Henry nodded in relief. "Thank god. It was a difficult position you put us in, Miss Peg."

I sighed. "I know and I'm sorry. If I had known the Druid knew the answer I would've never asked."

Dad looked at me expectantly. "So, who is this mystery person?"

I shrugged. "He wouldn't tell me. He said I had to find out for myself."

Dad and Henry shook their heads. Dad looked worried. "Sorry, babe ... we don't know either."

Henry's face was drawn with uneasiness. "I don't like this case. Morgan must be receiving help from someone on our side." He sighed. "Maybe your dad and I can nose around Morgan's stomping grounds and see what we can dig up."

"What stomping grounds?" There always seemed to be some new piece of information being presented—it was a little dizzying.

Henry shrugged. "College friends who he hangs around, and the clubs he belongs to."

I was a little surprised to hear this. "Clubs? Morgan joined a club?"

Henry grinned. "I have no idea, but I reckon it's worth a look."

I nodded. "Nose around all you want, but Morgan doesn't seem to be the club joining type. If he's planning to topple Lombardi, my bet is he doesn't allow himself to get too friendly with anyone."

Dad looked at Henry. "Do you think Elaine is still helping him?"

Henry shook his head. "That woman was so focused on her own problems, I doubt she bothered to try to contact Morgan. We also don't know if Morgan has the same ability to hear us that his grandfather possesses."

I pulled my lower lip as I digested Henry's analysis. His theory concerning Elaine fit—she was so self-absorbed that I doubted she gave her uncle a second thought once she woke up in Deadsville. Bob shared how pissed she was once she discovered that she was pushing up daisies. She became consumed with finding out how to get back to life. "Maybe Morgan's wife knows some nugget she hasn't shared."

"Possible ... but not probable," Dad said thoughtfully. "She doesn't strike me as the type to bother with her husband's business dealings."

I nodded. "True, but it won't hurt to ask a few more questions."

"Doesn't the mayor know them socially?" Dad asked.

I shook my head. "He's not close with them. I think Morgan makes him a little nervous."

Henry laughed. "Morgan should scare the sh … um … crap out of the mayor." His face grew red at the near slip.

I kept my face straight but saw Dad's grin out of the corner of my eye. "Something's out of whack though. Morgan is a crooked art dealer, but it doesn't make him a murderer. So far, we haven't found an ounce of evidence … certainly not enough to bring him in for questioning. Jack has to be foaming at the mouth by now."

"Anthony and Morgan both wanted to take over their family businesses," Dad reminded me. "Anthony had no problem removing people who were in his way."

I shook my head. "Anthony's nuts … there's no sign Morgan is emotionally challenged."

Henry was twisting his hat so hard, I thought he'd ruin it. I pointed to the mess he was creating. "Are you worried?"

He looked at me. "If Morgan isn't the killer … who is?"

I shrugged. "I have no idea. Maybe we should check with Cindy Morgan … she may be able to shine a light on the issue."

"I think it's a waste of time." Dad was insistent on the point.

I watched him carefully. "Probably, but I'd rather be safe than sorry. Wives have a way of knowing more about their husbands than you'd think."

Dad laughed. "Your mother never knew a thing about me."

I scoffed. "Mom is the exception to the rule … she was too selfish to pay much attention to you."

He grinned but refrained from a remark.

I grabbed my purse. "Are you guys coming along?"

Henry's eyes widened. "Absolutely! I'm not letting you out of my sight."

I nodded, then we headed out the door. The drive was quick—we didn't have much traffic in the township during the day. We pulled up in front of the Morgan's house. Once I parked, we sat and stared at the front door.

Dad smiled slightly. "Are you planning on seeing the wife or sitting here?"

"I'm trying to decide how I want to approach the situation. I don't dare say too much without flying it by Jack first, but I want to know if Cindy realizes her husband is involved in stolen art."

"Do you think she would lie?" Henry asked.

I shrugged. "Everybody lies to some extent."

"Peg, not everybody," Dad chided.

"You'd be surprised. Even I've been known to fudge the truth if I believe someone I love is at risk." I knew deep down I would lie myself bald if I thought Andy was in trouble.

"Let's get the ball rolling," Dad advised.

I nodded, then stepped out of the car. The front door opened before I could knock.

Morgan's wife looked me over. "May I help you?"

I quickly assessed the women standing in front of me—expensive clothes, great hair style, and pretty ... in a clean-cut sort of way—not much makeup needed or used.

"I hope so. I have a few questions." I held out my hand. "I'm Peg Shaw. I work with the Bath police department."

She frowned. "Is there a problem?"

I watched her face closely. If she was faking concern, she was damn good. "There have been a lot of burglaries in the area, and we wondered if you had any information."

Her frowned deepened. "Such as?"

I was tired of standing on her front porch, but it was obvious she wasn't letting me through the doorway. "Have you seen anyone hanging around the neighborhood or strange cars driving around?" It was the best I could come up with, and I wished a little more thought went into my decision to confront Cindy.

She shook her head. "I'm sorry but I haven't noticed anything unusual. I wish I could help."

I watched her face, deciding if she was lying, she deserved an Academy award for her performance. She was a quiet woman, her feathers never seemed ruffled. I started to wonder if she had a personality at all. She was very bland but good looking—maybe Morgan married her as a trophy wife.

I thought back to when I first met another quiet woman ... Laura Spanelli. She was very composed, beautiful, and guarded, but she had underlying emotions that could be felt a mile away. The woman in front of me gave me the feeling her emotions weren't hidden but rather nonexistent. I suddenly wished I dragged Amy along. She could spot a phony in a second. For the time being, I decided I gleaned as much from Cindy Morgan as I could. "Thanks for your time. If you see anything suspicious, please call the Bath police. We need to find whoever is breaking into homes before another tragedy occurs."

She smiled and nodded. "Of course, anytime." As she closed the door, she moved enough so I was able to see the room behind her was filled with moving boxes.

"Oh ... are you moving?" There was no sense letting her know I was well aware of the Morgan's intended move.

She frowned, then glanced back at the apparent moving style—boxes everywhere, clutter, and general disarray.

"Oh ... yes." She seemed to be caught off guard, but I chalked her attitude up to the fact that I was intruding on her time. "I'm tired of cold and snow. We decided to move to a warmer climate."

"I don't blame you ... winters can be brutal." I smiled, hoping she would share a bit more with me—I wasn't that lucky though.

"Yes. I'm sorry I couldn't help, but as you can see … I'm quite busy."

My eyes narrowed a tad at the brush-off I received, but I had to admit, I also hate to be interrupted during a project … damn.

I plastered a smile back on my face. "Good luck on your move."

She nodded, then closed the door.

Once I sat my butt back in the car, I turned to Dad. "See anything useful?"

He shook his head. "Moving boxes everywhere, but not much else interesting."

I glanced back at Henry. "Well?"

He frowned thoughtfully. "She's odd."

I nodded. "No personality at all. Morgan must've married her for her looks and not her brain."

"Just because she's pretty doesn't mean she's stupid," Dad argued.

I looked at him confused. "Did you watch the woman? She had zero charm."

Dad looked back at the house. "That doesn't mean she's stupid."

I sighed. "That also doesn't mean she's not."

CHAPTER 23

Once we were back home, safe and sound, Dad looked at me. "You should give Jack a call. Let him know we paid Mrs. Morgan a visit."

I nodded. "I agree. He'll blow a gasket if he finds out before I tell him."

Henry was standing at the window, watching my gang out back mill around looking bored.

I looked over at him. "Anything I should know?"

Henry briefly glanced at me. "Something doesn't fit, and I've got a feeling we've been barking up the wrong tree."

My mouth fell open. "What the hell are you saying?"

Henry shook his head. "I don't want to go off half-cocked and down some god forsaken bunny trail. I'm tellin' ya … something's off."

My mouth opened, shut, and opened again. I should've kept it shut. "There is no way we are wrong about Morgan. His own grandfather knows he's a bad egg. You're out of your mind."

Dad sighed. "Peg, Henry may have a better feel for the situation than either of us. Remember, he was a private investigator for a long time, so his perspective is nothing to be ignored."

I dug in my heels. "Morgan has to be at the center of this mess. No one else popped with background checks. Hell … even Lombardi looks squeaky clean next to Morgan."

"I never meant to infer Morgan was innocent or to be ignored." Henry continued to look out the window. "I reckon there's more going on with this mess than we counted on."

I started to argue with him, but Dad shook his head. I looked at the ceiling as I controlled my frustration with the old, southern guy. After a few minutes of silence, I gave in. "Henry, you could be right. However, nothing has surfaced to point us in another direction. Morgan is the key."

"I never said he wasn't." Henry's voice was so quiet, I had to strain to hear him.

I stomped my foot. "You said we were barking up the wrong tree!"

He turned to face me. "Yes, ma'am … I did. I still believe I'm right, but we don't need to be going off half-cocked. We need hard facts and so far, we don't have them. I have a feeling there's someone else involved."

I narrowed my eyes. "Dead or alive?"

He shook his head. "I'm not sure. Either way … it's a problem. They are invisible to us, and we need to force their hand in order for someone to step out of the shadows."

Just what I needed … a complication. My gut told me that Henry might have hit the nail on the head. Someone out of sight was involved, and I had no idea to what degree their involvement would complicate the investigation. I sighed. "I'd better call Jack. He's going to hit the roof."

Dad nodded. "The sooner he knows there may be another person involved, the better … maybe he's already come to the same conclusion."

I made the call and wasn't surprised by Jack's reaction. "Damn it! Why can't we have one case that's simple from start to finish?"

I sighed, trying to keep my patience intact. "Calm down. We'll sort out the mystery person. It might even be someone already working for Morgan."

Jack snorted. "I doubt it … we would've already found them."

I kept my trap shut, allowing Jack a few moments to reign in his frustration.

He finally sighed. "On a happier note, Dougal found a few interesting facts about our dead couple in Hudson."

"Great! What did he discover?" I was relieved by the subject change.

I could hear papers shuffling. "To begin with, Edith Peters Wilson wasn't Jewish. She and her entire family were in Dachu due to the fact that her parents were helping their Jewish friends hide assets from the Germans."

I was a little surprised by this new bit of information. "So they were political prisoners?"

"Yep. The Nazi's were furious once it was discovered quite a bit of art and expensive household items were being smuggled out of Germany.

Edith's father was a businessman, and he had good relations with local, Jewish business families. Once Hilter's plans became clear, Mr. Peters began helping them hide their paintings and silver in Switzerland." The satisfaction in Jack's voice was evident.

My eyes widened. "The Swiss bank key!"

"Yep. Knew you'd hop on that clue."

I was silent for a moment as I considered everything. "It explains the key but not what the Wilson's were doing."

Jack chuckled, then grew serious. "Finding the rightful owners of everything in the bank vault. It's taken decades to locate survivors or their families ... most didn't make it out of the camps."

"How did they manage to smuggle so much out right under the Nazis' noses?"

"Mr. Peters had an import and export company. It seems they falsified the documentation on crates, and no one knew for years. He was finally caught once the Nazis began raiding wealthy, Jewish homes and nothing of value was in sight. The bastards even tore walls out looking for stuff."

My stomach turned as pictures filled my mind. I could feel tears threaten, but I shook myself to control the urge to let them flow. "How'd Dougal discover the nitty gritty?"

"He kept digging. It seems there are a few websites preserving the stories of what these families endured, and he read every damn one of them. The Peters' name appears in many of the stories as a hero. Edith and her husband spent a lifetime tracking down families for the sole purpose of returning items her father hid for them."

"Wow ... that's all they did? Didn't Mr. Wilson have a job?"

"Nope. Her father hid enough of his wealth in Swiss banks to sustain whoever in the family survived. Edith was the lone person to make it out alive."

We were both silent, a sort of tribute to the heroic measures of a kind man.

Finally, I broke the silence. "It took a lot of guts for Mr. Peters to do what he did. The Nazis were brutal to anyone who thwarted their plans."

"Yep, hence Dachu for the Peters family. Not just Mr. Peters, but the whole family ... it's sick."

I remembered the tattooed numbers on Mrs. Wilson's arm and shuddered. "Do you know how much was stashed in Switzerland? Or what amount that has been returned?"

More papers rustled. "According to Dougal, about half of what was hidden has been returned to families. There was a notebook cataloging each item and family. It was coded, but Dougal managed to break the code."

I frowned. "How on earth did he figure out a code from the thirties?"

Jack laughed. "He told me he loved numbers. After a few hours of playing around with the notebook's entries, he was able to find the key number … whatever the hell that is."

"Do you think they were killed for the codebook and key?"

"It looks that way. If Morgan is selling stolen art from World War II, it stands to reason his supply is diminishing. He could need new artwork to sell. Somehow, he found out about the Wilson's and decided he wanted whatever is in the Swiss bank."

I frowned thoughtfully. "But the house was torn up everywhere except the bedroom … that doesn't make sense. The robbers didn't even bother to look for a wall safe."

"They may have looked but couldn't find it."

I shook my head. "Nope. I found the wall safe easily."

"A few of the floors were pulled apart, so they probably thought a wall safe was too obvious."

"Maybe." I wasn't convinced. How on earth did they miss the wall safe.

"Has anyone found her emerald ring?" The fact that the ring was missing didn't sit well with me.

"Nope. It's probably at one of the local pawn shops. We put the word out to be on the lookout for it."

I knew I missed a vital piece of the puzzle, but I couldn't, for the life of me, zoom in on it. I hoped my brain would realize the vital piece before I ended up deader than dead. "That ring could lead us to the culprits to the burglaries around the area, but I think the murders are in a different category."

Silence met my statement, and I wasn't surprised. Jack wanted everything connected for an easy solution.

Finally, he sighed. "I was afraid you would say something along those lines."

I pulled on my lip as I thought about the crimes. "They don't feel like the same person is responsible. The break-ins are messy … the murders are strategic … different personalities."

Jack cleared his throat. "Have your shared your theory with Amy?"

"Not yet, but I think it's a good idea."

"Yep, her insight is needed." He paused. "I never realized how much we rely on Amy."

I smiled slightly. "I agree. I'll call her soon. I wish I had her with me when I talked with Cindy Morgan."

I heard Jack suck in a lungful of air. "You did what?"

I frowned. "Didn't I mention it earlier?" Hell … my brain wasn't up to speed. I could've sworn it was the first thing I mentioned when I called.

"No, you did not! Peg, what were you thinking?" he roared.

I felt my temper flare, and I struggled to keep it from overtaking the conversation. I won … barely. "I didn't want to miss any angle, and we have ignored her so far." I felt the need to defend myself.

I knew Jack was weighing my words. I waited in silence while he came to the conclusion that my decision, while not exactly sound, at least had merit. "I guess we were so focused on her husband that she fell through the cracks."

I smiled. "Exactly."

"Well, what'd you think?" he prodded.

I could tell from his tone of voice I was out of hot water, so I relaxed as I explained my hesitation about the woman.

He listened to my concerns, then spoke. "I'll have Dougal run a background check on her. While I doubt she's involved … it always helps to eliminate people from the suspect list."

"Don't let her brother discover you are having her innocence verified. As far as he is concerned, she is free from trust issues."

Jack sighed. "I agree … he'd have a meltdown."

We agreed to have a phone conversation later in the evening, and I was thankful when the call ended. Now, to tackle Amy's logic. I'm not necessarily known for my logical skills, her organized, logical thinking tended to irritate me. I had to admit though … the old gal didn't miss much.

I punched her name on my speed dial, then waited for an answer. After close to thirty rings, she still hadn't answered. My stomach knotted as I tried Sal's phone. He didn't answer either. Sweat began to form in places I'd rather not mention, and I could feel the panic start to rise.

I called Santino, but again, no answer. I tried my other two mob guys with the same results. It would've been odd with one not answering but I knew out of the five, I should've had success contacting *someone*. My hands began to shake, and I knew we had pushed a button somewhere, but where? My mind raced as I analyzed who was rattled by our snooping.

After a few moments, I decided I needed help. "Bob!"

I felt a pop and was thankful at how quickly he appeared.

He watched me hesitantly. "What's up?"

"Bob, we have a problem. I've called Amy, Sal, and the trio … no one answered their phones."

He shrugged. "They could be out on the firing range."

I felt a surge of relief hearing his words. "I never thought of the gun range. Could you pop over there and make sure?"

He smiled, reassuring me. "No problem. I'm sure everything's fine. Sal increased security not only at the house, but on the entire property."

I nodded. "Sounds good, but we should check."

"Yep, on it." He faded quickly.

I paced the kitchen waiting for his return. It didn't take long.

Bob returned out of breath. "Peg, I can't find any of them. Their phones are lined up on the kitchen counter."

I leaned against the wall for support. "Go tell Jack, and I'll have Dad and Henry start scouting around."

He nodded and left. I didn't even have to call for Dad or Henry … they both appeared, worry lining their faces.

Dad was the first to speak. "We heard. Do you have a plan?"

"Nope. Right now, panic is ruling my thoughts." I turned to Henry. "What should we do?"

He turned and pointed toward the woods. "First, I'm going to gather a few of the boys, and we'll spread out over the township." He faced me. "You call Lombardi and get a few of his men involved."

I opened my mouth to argue that Lombardi might not be our best bet. Henry held up a hand, cutting me off. "Miss Peg, trust me. We might need a few big guns, and Jack has to stay within boundaries that Lombardi can work around if needed."

I nodded, wanting to throw up. How did the situation become so sticky, so quickly? Everything was fine earlier.

Dad's voice broke through my muddled thoughts. "Don't blame yourself … you haven't done anything that would lead to the current situation. Remember … the bad guys have a plan, and we are clueless about their endgame. Just because we know Nazi art is involved doesn't mean we have all the facts. We know a fraction, and I have a feeling this is dirtier than anyone realized."

"Call Lombardi," Henry instructed as he faded. I knew I could trust him, even if I didn't always agree with the guy.

Dad looked down at me. "I'll go inform Logan. He has resources we don't have access to, and he'll use them."

I nodded.

"Make the call." Dad faded.

I felt a tad better knowing Logan would handle the crisis with calm and determination. I searched for Lombardi's number, finally finding it in a pile of paperwork on the table. My stomach was busy performing circus acts, but I made the call.

Lombardi answered. "You have a problem." It wasn't a question but a statement.

"Yep." I spent thirty seconds explaining the situation.

He listened, then sighed. "I was afraid a trick of this sort would arise. I will call you back." He disconnected, and I was left staring at my phone in shock.

What were the old mobster's plans? Why didn't he give me a hint about the strategy he planned to use? I had a million questions and not one damn answer. I began pacing again.

I didn't have long to wait, even though it seemed a million years passed.

The phone screamed, and I quickly answered.

"I'm tracking Sal's car. Please tell the police chief they are headed west on Route 18. There's a lot of open land once you clear Medina."

"You have a tracker on Sal's cars?" I was stunned by the revelation.

"Of course. He tracks me, and I track him. We have each other's backs." Lombardi actually managed to sound confused.

I shook my head. I doubted Sal would agree with the old guy, but I had bigger fish to fry at the moment. I frowned, realizing Lombardi was correct concerning open land. Medina is the county west of Bath. Once you pass through the town of the same name, it's pretty clear sailing as far as population is concerned. Nothing but open fields and country living with a few smaller towns dotted along the way. "Why Medina?"

Lombardi didn't answer for a few moments. "Mrs. Shaw, there is a possibility this may end badly. A lot of open farm land, and a good place to hide bodies."

I groaned, sliding down the wall I was leaning against. I shook from head to toe, unable to control the spasms.

Lombardi's voice broke through my panic. "I will handle my grandson and leave Sal to your friends. I will update you with the car's location if it changes direction."

My eyes widened in shock. "Wait! You can't 'handle' Morgan! It's illegal!"

He chuckled. "I don't want the boy dead, I want him *contained*."

Contained? What the hell did the old man mean? Before I could ask, he hung up ... damn.

"Peg, we will find them." Logan was standing just in front of me.

I was so relieved to see him, I burst into tears.

Dad squatted down next to me. "It's going to be ok."

I spoke when I finally felt like I could. "Lombardi has a tracker on the car. It's headed west towards Medina."

"Yes ... Henry was able to find the car. Jack has an alert issued." Logan's voice was cool as a cucumber.

"Why? What happened?" I asked as I blew my nose.

Dad smiled. "You poked at someone or something. It's what you do."

"But I haven't done anything but ask a few questions!"

Logan was smiling too. "It was enough."

"This isn't funny! My friends are in danger, and we have to save them," I snapped.

Logan nodded. "Yes."

I glared at Logan, hating his ability to remain calm in a crisis. It was not something I ever learned, and today wasn't going to change how I handled disasters. I'd work on fine tuning my responses at a later date.

Henry popped into view. He nodded toward me, then turned to Logan.

"Jack was able to stop the car." His eyes slid over to me and back to Logan. "Santino, Antonio, and Bill are all safe and sound … drugged … but safe."

Logan nodded. "Sal and Amy?"

Henry looked down at the floor. "They were not in the car."

My eyes widened. "What? They weren't in the car? Where in the hell are they?" I yelled. "Amy's injured, and she hasn't had time to heal. Sal is a bull in a china shop when it comes to Amy's safety. He'll get himself killed!"

Logan ignored my outburst, keeping his attention on Henry. "What are your plans?"

Henry jerked a thumb toward the woods. "Half your guys out back are scouring the area looking for them. The Druid and the Scotsman went to Sal's to see if their … um …" he stopped, glancing at me before continuing. "… bodies are on the property."

"Oh, my god! Bodies?" I groaned.

Logan shook his head, smiling. "Peg, they are alive. I would know otherwise."

I narrowed my eyes. "Do you have some sort of tracker on them that allows you to be informed if they die?"

His head inclined a fraction of an inch. "Your description will suffice. I would be aware if they passed over to my realm."

I looked over at Dad, noticing the surprise on his face. I was a little surprised. "You didn't know about Logan's tracking system?"

He shook his head. "It's news to me."

The back door opened, and Andy walked in. One look at our gathering and he was by my side in three long strides. "Peg, are you okay?"

I looked at Dad, and he smiled. "Thought it was a good idea for him to come home."

I nodded as fresh tears flowed down my face. Andy wrapped his arms around me, letting me sob. When I could finally talk, I took a deep breath and looked at Logan. "What do I need to do?"

Logan smiled. "A very healthy attitude."

CHAPTER 24

Logan looked at me for a second, and I knew he was weighing my mood and ability to work. Once satisfied I was done with the waterworks, he glanced toward the woods.

"Henry, your use of available resources was wise. I knew we needed a larger faction as Peg's work increases. This will not be the last time my friends will be utilized, and they are trustworthy. He turned to me. "Peg, Jack will be contacting you soon to bring you up to date. I am sure he will be engaged with police paperwork for a while. Dave, we must find Sal and Amy."

Dad nodded. "If they aren't dead, where are they being held?"

Logan shook his head. "I am not aware of their location." He sighed. "It is quite frustrating to see so much but so little of importance."

Henry looked at me. "Once your guys return from Sal's, we can cover a larger area."

I looked around the room. "Where's Bob? He's usually in the thick of things."

Logan looked at me. "I have sent Bob on an errand."

My eyes popped wide. "In the middle of this mess! What type of errand?"

Logan shook his head. "I will explain in due time."

The phone ringing interrupted my chance to argue with Logan. I grabbed it, and Jack's voice came on the line. "Peg, I'm sorry, but Sal and Amy weren't in the car. Your three friends are fine but doped up to their eyeballs."

"Doped with what?" I needed to ask questions to keep my mind busy.

Jack sighed. "I'm not sure … we'll have to wait for the lab results. Once the paramedics finished with them, I put a rush on their bloodwork."

"Are they conscious? Can they tell you what happened?" I was hopeful they could give us a clue about what happened to Amy and Sal.

"They're talking, but they have no idea what happened. They were all sitting at the table drinking coffee and the next thing they knew, we were dragging them out of Sal's car."

I frowned thoughtfully. "Some type of gas?"

"I have no idea. The blood tests will tell us what was used." There was a pause before he spoke again. "How'd you know there was a problem?"

"I tried calling all of them and worried when they didn't answer. Bob checked it out for me, and once he saw all five phones lined up on the counter, he knew there was trouble."

"How'd you know they were on Route 18?"

I pursed my lips, knowing he wasn't going to like the answer. "I called Lombardi for help. He has a tracker on Sal's car, so he was able tell me the location."

Silence greeted my explanation. I gave him time to digest the information and control his irritation since we had another mob guy involved with an investigation.

Finally, he sighed. "So, we owe Lombardi a favor now?"

I hesitated. "I'm not sure." I never anticipated owing Lombardi anything, but Jack brought up a point I hoped wasn't true. The last thing I needed was to be in Lombardi's debt.

Jack sighed. "I'll keep you updated. Watch your phone for text messages."

I didn't plan to be far from my phone until Sal and Amy were found. "Sounds good. Thanks for the call." After the conversation with Jack ended, I looked at Logan. "What do I need to do?"

"I believe it is time to connect the dots. You and Andy are both excellent at finding patterns. Who have you spoken with? What was the timeline and were there any activities which could narrow down those involved? Think through the evidence and draw conclusions."

"What if my conclusions are wrong?" I was worried I would make a mistake. "I'm not perfect."

He shook his head. "Even wrong ideas have value as they allow us to eliminate roads to examine."

"True. Amy's much better at this logic stuff than I am," I reminded him.

He smiled. "You do quite well yourself. I trust your abilities." He started to fade but stopped. "Peg, we will find Sal and Amy."

I nodded but didn't trust my voice to reply.

We watched Logan disappear, then Andy sighed. "Let's get started."

Dad looked at me. "While you two are busy with Logan's assignment, Henry and I are going to snoop around the township. They may still be close to home."

I nodded. "Good idea. You two can achieve results faster than Jack."

Dad nodded agreement. "My thoughts exactly. We'll check in later."

After the house cleared of my bloodless pals, Andy and I got busy outlining the case from the very beginning. The project took over an hour and when we were done, we sat back and stared at the graph Andy drew.

I sighed. "I can't find the pattern, even though I know there is one."

Andy watched me carefully. "What does your gut tell you?"

I scoffed. "I think it's on vacation."

Andy leaned forward, and I knew he spotted something. He grabbed his pencil and drew a fresh line on the paper. After a few moments, he sat back and grinned. "Morgan's customers."

"I knew that!" I snapped.

He shook his head, but his grin grew wider. "Every single crime scene is a customer of Morgan's lawn service. Even the couple in Hudson."

"The Wilsons?" I supplied.

"Yep." He nodded. "Even the Wilsons."

"There's nothing weird about the fact that they were customers. The lawn companies go all over the county."

Andy nodded again. "And every crew member has done time in the county jail. So they all know one another."

"So what?" My irritation was mounting, and I wished he would make his point.

"Each one has at least a year of probation." Andy smiled confidently. "I'd bet money their probation officer is on Morgan's payroll."

I frowned. "Jack was supposed to check into him. I never heard if they discovered anything important."

Andy shook his head. "Jack got busy. This case is moving pretty fast."

I nodded. "True. Who cares if his employees have records or even if the probation officer supplies Morgan with manpower."

"Morgan must be the kingpin for both operations," Andy said firmly.

Something was tugging at my brain, so I sat still, hoping it would pop for me—it did. "Oh hell … it's been in front of me the entire time!" I was disgusted with myself for not seeing it sooner. Amy would've spotted it immediately. I got up from my chair, then began pacing the kitchen as my brain went into overdrive. I was connecting dots so fast, I thought I'd fry what was left of my brain.

Jeez Louise! I snapped my fingers, then grabbed my phone, at the same time I was yelling for Dad and Henry. Andy sat staring at me, and I knew he worried I lost my mind. Maybe I did, but I'd bet money on my theory.

There was a pop in the air, but I held up a hand before they could ask any questions. Jack answered his phone. "What now?"

"I know who's behind everything."

"Sure … Morgan." Jack sounded a little confused.

I shook my head. "Nope. His quiet, arm candy wife!"

Andy's mouth fell open. "What?" He grabbed his graph and started tracing the evidence with his finger. After a moment, his head lifted, and he grinned.

Dad and Henry peered over Andy's shoulder. While he was explaining my idea, Jack interrupted. "No way! She was never on our radar."

"Exactly! We ignored her completely. She was too quiet and always in the background. Even the mayor described her that way … we never gave her a thought."

I noticed Henry's face. He had a faraway look, and I knew he was remembering our miserable visit with the woman. He knew something was off, and I had ignored his instincts. When would I learn to trust the good dead guys?

"She's packing up the house and moving. The mayor informed us they were leaving the country and moving to Argentina, which just happened to be a safe haven for Nazis after the war. I should've realized the second I heard where they were moving, but I didn't see the pattern."

"Oh shit … now I'll have to call in the Feds … Damn it," Jack muttered.

I shook my head. "The house is only partially packed. Unless she skedaddled as soon as we left her house, she's still in the township."

"I'll send a couple of squad cars right this second." I could hear him yell down the hall for Dougal.

My stomach knotted as a new thought flew in my brain. "You might need to start searching for Morgan's body."

My comment was met with silence.

Jack finally broke the silence. "Lombardi finally getting even with the shit?"

"Nope. Cindy may be tying up loose ends. Morgan is probably an idiot, and she won't risk her future leaving him alive to testify against her."

Jack whistled in shock. "Hells bells … where do you think we should search?"

"No idea. She fooled a lot of people, including her own brother."

Jack scoffed. "I'm glad he's Logan's problem. He's going to hit the ceiling when he finds out."

"It's not my problem that his sister is dirty. I bet she had her own parents murdered for the money. How they connect with the Peters family back in Germany is the one piece I can't decide on."

"Miss Peg?" Henry interrupted.

I looked over at him with my eyebrow raised.

"Have Jack check the Morgan house for Sal and Amy." He glanced at Dad. "Are you game?"

Dad nodded. "Let's go." They faded fast.

"What'd Henry say?" Jack asked.

I was so stunned, I couldn't answer for a moment. I took a deep breath. "Henry thinks Sal and Amy are at Cindy's house."

Jack was silent for a moment. "Wow … that's a leap of logic."

I thought about the woman's demeanor while I talked with her. She never allowed me to enter her home, and she kept the door pulled close to her body the entire conversation. She was hiding more than the fact that she was packing. "I think he could be right."

"I'll send two squad cars, and I'm on my way. Are you meeting me there?"

"Yep. On my way." I looked at Andy.

He nodded understanding. "Let's go."

Since I knew where the house was, I did the driving, breaking every speed limit along the way. I didn't care, and I knew Jack would understand, especially when his car blew past me on Ira Road.

By the time I pulled in front of Morgan's house, Jack was yelling at his officers. "Break the damn door down! Worry about warrants later!"

I was relieved he was moving full speed ahead. My gut informed me time was short. As Andy and I ran up the front walk, we heard three gunshots and I almost fainted. I'd kill the bitch if she harmed one bouncy, gray curl on Amy's head. I ran past Jack as Dougal forced the door open.

"Amy! Sal! Where are you?" I screamed.

"In the basement," Sal yelled back.

I was thrilled to hear his voice, noting his anger vibrating through the house. Good … anger can save a person.

We all hustled down the basement stairs and was shocked by the sight. Sal was tied up and fuming. Amy, disheveled and filthy, had an expression of pure spite on her face. I heard a groan, so I began to search for the owner. Cindy Morgan was lying on the basement floor, blood pouring out of her at an alarming rate. I heard one of the cops call for the paramedics. I was shocked at myself when I realized I was hoping they wouldn't get to her in time.

I rushed over to Amy while Jack made a beeline for Sal. I looked at Amy. "Are you okay?"

"The bitch was going to kill us," Amy declared.

I sat back on my heels in shock. I never heard Amy use a bad word in all the years I'd known her. "Wow ... you must be mad." I helped her to her feet.

Once Jack untied Sal, he rushed to Amy's side and wrapped his beefy arms around her. "Good girl!"

She looked up at him, but her face wasn't the usual gush of romance ... she was furious. "Why wouldn't you let me take the kill shot?"

Jack and I exchanged looks of disbelief. Kill shot?

Sal smiled. "We need her to explain everything. A dead woman couldn't answer any questions."

Amy's gray curls bobbed as she shook her head. "Bullshit. I don't care about the answers."

My mouth dropped open, then snapped shut. Amy was picking up bad habits. I'd have a talk with Sal concerning his influence over Amy's choice of vocabulary. A woman her age had no business developing a potty mouth. Hell ... a woman my age should be damn careful.

I looked at the gun in Amy's hand. "Is that *your* gun?"

She glanced down. "Yep."

I frowned. "How did you manage to keep it? Didn't Cindy frisk you?"

Amy shook her head. "Nope. I had it hidden in my sling, and she never bothered to check. I guess I didn't appear to be much of a threat."

Jeez Louise.

Sal looked at Jack. "If they had us, they have the boys. I need you to find them."

Jack patted Sal's shoulder. "We already found them ... they are at the hospital."

Sal's eyebrows flew north. "How bad?"

Jack shook his head. "Not bad ... just drugged. The doctors want to flush their systems before they release them."

Sal nodded. "I figured we were drugged. They took out all five of us in one swoop."

We heard the scream of sirens, so Andy ran up the stairs to direct the paramedics to the basement. I didn't offer Cindy a bit of help as I watched her blood pour onto the floor.

Suddenly, I was hit with an awful smell. My adrenaline kept me from noticing sooner, but it was horrible.

I covered my nose and mouth. "What am I smelling?"

Sal nodded toward the corner. "Morgan. His body was here when we became conscious. From the looks of him, I'd say she killed him a couple of days ago."

Jack walked over to Morgan's still form, then turned to one of his officers. "Get the equipment and start processing the crime scene."

I took the opportunity to explore the underground room. It was a huge room without the normal basement clutter. The walls weren't the concrete block I expected, but thick metal. I used my knuckles and rapped on the wall … sounded solid. The floor wasn't concrete, but I had no idea what it was. Usually, a finished basement had carpet or flooring of some type, this was neither. I started to wonder if it was also metal.

I turned and saw Dad and Henry. Since the basement was full of cops, I jerked my head toward the stairs. They both nodded, and I made my way past the paramedics as they cared for Amy and Sal. Once outside, I turned to both men. "You didn't find them before we did. What happened?"

Henry shook his head. "We didn't know about the basement. Couldn't find a door that suggested there even *was* a basement."

Dad was visibly upset. "My guess is that it was soundproof. We heard the shots the same time you did and came running."

Henry was furious. "I should've paid more attention to the woman. If Miss Amy or Sal had been hurt …" He couldn't finish his sentence, and I knew exactly how he felt.

I looked back at the house. "She must've opened it when you were somewhere else in the house. It was part of the floor to ceiling bookshelves."

Dad was thoughtful for a moment. "I think it was a bomb shelter."

"Bomb shelter?" I remembered my quick survey of the room. "From the Cold War?"

Dad nodded. "It was all the rave back in the fifties, and I remember hearing rumors wealthy people were building them in their backyards or making their basements into a shelter. You have to remember … the Soviet threat was real."

I nodded. "Yeah … I do remember hearing talk when I was a kid." Along with the worthless fallout drills we had to perform each semester in case of a nuclear attack. Hiding under our desks was fine for tornadoes, but I doubted it would've been much help shielding a bunch of kids from radiation.

The paramedics rushed past us with Cindy on a gurney. I watched as they loaded her in the ambulance and roared away.

I looked at Dad. "Do you think she'll make it?"

"Hope so." Dad sighed. "She has a lot to answer for, and I would like to know the story behind this mess."

"She will survive." Logan's voice came from behind us.

I turned and saw him standing next the police car. "Are you sure?"

My old Indian nodded. "Yes. She will find life can be difficult."

I watched him carefully. "Are you going to tell her brother?"

"He has already been briefed, and he is meeting her at the hospital. There is little he can do to help her, either health wise or legally. He felt he should be present though, and I agreed."

"What did his parents tell you?"

Logan shook his head. "Now is not the time. Please convince both Sal and Amy that they need to have medical attention. Amy is being rather difficult."

I grinned. "She's furious."

The Indian smiled. "Yes. That is quite the understatement. She will listen to you."

I headed back to the house. I heard Jack arguing with both patients. "I need you both healthy to testify against the woman … please go with the paramedics."

"I'm fine," Amy snapped. She could bluster all she wanted, I heard the quiver in her voice and stepped forward.

"Amy, you are both going … no arguments." I nodded to the paramedics, and they pulled the gurney close to Amy.

"I can walk!" she protested.

I shook my head. "Nope. Hop on, and let these guys give you a free ride outside. Sal, you too."

It didn't take much to convince Sal. He looked worse than Amy, and I feared the strain was taking too big of a toll on the ex-mobster.

He saw my look of concern and gave me a small smile. "I'm tired."

I nodded understanding. "All the more reason for you both to head to the hospital. The faster the drugs are flushed out of your system, the better you'll feel."

I watched as both were wheeled away, then I leaned against the wall. After a few moments, I decided searching the house would occupy my mind, so I began wandering around the Morgan home. As I drifted from room to room, I realized there was nothing spectacular in the furnishings— good furniture, nice decorating, but nothing flashy.

Jack joined me, and we walked through each room. "She was careful. Nothing to indicate they were doing anything sketchy."

I nodded, but I didn't say a word. I was more interested in finding any special hiding spots Cindy might have. I walked on a small carpet and heard a creak in the floorboard. I glanced at Jack. "Did you hear that?"

He nodded. "Yep."

"Do we need a search warrant?"

"I have one on the way. It shouldn't take long." Jack smiled. "The mayor expedited it once he heard the story. I think he's thrilled he didn't get dragged too deep into this mess."

I thought about the mayor for a moment. "I don't think he knew much about Morgan, but he was cautious. He knew instinctively the guy was rotten. Was he surprised about Cindy?"

Jack nodded. "Just about dropped the phone. It seems no one ever gave her much notice."

I nodded. "Sounds right. I think she purposely stayed well in the background and played the subdued wife of a bully. Turns out, she was the bully, and Morgan was just a greedy jackass."

One of his officers ran in with a piece of paper. "Here's the warrant, sir."

Jack grabbed the paper and checked to make sure it was in order. Nodding, he handed it back to the officer, then turned to me. "Now we're legal." He looked down at the floor. "I'll need a crow bar to lift the flooring."

My eyes flew around the room looking for something to use. My patience was worn thin, so I grabbed a letter opener from the desk. "Try this."

Jack took it and nodded. "It should get the ball rolling." He knelt down and began prying up the wooden flooring. It was only a few moments before he had success. Lifting the panel, he peered down. "Well, I'll be damn. It's a floor safe."

"Hells bells … another safe. I won't be able to guess the combination this time." I was disappointed, but I knew we'd have to wait for a locksmith to be called.

"I might be able to help." A familiar voice spoke up from behind me.

I turned and was stunned to see David Peters. "I thought you were at the hospital."

"She's in surgery. There's nothing I can do for her." He shook his head. "I knew Mom and Dad were worried about her, but I thought they were being over-protective." He sighed. "We were close as kids, but we drifted apart while I was in college. She's younger than I am, so she was still in high school. I have no idea what happened to make her turn out so rotten."

Jack pointed to the hole in the floor. "Do you know the combination to this safe?"

"She's used the same numbers for everything since she was ten years old." He rattled off the numbers, and Jack's fingers twirled as he tried to keep up with David. I heard a click and knew we hit the jackpot.

Jack was shocked. "Well … I'll be damned. Who uses the same combination for over twenty years?"

David sighed. "It's her birthday. She was worried about forgetting a combination, so she used the one thing she was certain she would never forget."

I nodded. "I use the same password for everything."

Jack frowned. "Peg! You shouldn't do that! If a crook discovers your password, he could use it to break into all your accounts or online sites."

"I would never remember a different password for every single online site or account," I snapped.

Jack shrugged. "I keep a list in my drawer."

I burst out laughing. "What's the difference? A burglar would find a list in a split second."

Jack's face was beet red as he turned his attention back to the floor safe. He reached in and started pulling out ledgers and paperwork. He handed me piles, which I stacked neatly on the floor to be entered into evidence. By the time we finished, I had five piles stacked on the floor. Jack and I took a few minutes and quickly scanned a few documents.

I looked up at Jack. "She had a list of stolen artwork and the original owners."

"Just like the Wilsons." Jack held up a few papers. "She also had the rap sheets on every criminal she hired. She knew they were ex-cons."

I shook my head in disbelief. "I don't think Morgan was the culprit here. I know he wanted to overtake his grandfather's position in the mob, but Cindy was the mastermind."

David was watching us with shock. "I had no idea she was capable of this behavior."

I narrowed my eyes. "You must've suspected *something*."

His eyes widened. "I didn't have a clue … I swear. She always had her head in the clouds as a kid, so I assumed not much had changed."

I shook my head. "People never cease to amaze me."

"Human nature has not changed in thousands of years," Logan said from somewhere in the room. I glanced around until I spotted the Indian. He nodded to David. "Your sister will be out of surgery soon. I would appreciate your presence when she regains consciousness."

David nodded, then faded slowly.

I looked at Logan. "He's not handling his sister's criminal activity too well."

Logan gave a brief nod. "It is understandable. He will recover once the shock has worn off."

I shrugged. "Maybe … I think he feels guilty."

Logan watched me carefully. "Time will heal his wounds."

I sighed. "What's next?"

"We will have a meeting once the legal issues concerning Mrs. Morgan are under control. I also want Amy, Sal, and your trio to recover from their ordeals."

I nodded. "Logan, go easy on David for a while. He's upset about his sister. I'm pretty sure she killed their parents, and that information is going to hit him hard."

He nodded. "I agree." He faded before I could add anything.

Jack looked at me. "You really think she was responsible for the parent's accident?"

I nodded. "Yep."

He shook his head. "Damn."

CHAPTER 25

Two weeks passed before we could have Logan's little get together. Cindy Morgan was in critical condition for most of that time. Jack had a ton of paperwork to plow through concerning the robberies and James Morgan's murder. We had to attend Morgan's funeral as a sign of respect to Lombardi. He wasn't very upset, he was relieved. I didn't think his grandson was the monster he thought. The guy was a jerk but not horrible … Cindy won that particular award.

Sal and Amy, along with my favorite mob trio, were back to normal within days. Amy was still fuming, but Jack finally convinced her we needed Cindy alive. Sal made the correct call concerning the 'kill shot'. Jack ignored the fact that Amy was armed without a concealed weapons license since her hidden gun saved their lives. The prosecuting attorney agreed but insisted if Amy was determined to haul her gun around, she had to go to the classes and get the damn license. I knew I'd be dragged along but so far, she hadn't mentioned it.

Once everyone with a heartbeat arrived at Sal's, the dead began to appear. Lined up next to the window stood Henry, hat in hand since there were ladies present … Dad, who looked relaxed but watchful … and Bob, disheveled as usual. Even David was present, but he was standing alone, off to the side. I was surprised when the Druid and the Scotsman joined us. I decided that since they were part of the investigation, Logan asked them to join our little gathering.

Amy was serving her concoction of various teas, and I ended up with the ghastly green crap I detested. She was determined to make me healthy, and she was convinced green tea was the answer. I disagreed, refusing to touch the cup. She shook her head in dismay. I was surprised there was no coffee in sight … even Jack was served a cup of tea, which he took with rare thanks. He obviously didn't realize what she gave him, so I knew he'd blow a gasket with the first sip.

Logan was the last to arrive, and he made a quiet entrance. No need to awe anyone in the group, he was dressed in what I called 'Indian casual'— one bare braid hung perfectly down the side of his head, and his clothes were subdued. He could make quite the arrival when it suited him but not today.

He looked around the room at everyone. "I want to thank each of you for your help in the recent matter." His eyes rested on David. "I realize the circumstances have been shocking to you, but the truth can be painful."

David looked startled to be addressed, and merely nodded.

"This investigation had elements from the past many of you were unprepared for, and I understand the surprise you felt." He paused as his eyes surveyed each of our faces. "The story began many years ago. Before the war in Europe, many people were aware of the pressure placed upon Jewish families. Some tried to help them by hiding their children, their possessions, and they even smuggled many families out of Germany." He shook his head. "Those were the lucky ones. Others found themselves less fortunate."

He looked at David. "Your family played a compassionate role leading up to the war. I believe you were completely unaware of the part your family had in aiding friends and neighbors."

David nodded. "Until recently, I never heard anything. My parents didn't discuss their families. We never questioned them, and they never offered any information." He paused. "I've learned more now that I'm dead than I ever knew living."

Logan nodded. "They had been sworn to secrecy, and they understood the consequences should anyone have access to the family legacy." He turned to face the rest of us. "David's family hid many items for their Jewish friends and business acquaintances. Family fortunes were included … had David's family been less virtuous, they would have been very rich indeed. However, they kept meticulous records, and they had plans to return each families' belongings to them at the end of the approaching war." He paused. "No one could envision the coming events."

We hung onto every word Logan said. No one uttered a word or made a sound while Logan revealed the background that led up to the recent crimes.

"Edith Peters' father was responsible for much of the Jewish belongings being hidden from the Nazis. He traveled frequently for his business, and he had the necessary resources to smuggle art and valuable household items past the Nazis." He turned to David again. "Edith was your mother's cousin and at one time, they were close friends. They stayed in contact through letters, which your mother kept secret from everyone but your father. Edith's father was eventually suspected by Nazi spies, and the entire family was taken into custody. Unwilling to turn his back on his friends, he refused to give his captors any information, which led to every family member being sent to Dachu. Edith was the sole survivor." Logan let that tidbit sink in to our minds before he continued. "She knew where her father hid the ledgers cataloging every item he hid in a Swiss bank."

Sal coughed. "I hate to interrupt you Logan, but I'm still confused. What does Nazi plunder have to do with Vito, burglaries, and Morgan?"

Logan smiled. "Historical events have long arms that reached through to current times. Many pieces of art were priceless, and there are people who would take great pride in owning artwork thought to be destroyed during the war."

"Anthony," Sal shook his head, disgusted. "I'm still trying to track down the owners of a couple of his paintings."

Logan nodded. "Yes … but Anthony was a small player in the game. However, he was able to direct Morgan to potential buyers."

I decided to ask a question of my own. "Why would Morgan even consider the black market of stolen art? It isn't on the mind of most people."

Logan smiled. "Morgan wasn't most people. He wanted to be important and that requires money."

David sighed. "How did my sister get involved?"

"Excellent question. Your parents tried to protect your sister from anyone they considered unworthy." He held up a hand as David began to defend his parents. "No disrespect intended. Your sister considered their protection as a way to control her, so she rebelled. She was young, and she wanted to be free from their domination."

I frowned. "She was out of college … at least twenty-two. That's not extremely young."

David nodded. "They sent her away to college, so she could have freedom and grow up."

Logan shook his head. "They sent her to an exclusive, all girls college in the mountains of New York state. I am sure she did not consider it to be the experience she craved."

David sighed, shaking his head. "I did warn them not to hold on too tight."

"It would not necessarily changed where we are today. I believe you will discover that your sister has character flaws which your parents were quite aware of, and that knowledge was the reason they were so controlling." Logan shook his head. "Raising a child to be a productive member of society does not guarantee a satisfactory outcome. Personalities are born and cannot always be molded."

David's mouth dropped open. "Your saying she's a bad apple?"

I thought I would have to explain David's phrase, but I was surprised by Logan's response. "While I may not have expressed myself in those words … they suffice."

David sighed again, and his shoulders dropped. "I thought I was protecting her from an ass, and it turns out she was the problem."

Logan studied David a moment before continuing with his story.

"Sal, I believe you will discover in Anthony's paperwork a list of paintings he purchased."

Sal nodded. "Yep. I've been working to find the owners, but no luck so far."

Logan nodded. "I believe Jack will find a ledger containing the information. Mrs. Wilson had access to long lost artwork, which was suspected to be in Argentina. I believe that information is one of the reasons Cindy Morgan murdered them."

Everyone began talking at once. Logan held up his hands for quiet and mouths snapped shut.

"Cindy Morgan was the person who not only murdered the Wilson's but also her own brother."

"No way! I would have recognized her!" David shouted.

Logan shook his head. "She did not trust anyone to perform those vicious acts, and she refused to allow someone else to be privy only to have a hold on her later. She disguised herself well. You would never have believed it was her in your house."

"I still don't believe you," David sulked.

"She saw you at the gas station, and she knew you were investigating Morgan. She played the part of the innocent wife well, even fooling the mayor."

"I've known her our entire lives! I would've spotted her in a second," David countered.

Logan watched him carefully. "Do you know what classes she attended while at college?"

David frowned. "I have no idea."

"Theater … she learned how to alter her appearance for stage productions."

"But the guy who attacked me was …" He paused. "Oh shit."

"Exactly. She knew how to change every recognizable feature." Logan's expression was bland, but I knew by the tone of his voice that he felt sorry for David.

Jack cleared his throat. "What about the burglaries in the township?"

"Cindy controlled the lawn service business. Morgan was merely a figure head. She hired only former convicts, then used them to look for paintings she could sell on the black market."

"Wait a damn minute," I cut in. "If you have access to millions of dollars worth of stolen art … why bother with robbing houses?"

Logan smiled. "Cindy had access to very little lost art. The reason she went after the Wilsons is because she heard conversations between her parents about the bank in Switzerland. She was hunting for the list and key for the bank. The bulk of homes robbed were bonuses for her employees. They could keep anything she personally did not want." He shrugged. "Once she found the Wilsons and realized they lived so close, she had her employees rob various houses on their work schedules to throw law enforcement off track." He paused. "It was, in all honesty, an excellent plan."

My brain was spinning as I listened to Logan's speech. An idea hit, so I spoke up. "The guys in the woods told me the break-ins weren't done by local people."

Logan nodded. "They were correct. None of the men hired by Cindy were from Bath or surrounding areas."

David interrupted. "Logan, if Cindy was willing to murder me, her husband, and the Wilsons, then she killed our parents too … didn't she?" He sounded sick to his stomach, and I didn't blame him.

"I am very sorry, but yes. She caused the accident that killed them. I have not been able to determine how she managed the accident, but I do know she is the sole person responsible."

David shook his head. "Why? Why kill all these people? For money?"

Logan nodded. "She needed the money from your parents' life insurance policies to form the lawn business but more importantly, she wanted those letters from Edith Wilson. Your mother kept them, but she had them hidden. Cindy could not obtain them as long as your mother was living."

I didn't think David could be any more distressed, but Logan's words hit him like a brick. Tears began streaming down his face. "I should have protected them."

Logan shook his head. "You had no reason to suspect your sister, and she guaranteed your suspicion of her husband by her demeanor. She played her part extremely well."

I thought of another question I had and decided to speak up. "Why the sudden decision to move to South America?"

Amy smiled. "She had what she wanted … the list. Once out of the country, she wouldn't have to worry about the FBI on her trail. No one connected her to the artwork."

I looked at Logan. "She made a mistake killing the Wilsons."

"Yes. If only robbed, law enforcement would have assumed the crime was part of the burglaries in Bath. They never would have looked further. Once the safe was discovered, the hidden ledgers were the clue needed to point a finger at her."

I frowned thoughtfully. "That safe wasn't well hidden. Hell … I found it in seconds. Why couldn't she?"

Logan shook his head. "I am not positive, but I believe she feared neighbors would call the police, and she ran out of time. Remember, the bedroom was not searched."

I was in a stubborn mood, so I shook my head. "She killed them in the bedroom. She could've started her search there."

Logan shrugged. "Her own safe was located in the living room. It may never have occurred to her the Wilson's safe would be in their bedroom."

"Why kill her own husband if he was her partner in crime?" I had so many questions that needed answering.

"He became nervous once he realized Cindy was murdering people. He worried she would steer the blame fully on him."

I narrowed my eyes. "How do you know so much? A few days ago, you knew nothing of worth."

His face became a blank slate. I stared at him a few moments until my brain notified me of the answer. "You have Morgan! You must've scooped him up the second he was killed!"

He refused to answer, but I knew I hit the nail on the head.

"Then answer this question … were Morgan and Elaine hooked up as partners in the past?"

He relaxed as he glanced at Bob. Bob's face was scarlet, but Logan nodded. "Elaine and Morgan were both disliked by the family. They decided to take over Lombardi's position. Once Bob and Elaine were murdered, he had to rethink his strategy. He believed Cindy was the answer."

"Why marry a young girl? What did she bring to the marriage?" I pressed.

"Respectability. She was beautiful, well educated, and quiet. He believed she would inherit a fortune. He still had plans to overtake Vito's position within the family."

David frowned. "Our parents weren't rich. Comfortable, yes … but not rich."

Logan smiled slightly. "Morgan was not known for his intellect."

My eyebrows raised slightly. "How much did he actually know?"

"He slowly began to suspect Cindy of the robberies. He was aware of the art and her desire to control it, but he was ignorant of her ability to murder another person. Even Morgan balked once he realized she killed her own parents. His reaction caused his death."

"I assume you've talked with Vito about Morgan. He was calm at the funeral."

Logan's face became bland again, and I sighed. "Jeez, Logan … we all know Vito can see and hear dead people."

Logan looked out the window but remained silent.

I looked at Dad, and he shook his head.

I noticed the Druid looking around the kitchen and frowned.

I looked back at Logan. "Why are those two here?"

He turned to Sal. "You have an announcement I believe."

Sal grinned, and Amy blushed … uh oh. "Amy and I are getting married."

There was stunned silence for two seconds before everyone talked at once. Everyone but me. I dreaded this moment from the second I knew they were dating. "So, you're moving here permanently." It wasn't a question, but a statement.

"Oh, yes," Amy beamed.

I felt tears well up. "Amy, you've lived next door to us forever. I don't want a different neighbor. Plus, you're protected by our dead gang in the woods."

Amy smiled. "Peg, you'll be fine. We already know who will rent the house. I'm not ready to sell, and Sal agrees."

I narrowed my eyes. "Who's going to be living there?"

Sal grinned. "Eric Spanelli. I believe you've met him?"

My mouth fell to the floor. "The doctor? The guy who took care of me when I was shot a few months ago?"

Sal nodded. "I thought you would feel safer if someone you knew rented Amy's house."

"Think how convenient it will be to have a doctor next door," Amy added.

I knew I was pouting, but I didn't care. "Fine."

Everyone began talking, and I used the opportunity to slip out the door to find some peace and quiet. I sat in one of the comfy patio chairs. I felt a presence beside me.

I didn't need to look to know it was Logan. "Andy is not present."

It wasn't a question, but I answered. "He had some big meeting at work."

Logan seemed to think this over for a moment, then he nodded. "Are you pleased the investigation is over?"

"Yep. It was nice not to be the one in danger this time, but I worry about Amy."

He smiled. "She will be well guarded from this point on."

"Ha! If Sal can't keep her safe … who can?" I snapped.

Logan remained silent. After a few moments passed, I realized he wasn't keeping secrets, he was waiting for me to connect the dots. "Oh hells bells … the Druid."

He smiled. "And the Scotsman … they are fierce protectors."

I shook my head. "Does she know?"

Logan nodded. "Yes. I believe Sal feels safer knowing they will have their own protectors roaming the property. He decided security alarms are not reliable."

Another question popped into my mind. "How were all five of them drugged?"

"Sal's love for his special blend of coffee is well known. When the house was broken into previously, they merely poured the drug in the coffee."

My mind flashed back to Lombardi recognizing the coffee as Sal's favorite when he was at the house. I decided anyone who knew Sal was aware of his love for his special blend. He would never suspect the coffee being tainted.

"What about Morgan. He's a slime ball."

"True. However, he has yet to break any of our laws. He will be watched, but I believe the man has learned valuable lessons these past few weeks."

"Ha! Personality defects can't be cured," I reminded him.

"No," He agreed. "However, greed has little use in our world."

I sighed. "Power hungry could be a problem for all of us.".

Logan smiled confidently. "We will handle him."

"Maybe." I could be damn stubborn when I wanted to.

He watched me carefully. "Are you pleased Amy and Sal are to be wed?"

I cut my eyes over to him. "She deserves to be happy."

"Your statement is not an answer to the question." The amusement in his voice was evident.

I sighed grumpily. "I don't like change."

"No. However, the past few months have brought much change to your life."

"Don't remind me," I snapped.

I heard his laughter long after he faded … jeez Louise.